Peter was looking at her, and she couldn't bring herself to meet his gaze. Those hazel eyes would steal every thought from her head. So she looked at her hands, her boots, the pew, anything but him.

"Did you find an envelope at the garage?"

His brow pinched. "What kind of envelope?"

"A regular one. Full of papers and such." She didn't exactly want to admit that she'd lost actual money, not when some of their customers were standing within hearing distance.

"No."

Her hopes died. "Oh. I'd hoped…" Her voice trembled so she stopped.

His expression softened. "I didn't look around, though. Wanna go check?"

"Can we?" In her excitement, she made the costly mistake of looking into his eyes.

They twinkled. "Sure." He held out an arm. "Let's go now."

Warmth came back to her fingers and toes. She told herself it must be due to her renewed hope that they'd find the money, but deep down she knew it was something else. Or rather *someone*, who just so happened to have twinkling hazel eyes.

Books by Christine Johnson

Love Inspired Historical

Soaring Home
The Matrimony Plan
All Roads Lead Home
Legacy of Love
The Marriage Barter
Groom by Design
Suitor by Design

*The Dressmaker's Daughters

CHRISTINE JOHNSON

A small-town girl, Christine Johnson has lived in every corner of Michigan's Lower Peninsula. She loves to visit historic locations and imagine the people who once lived there. A double-finalist for RWA's Golden Heart award, she enjoys creating stories that bring history to life while exploring the characters' spiritual journey—and putting them in peril! Though Michigan is still her home base, she and her seafaring husband also spend time exploring the Florida Keys and other fascinating locations.

Christine loves to hear from readers. Contact her through her website at christineelizabethjohnson.com.

Suitor by Design

CHRISTINE JOHNSON

HARLEQUIN® LOVE INSPIRED® HISTORICAL

Recycling programs for this product may not exist in your area.

LOVE·INSPIRED BOOKS

ISBN-13: 978-0-373-28284-5

SUITOR BY DESIGN

www.Harlequin.com

Printed in U.S.A.

That they might be called trees of righteousness,
the planting of the Lord, that He might be glorified.
— *Isaiah* 61:3

I must thank my father,
who answered many, many mechanical questions.

Any mistakes are mine alone.

No expression of gratitude would be complete
without acknowledging my husband, who
endured all my strange questions and pleas for
solitude with patience, if not full understanding.

Most of all, every iota of glory belongs to
my heavenly Father, the Author of everything,
without whom there would be no stories.

Chapter One

Pearlman, Michigan
February 1924

"It's hopeless." Minnie Fox stared at her reflection in the mirror behind the drugstore soda fountain, her cherry soda temporarily forgotten. Only three weeks shy of her nineteenth birthday, she should at least have a beau. Most of the girls her age were either engaged or married. Minnie had no one.

It must be her looks. She bore no resemblance to the motion-picture actresses on the covers of *Photoplay*. They sported glamorous bobs. How would she look with that hairstyle? Minnie pursed her lips, stained red from the soda, and rolled her long, wavy hair up to her jawline. The fat rolls of hair on either side of her face looked like loaves of bread sitting atop her threadbare brown wool coat.

She let her hair drop. "It *is* hopeless."

"What's hopeless?" Minnie's next older sister, Jen, plopped onto the stool next to her.

"Nothing." Minnie twirled the straw in her soda, took a sip and lingered while the bubbles fizzed against her lips. "I don't know why I care. There isn't a sheik within fifty miles."

"Sheik?" Jen's lip curled in distaste. "Stop talking like them." She poked a thumb toward Kate Vanderloo and her college girlfriends a couple stools away. Born to wealth and privilege, Kate was pretty enough to grace the cover of *Photoplay*. So were her girlfriends. All were here on midsemester break and to attend the Valentine's Day Ball.

"Shh! They'll hear you." Minnie scrunched a little lower. "For your information, that's what everyone calls guys who try to look like Rudolph Valentino." She flipped through the magazine until she found what she'd read earlier. "It says here that the college campuses are full of sheiks. It's quite the rage."

Jen rolled her eyes. "What do we care? None of us will ever go to college. I can't even save enough money for flight lessons. Besides, other things are more important, like getting Daddy well."

Minnie flinched at the reproach. "I'm sorry. You're right." Daddy's heart had been weak from childhood, but last summer he'd suffered a seizure that left him even weaker. He'd recovered enough to walk her older sister, Ruth, down the aisle in October but soon after retreated to his bedroom. "I want that, too." Minnie outlined the glamorous actress on the *Photoplay* cover with her finger. "That's why I'm hoping for a rich and famous husband."

"Sure," Jen snorted. "Where are you going to find that in Pearlman?"

"There are a few well-off bachelors."

"One or two, and they're much older than you."

"I suppose." Minnie couldn't give up her dream that easily. "Maybe he'll be new to town. Like Sam. He came to town to open the department store and ended up marrying Ruthie. It could happen again."

"That happens only once in a lifetime. Besides, Sam had to give up his inheritance to marry Ruth. They're just as poor as we are."

"Unless she sells her dress designs. Sam says that'll make them rich."

"Sam's a dreamer. How many manufacturers have they tried? Every one has turned down her designs."

"Maybe this time they'll get good news."

"Maybe." But Jen didn't sound hopeful. "They're supposed to get word today."

Rather than dwell on something she couldn't control, Minnie watched Kate flirt with the soda-fountain clerk. Kate Vanderloo always seemed to have a new beau. Even in high school, she'd been able to capture every guy's attention. Minnie, on the other hand, could only imagine what it would feel like to have every man's gaze follow her across a room. She glanced again at the magazine cover. Maybe if she looked more like a movie star. "Should I get my hair cut?"

"Why?"

Minnie pointed to the cover. "So I look like a star."

"You can't even act."

"I can sing. I was second soprano in the school choir."

Jen shrugged, as if that accomplishment meant nothing. "Are you almost done with that soda? We need to close the shop. Ruth wants to go with Sam to the telegraph office. The call's supposed to come in around five o'clock." The telegraph office was also the telephone exchange. Since neither the dress shop nor their house had a telephone, they had to place and receive long-distance calls there. "Ready?"

"I suppose." Minnie sucked more of the fizzy liquid into her mouth, but she couldn't gulp down a soda, and she wouldn't waste it. At five cents apiece, they were a rare treat.

Down the counter, the soda clerk leaned close to Kate and gave her a dazzling smile. "I'd take you to the ball."

Kate giggled and fluttered her eyelids. "If I didn't already have an escort, I might consider the offer."

Now, *that* was ridiculous! Kate Vanderloo would rather get run over by a train than go to the Valentine's Day Ball with a soda clerk.

Jen gave Minnie a look of disgust. "Let's go." She spun around to leave.

Minnie slurped up a mouthful of soda and swallowed. The bubbles tickled her nose, and she sneezed.

That drew Kate's attention. "Oh, Minnie. I didn't see you there. Sally tells me you are serving punch again at the ball. I hope you don't spill it this time."

Minnie wanted to disappear. It was bad enough that she had to dress in a maid's uniform and wait on Pearlman's elite, but she couldn't bear doing it in front of her former classmates. She stared at the *Photoplay* cover. If only...

The bell above the drugstore door signaled a new arrival and drew the attention away from her. Tall Peter Simmons entered. He cast a quick look at the counter and swiped off his cap before stomping the snow from his old work boots.

"Oh, it's just Peter." Minnie turned back to her soda.

"Just Peter? What do you mean?" Jen sat back down. "I thought you were friends."

"A little, but he's been acting strange lately."

"How? He seems perfectly normal to me."

"I don't know." Minnie had run into him more than once in the alley that ran behind her house. He could take that route from work to home, but he seemed to always time it for when she was coming back from work. Then he wouldn't say anything intelligent, just mutter something about the weather or ask how work had gone. "He just acts different."

"Ahhh."

Minnie knew exactly what her sister was thinking. "Don't get any ideas."

"Did I say a thing?"

"You don't have to," she muttered low enough so no one could hear. "Between you and Ruth, you practically have us married. Stop it."

"All right, all right. The subject's closed." Jen stood. "Are you ready yet?"

As Minnie drank the last of her soda, Kate snickered and whispered something to her group of friends. The giggling girls were all watching Peter, who had asked for a bottle of Lydia Pinkham's tonic from the druggist. At their laughter, embarrassment bled up his face clear to the roots of his tousled brown hair.

Minnie felt sorry for him. Peter was a decent guy. It wasn't his fault he'd lost his parents and got sent to Pearlman by that New York orphan society. He'd gotten a good home with Mrs. Simmons, but then she lost her house and had to move in with her daughter. That meant Peter had to stay with his foster brother's family at Constance House, the local orphanage. That must have reminded him every day that he was an orphan, too. Poor guy! He could act like an idiot sometimes, but he didn't deserve Kate's ridicule.

"It's for Mariah," Peter explained while he waited for the druggist to fetch the tonic. "She's not feeling well."

Peter's sister-in-law had her hands full running the orphanage. Peter helped out when he wasn't working at the family's motor garage. He was good with his hands. He'd built the shelving and counter at the bookstore, helped out in Sunday school, and was the first guy to set up tables and chairs for any church function. He deserved Kate's respect.

Instead, the girl laughed at him.

With every passing second, Minnie got angrier until she couldn't stand it anymore. "Mariah's lucky to have a brother like Peter helping her out."

If anything, his face got redder, but it did draw Kate's attention away from him.

The girl's mouth curved into a smirk. "Minnie's sweet on Peter."

Her girlfriends seconded the proclamation.

Minnie felt her cheeks heat. "Am not!"

The girls giggled harder.

"Then why are you blushing?" Kate asked.

"Am not!" But that wasn't true. Her face burned and was probably as red as Peter's. Her gaze dropped to the magazine cover. If only she looked like Clara Bow, she could command respect. The fashionable guys would notice her. All it would take was a new hairstyle. She jutted out her chin. "For your information, I'm going to marry a sheik."

Kate snorted. "A sheik? You? What a laugh. No sheik would look twice at someone like you. If you want my advice, you had better settle for a local guy." She inclined her head toward Peter, making her point perfectly clear. "Come along, girls. We wouldn't want to interfere with Minnie's romance."

The girls headed for the door, singing, "Peter and Minnie, sweet as can be…"

Minnie wanted to throw her soda at them, but the Bible said to turn the other cheek. It didn't mention how hard that was to do. She slurped up the melted ice that tasted faintly of cherry soda. It was hopeless. She had only a hint of flavor, while girls like Kate sparkled.

"Forget them," Jen said. "They only care about themselves."

"I know." And deep down she did know that, but would

it really be such a terrible thing to be attractive and important for once? *Just one day, Lord. One little day.*

"They should get their mouths washed out with soap," Jen added. "Let's go."

Minnie dug around in her pocket for the nickel to pay for her soda but came up with nothing. She frowned and hunted in her other pocket before a sudden thought distracted her. She *could* look like Clara Bow. Oh, she couldn't afford a real hairstylist, but Jen had cut her own hair. It didn't look that great, but then it had to be easier to cut someone else's hair than your own. "Will you cut my hair?"

"Me?" Jen's eyebrows lifted with surprise. "Mother always cuts your hair."

"She won't give me a bob. I want my hair to look like this." She pointed to the *Photoplay* cover. "It shouldn't be too difficult. Easier than cutting your own hair, and you did a pretty good job on that."

"After Ruth straightened out all my mistakes. Why don't you ask her?"

"Because she'd take Mother's side. Will you do it? Please?"

"All right, then, but no promises you'll look like that cover."

"Good!" Minnie clapped her hands together.

"And you have to take the blame when Mother sees it."

Minnie had no choice but to agree. Mother would throw a conniption fit. She loved Minnie's long hair. Well, times were changing, and Minnie intended to change along with them. She was going to become a modern woman, and modern women wore both their hair and their skirts short. Modern women had guys, not beaus. They dated instead of being courted.

She sneaked a glimpse at the register. Peter had finished and was headed their way, tonic safely hidden in a paper sack.

"That'll be five cents, miss." The soda clerk tapped the counter.

Minnie dug around in her other coat pocket. Where had she put that nickel? "Just a minute." She tried her skirt pocket. Nothing there, either. "I had a nickel in my coat pocket." She reached in again and found a hole. "Oh, no! It must have fallen out. Jen?"

Her sister shook her head. "I don't have any money with me."

Minnie bit her lower lip. At least Kate wasn't here to witness this embarrassing moment. She turned to the soda clerk. "May I pay you later?"

"You don't have five cents?" He looked shocked.

"Here." Peter stepped up and placed a dime on the counter. "Keep the change."

The soda clerk snatched it up and went to the cash register.

Peter Simmons paid her bill? If Kate ever found out, she'd hound Minnie to death. "I'll pay you back."

He shuffled his feet, halfway looking down and half of the time peeking up at her. "Don't need to."

"Yes, I do." She took a deep breath and remembered her manners. "Thank you." She even managed a smile. "I found a hole in my pocket. It must have fallen out on the way here."

"That happens." Still, he stood there.

"I guess we should be going," she suggested.

"Yeah, I suppose." He stuffed the tonic into his coat pocket. "Look, Minnie, I was wondering—" He stopped abruptly, and his face got red.

She panicked. He was going to ask her to go with him to something. Not now. Not when she had discovered the means to interest a real man—one who could both help her family get out of debt and fulfill her dreams. "I need to get going." She backed away. "Ruth is waiting for us."

"Yeah. I should go, too. Mariah needs the medicine."

"See you later, then. And thanks again." She edged behind her grinning sister.

"Anytime." He glanced at Jen before striding to the door. He yanked it open and let it slam shut before hurrying off toward the orphanage.

Only then could Minnie take a breath.

Jen was still grinning. "He *is* sweet on you."

"No, he's not." Minnie felt the unwelcome flush of heat coupled with an odd slushy feeling inside. "He was just helping me out, like a brother would help a sister."

Jen laughed. "Think that if you want, but I'm telling you that he is definitely interested."

"Well, I'm not." That should put an end to this. "I don't feel anything romantic for him. Besides, he can hardly talk around me."

"Ahhh."

"And he's not my type. I'm looking for more out of life than settling down with a local guy. I want to go places and see things. New York City. Maybe even Hollywood. I'm looking for a real hero."

Jen dug in her coat pockets and pulled out some gloves. "You don't want much, do you?"

"I just won't settle. Kate Vanderloo can say what she wants, but I'm never going to marry someone local."

"All right, then." Yet Jen still had that impish grin on her face. "Let's go."

Minnie finished buttoning her worn hand-me-down coat and followed her sister. The moment she stepped outside, a blast of icy wind knocked her hat off her head. It tumbled and rolled toward the street. Before she could retrieve it, a fancy new car glided past. Its deep blue finish gleamed. The chrome grille sparkled. Every inch of it looked fast and expensive.

She grabbed Jen's arm, her hat forgotten. "Look at that. I wonder who owns it. He must be rich to afford an automobile like that."

Jen dug her hands deeper into her coat pockets. "I suppose."

"I've never seen the car before," Minnie mused. "It's not Mr. Kensington's or Mr. Neidecker's or anyone else's from the Hill." Everyone referred to the wealthy neighborhood above Green Lake as the Hill. "He must be a newcomer. He could be a motion-picture actor."

Jen rolled her eyes and started toward the dress shop. "In Pearlman?"

"Why not?" By the time Minnie retrieved her hat, the frigid air had numbed her cheeks and fingertips. She hurried after Jen. "Maybe he's a new student at the airfield."

"There won't be any new students until spring."

"Then who could he be?" Minnie leaned over the frozen street, trying to see where the car went, but she lost sight of it after it passed the bank. "Maybe he's just passing through."

"No one just passes through Pearlman."

Jen had a point. That meant a newcomer in town—an important newcomer. Hopefully, he was a bachelor.

Minnie had smiled at him.

The thought warmed Peter on the short walk to the orphanage. Not only had Minnie smiled at him, but she'd also said nice things. *Mariah's lucky to have a brother like Peter.* That was just about as close as Minnie had ever gotten to giving him a compliment. Didn't matter that Mariah wasn't really his sister or even his real sister-in-law. She'd married Peter's foster brother, Hendrick. Seeing as Peter didn't have kin—leastways none he wanted to acknowledge—that made Hendrick and Mariah as good as family. He'd do anything for them. Still, it was good of Minnie to notice.

The orphanage was in chaos, the older kids chasing the younger ones around. No wonder Mariah had reached the end of her patience. Those kids needed something to keep them busy. When he'd been in the New York orphanage, he'd learned carpentry and how to fix things. The older kids needed something like that—a place to go and someone to teach them. But this was Pearlman, not New York. There just weren't that many places a kid could go.

Peter dropped off the medicine and scooted out, saying he had to get back to the garage. That was kinda true. He'd closed the doors while he ran the errand and hoped Hendrick would understand. Business was slow this time of year, both at the motor garage and in the factory. His almost-brother had gotten edgy lately, but he refused to take a cent from Mariah's family. Peter respected that. A man had to have his pride.

He dug his hands into his jacket pockets and trudged down Main Street. Kate Vanderloo and her friends entered the new department store, still giggling and chattering like a flock of blackbirds getting ready to head south.

Why did Minnie have to see him fetching female tonic for his sister-in-law? He didn't mind the likes of Kate Vanderloo snickering at him. She was a selfish snob. But Minnie was good, through and through. He was gonna ask her to join him at the church supper on Wednesday, but after the way those girls teased her, she got all jumpy. Minnie couldn't seem to hold up to that kinda talk. She was always wanting to look like some movie star, but to his way of thinking she had them beat a hundred times over.

A throaty car horn jerked Peter out of his thoughts. He knew every car in Pearlman, and none of them had a horn that sounded like that. This blast came from a gleaming new Pierce-Arrow touring car that inched down Main Street alongside him.

"Hey there, Stringbean," shouted the man behind the wheel.

Peter squinted into the glare of the late-day sun. No one had called him Stringbean since the orphanage. Even there, only one person used the nickname.

"Vince?" The driver sounded like Peter's old friend, but this man had slicked-back hair and a fancy suit. Gold cuff links flashed in the sun. "Vince Galbini?"

"You got it, kid. I said I'd look ya up, and here I am."

Peter couldn't get over it. "How'd you find me? Mariah said Mr. Isaacs closed the orphanage."

"I got my contacts in the old neighborhood. They told me you were sent here."

That made sense. Mariah had gone back to the orphanage after all the orphans on the train were placed in families. She'd probably told everyone working there that he'd found a home with the Simmons family. From there, the news would have spread through the neighborhood.

"You kept your promise," Peter said in astonishment. "I can't believe it. You said you'd find me again, and you did." Pleasure surged through him at the thought. "You remembered."

"'Course I did, kid. Vincent Galbini always keeps his promises."

Vince rapped his hand against the car door, a gold ring clinking against the metal. "Let's catch up on old times. Where do you call home?"

Peter didn't want his old pal to see that he was living in an orphanage, even though he wasn't there as an orphan.

Vince had clearly risen in the world. Peter, on the other hand, was just trudging along.

"I'm headed back to the motor garage." Peter pointed down the street and puffed out his chest. "I'm a mechanic now, and I manage the place."

Vince whistled. "I heard you were working on cars, but I didn't know you were the man in charge. You're doing all right, kid."

Peter stood a bit taller under the compliment. Vince was proud of him. Vince Galbini, the man who'd taught him how to measure and cut two pieces of wood so they joined without a gap. Peter had learned how to plane and sand and finish from him. Most of all, he'd learned to respect each piece of wood, to feel the flow of the grain and use that to make the perfect cut.

Vince had sure changed in four years. He'd been a hard-luck carpenter from the neighborhood who liked to help out at the orphanage. His trousers were always patched. His stained shirts looked more gray than white. His cap had hidden a mop of wiry hair that rarely saw soap and water, but he'd always had time for the kids, especially Peter.

A couple months before the orphan society plunked Peter on that train, Vince had stopped by to tell them he was leaving.

"I got a real good job," he'd said with a grin. "They'll be throwin' buckets of money at me."

Vince loved to exaggerate. No one believed he'd really get that kind of money. Except Peter. When Vince promised to come back for Peter after making his stake, Peter clung to that promise. He waited at mail call. He prayed for a telephone call. He sat in the front window and watched the street. No letter, no call, no Vince. Then Mr. Isaacs put Peter on the train, and he figured he'd never see his friend again.

Yet here Vince was, and it sure looked like the company had thrown those buckets of money at him after all. A new Pierce-Arrow cost more than Peter could earn in a decade. Its quiet, powerful engine was the envy of every man who longed to show others he'd made it big. Vince had done just what he'd promised.

"Hop in, kid," Vince said. "Passenger seat's empty."

As he rounded the car, Peter's pulse accelerated. Maybe Vince hadn't just shown up to keep a promise. Maybe he was gonna spread a little of his good fortune around. That sure would get Minnie's attention.

By the time they reached the garage, Peter and Vince were chatting as if it was old times.

Vince whistled when he pulled up in front of the garage. "Nice place. You're doin' good for yourself, kid. How many cars can you work on at once?"

"Two inside. Three if they're small. Let me show you around."

"Sounds like a good plan." Vince pushed open his door.

Peter hopped out, taking care to close his door without slamming it, and then hustled to pull open the big doors to the work bay.

His friend moseyed forward. "Looks like you do a good business."

"Good 'nuff." Peter dug his hands into his pockets and kicked an ice ball toward the gasoline pump. It banged against the metal case and stopped. Compared to Vince, he'd come plumb against a brick wall. No gal. No fancy car. No car at all. He'd been reduced to fetching female tonic for his sister-in-law.

Vince took a gold cigarette case from his inside jacket pocket. He flipped it open, removed a cigarette and offered it to Peter.

"No thanks. Don't smoke. Yet." Peter was too embarrassed to say he found the habit disgusting. His uncle Max smoked, and he wouldn't do anything that rotten man did.

"Give it a try."

Peter shook his head and toed the ground. "Maybe some other time."

Vince snapped the case shut, slipped a lighter from another pocket and lit the cigarette. After a couple draws, he pointed to the garage. "Let's take a look."

Once they got inside and Peter started showing off the machine shop and all his tools, the old Vince came back. Excitement lit his eyes, and he asked dozens of questions. He got especially excited when he saw Peter's wood shop and heard how Peter made the shelving and counter at the bookstore.

"Sounds like you can build anything."

Maybe it was the lighting, but Peter thought he saw a gleam in Vince's eye. "Most anything. Can't make a spark plug, of course."

Vince laughed and ran his hand over the fender of Mr. Kensington's Packard. "Have you ever done custom work on the body of the car?"

Peter thought back to the luggage rack Mariah had insisted they make for her Overland after returning from Montana. "Some."

"Think you could redo an interior?"

Peter wasn't sure what his friend was getting at. "Not the upholstery."

"But anything in metal or wood?"

"Sure." He tried to sound more confident than he felt.

Vince's grin broadened, and he clapped Peter on the back. "Then I've come to the right man. I told the boss that I knew someone that could do the job."

"What job?"

"It's more like an opportunity, old sport, a chance to get

yourself some of this." Vince flicked his gold cuff links. "My boss is lookin' to get his car customized to his particular needs."

"What kind of needs?"

"He needs room for…er, luggage."

"I made a luggage rack for an Overland." Though many touring car manufacturers offered luggage racks with a trunk, Peter figured the car in question must not have that option.

Vince shook his head. "My boss don't want a trunk outside, where his stuff might get wet. Do ya know what I mean? He wants storage inside the car."

"There's storage under the rear seat if it's a sedan."

"But it's not quite the right size. And he wants a place for his valuables, say underneath the main luggage compartment. Is that something you can do?"

"You mean a hidden compartment?"

"That's it," Vince said with a grin. "Glad we understand each other."

Peter supposed a man rich enough to run a company that paid Vince high wages would want to hide his valuables. "Depends on the car. What make we talking about?"

Vince motioned to the Pierce-Arrow. "How about that one?"

Peter ambled over and peered inside. The rear seat was spacious and had decent depth. He popped his head out and wiped his fingerprints off the polished door. "I can do it, but it wouldn't fit a full steamer trunk."

Vince waved that off. "The boss wouldn't bring anything that big. I'm thinking about like this." He demonstrated something almost twice the size of a vegetable crate.

"That'd fit, but I might have to raise the seat a bit depending on the size of the hidden compartment. How big do you need it?"

Vince explained the dimensions. They even pulled out the seat cushion, and Peter measured the space. He penciled the figures on a piece of paper and sketched a rough design.

"Look all right?" Peter asked.

"Perfect! Just what the boss wants."

For some reason, Peter got a strange feeling in the pit of his stomach. Maybe because Vince never said who he was working for. "Your boss?"

"An up-and-comer out of Brooklyn. He moved to Chicago a few years ago and set up shop. Furniture. Antiques. That sort of thing. Since coming to these parts, business took off, and he's setting up other locations." Vince wandered around while he talked, seeming too fidgety to stand still.

That made sense, but the strange feeling wouldn't go away. "Is this a paying job?"

"Of course." Vince laughed. "Would I ever cut you short?"

Peter thought back to those long days waiting for Vince to come back to the orphanage. "I guess not."

"Tell ya what, kid. Do a good job, and the boss'll make it worth your while." Vince pulled out a money clip fat with bills. "Maybe he'll even have more work for you."

Peter's jaw dropped. The outside bill was a hundred. There had to be fifty of them in the wad.

Vince grinned. "That's right, kid. I seen the way you worked with your hands back in New York. Figured you still had the talent, but I had no idea you got a shop like this." He whistled. "Far as I'm concerned, you're the man for the job." He pulled one bill off the clip and slipped the rest back into his pocket. "Is this enough to start?" He waved the bill before Peter and then snatched it back. "One question. What about the upholstery? You got anyone who can handle that if you gotta change the seat?"

Minnie's face flashed into Peter's head. She did sewing at the dress shop, and her family could sure use the extra money with her pa sick and all. Maybe if he got Minnie some work, she'd be so grateful she'd see him as more than a friend.

"I know someone who could do it."

"Good." Vince grinned and handed him the hundred-dollar bill. "We got a deal, then, Stringbean?" He extended his hand.

Peter hesitated. Something still didn't feel quite right, but it was a lot of money. It would help at the orphanage, and Minnie's family could use a little extra. Maybe she'd even stop chasing after no-account swells and notice him. Besides, Vince was a good guy. Peter had known him for years.

He grasped Vince's hand and shook. "Deal."

Chapter Two

Minnie didn't spot the sleek new car again until they reached the dress shop. From there she could see it parked half a block ahead in front of Simmons Motor Garage. The driver leaned against it, his back to her, as he talked to Peter. The man wore a slick wool suit in the latest fashion. The cold didn't seem to bother him. No overcoat. No gloves. No scarf. Just a black fedora. His cuff links flashed in the sun. Could they be gold?

Her pulse quickened. Had her unspoken prayer been answered that quickly? A wealthy stranger in Pearlman. In February. That simply didn't happen. Now, if he was a bachelor who happened to be looking for a wife…

"I wonder who he is," she mused.

Jen paused at the dress-shop door. "Who are you talking about?"

"The man driving that fancy car. He's talking to Peter. Either they know each other or the man has car trouble. Must be the car. How would someone like that know Peter?"

"I don't know." Jen opened the door. "Are you coming?"

"In a minute." Minnie couldn't let this opportunity pass.

"Will you start closing up? I promise to be back just as soon as I find out who he is. Please?"

Jen relented. "All right, but hurry."

"I will," Minnie called over her shoulder as she hurried toward the garage.

When she reached the end of the block, she lingered on the corner, pretending to wait for an opportunity to cross Main Street. A quick glance revealed nothing had changed. The man still stood with his back to her. He gestured with his arms as he talked. A few heavily accented words drifted her way. To her disappointment, he was shorter and stockier than Peter. But that suit! Even Hutton's Department Store didn't carry one that fine.

A cloud of steam rose above his head, and he lifted a cupped hand to his lips. Oh, dear. That wasn't steam. He was smoking a cigarette. A wave of nausea rolled over her. She hated their stench, but they were growing more and more popular thanks to the movies.

Peter looked her way, and she darted behind a nearby maple. Peeking around the trunk, she noted that the two men continued their conversation. Neatly trimmed dark hair peeked from under the brim of the driver's hat. From the way the hair gleamed, he must use a treatment. One of those nice-smelling ones, she imagined. She hugged her gloved hands to her chest, torn between wishing he would turn around so she could see his face and terrified that he'd turn around and see her spying on him.

She chewed on the fingertip of her glove.

The man acted as if he knew Peter. The two laughed, and then the man clapped Peter on the back. They shook hands, and the man climbed into his car. He was leaving? Then he couldn't have car trouble, at least not bad enough to leave the vehicle at the garage.

As the man backed the car away from the building, the

sun reflected off a thick gold band on his finger. Minnie squinted. A ring! Oh, no. Worse, it was his left hand. The car turned, and she saw his hand clearly. What a relief. The ring was on the pinkie, not the ring finger.

Minnie slid around the tree as the man drove down the side street. She didn't get a good look at his face, so she couldn't tell if he was handsome or not, but he didn't seem terribly old. The car turned left on State Road and headed out of town. He was leaving, and she would never know who he was or why he'd come to Pearlman.

She pressed a cheek to the prickly bark. Why did every opportunity elude her? For ages she'd pined after Reggie Landers, although he not only wasn't interested in her, but he'd also gone and gotten engaged to that nasty Sally Neidecker, who bossed Minnie around as if *she* was the mistress of the house. Mrs. Neidecker was much kinder and even gave Minnie a little extra money at Christmastime. Still, Minnie longed for the day when she wouldn't have to clean houses.

This man could have been her chance.

She bit her lip. Maybe he still could be. If he knew Peter, he might come back. Moreover, Peter could tell her if he was married or not. A smile settled in place. Peter liked her. With a little encouragement, she could get him to tell her anything.

She flounced across the street, passed by the fueling pump and stepped into the office of the motor garage. The nasty smell nearly sent her right back out. Grease. Exhaust. She fought the urge to press a handkerchief over her nose.

No one was in the office area, if it could be called that. The tiny room had lots of shelves and hooks filled with automobile parts, like belts and hoses and stuff that Jen would love but Minnie didn't recognize. A single desk with a small cash register and a messy pile of papers dominated the room. To the left, an open doorway led to the work area. A couple of cars filled the dirty space, but Minnie couldn't see Peter. He must be underneath or inside a car.

Should she wait or call out for him? As she nibbled on the glove and debated what to do, she happened to notice that the papers on the desk were work orders and bills. If the man needed work on his car, then one of these might have his name on it. She turned the top piece of paper around. No, that wasn't it. Mr. Kensington's name was at the top.

"Can I help you?" Peter said.

"Oh!" Minnie jumped away from the desk, paper still in hand. "I was just…" She didn't have a good explanation, but maybe a smile would distract him from the fact she'd been snooping. She slipped the paper behind her skirt and gave him her biggest smile. "I thought maybe we could talk."

"About what?" Peter stood in the open doorway between the office and the work area, rubbing his hands on a filthy old rag.

"That rag must be putting more dirt on your hands than taking it off."

"You came all the way here to tell me that?"

"No." She gave him another smile, swished in front of the desk and covertly replaced the invoice on the desktop. "I wondered what kind of car that was."

"What car?"

"The one your friend just drove away in."

"A Pierce-Arrow."

"Ah." Minnie noted that he didn't contradict her assumption that the driver was a friend of his. "It looks expensive."

"It is."

"Your friend owns it?"

Peter looked suspicious. "Why do you want to know?"

"No particular reason. Just making conversation." Out of the corner of her eye, Minnie saw the invoice slip off the stack. Before it slid to the floor, she nudged it toward the center of the desk. Though Peter hadn't answered her question, he hadn't contradicted her assumption, either. That was good enough for her. Now all she needed to know was his marital status. "Is your friend staying long?"

"Just the night. Why?"

"I just figured you would want to talk with him. You know, catch up on family and all."

Peter didn't bite. "What are you getting at?"

This time Minnie couldn't explain away the heat in her cheeks, so she stared at her feet. "Just wondered who the stranger was. We don't get many newcomers in Pearlman, especially someone with such a fancy car."

"Vince is an old friend from New York. He used to help out at the—" he hesitated, and his neck flushed red "—at the orphanage."

"Like volunteer work?" Maybe this Vince was like Pastor Gabe and his sister. They did a lot of work for the orphan society that had sent Peter and a handful of other orphans to Pearlman almost four years ago.

"I suppose he volunteered, but I don't really know. It didn't matter to the kids if a person was paid or not."

"Oh." Embarrassed, Minnie struggled to turn the conversation back in the right direction. "But he became your friend."

Peter smiled at that. "He taught me carpentry."

Relieved, Minnie seized the opening. "He's a carpenter? He doesn't look like one." The only carpenter she knew dressed in work clothes and drove a Model T truck. "Is that his regular job?"

"I don't know. Why all the interest in Vince?"

Minnie had come too close to revealing what she wanted. "Oh, just curious. It gets so dull here that anything new is welcome." She tossed him another smile. "Besides, he did a good job teaching you carpentry. You make beautiful furniture."

He beamed. "I like working with wood. It's kinda creative. More'n fixing cars." He flushed again. "I mean, *more than* fixing cars."

In a way, Minnie appreciated that he tried to speak correctly around her, but it made him nervous, and a nervous Peter wouldn't divulge what she needed to know.

"I'm glad he taught you. Be sure to thank him for me and for my father. Daddy appreciates the bed table that you made for him. The casters make it easy to move into place, and it lets him work on the accounts. It helps him feel—" her throat swelled before saying the last word "—*useful.*"

Peter shrugged. "I liked making it." He shifted his weight, telling her this conversation had gone on too long.

"Well, I suppose I should get home."

"Me, too."

Minnie wouldn't exactly call Constance House a home, but Peter had moved in with his foster brother and sister-in-law a couple of years ago to help out at the orphanage.

"See you later." Peter headed back into the garage.

If she didn't get the answer she needed now, she'd never know. "I hope you get to spend time with your friend tonight."

Peter halted, his expression quizzical.

"Before he has to go home to his family," she added and then held her breath.

He shrugged. "Oh, he'll be back on Saturday." Then he returned to work.

Minnie didn't follow. He hadn't told her what she wanted to know, but she had time to find out. Between now and Saturday, she would transform herself into a woman who would dazzle Peter's friend.

Peter had let an opportunity slip away to ask Minnie if she would help with the upholstery, but he didn't realize it until he sat down to supper and Mariah asked about his day. Long ago, they'd learned to feed the children first and then have the older orphans read to the younger ones so the adults could eat in relative peace. That gave them the chance to catch up and take care of any pressing business.

"Anything interesting happen today?" Mariah asked him.

Hendrick looked up hopefully. "Any new business?"

Peter swallowed a mouthful of mashed potatoes as his mind flitted over the surprising events of the past several hours. "An old friend stopped by after I dropped off your medicine. Do you remember Vince?"

She shook her head.

"Vincent Galbini. He helped out around the orphanage in New York."

"Oh, yes. I remember him now." Mariah set down her fork. She still looked a little out of sorts. "He used to do odd jobs, carpentry and repair work, right?"

Peter nodded. "He's the one who taught me to work with wood."

"At least one blessing came out of his work there."

The strange feeling that something wasn't right returned, but Peter shoved it away. He must have misread his sister-in-law. "Yes, ma'am. I'm sure grateful for that. Having something to do kept me out of trouble."

Mariah smiled briefly before her brow furrowed again. "The last I heard, he found work somewhere, but I can't quite recall where he went. Brooklyn? New Jersey? Baltimore?" She shook her head. "I can't remember, but that's not the point. Whatever would bring him to Pearlman?"

"He promised." Peter gulped down a swig of milk. "The day Vince left the orphanage, he promised to find me once he got ahead."

"He did?" Mariah glanced at Hendrick before returning her attention to Peter. "That's quite a commitment for someone with Mr. Galbini's prospects."

Her words rubbed Peter the wrong way. "He told me he was going to get a good job, one that paid a lot."

"Money does not bring happiness."

But it sure doesn't hurt. Peter bowed his head to hide his feelings. Mariah had never known hunger. She hadn't scavenged through garbage or risked jail for a bit of bread. She hadn't slept on the sewer grate hoping for a little warmth when the snow fell. The raw pain of those months on the street came back as if they had happened yesterday. "He's doing good for himself. He's got nice clothes, and the job pays good."

"Well," Mariah corrected.

"Well," Peter repeated, though he wasn't quite sure what part of his sentence he'd gotten wrong.

Mariah picked at her potatoes before leveling her gaze at him again. "How did he find you?"

"He said he talked to friends back in New York who knew I'd been sent here."

"Hmm. I suppose that's possible. We never kept it a secret that you and the other children found good homes in Pearlman." An impish smile curved her lips. "So you're telling me that he came all this way to fulfill a promise, and you didn't invite him to supper?"

"Uh, he had to leave." Peter didn't want to admit he'd been ashamed to invite Vince to the orphanage. He shouldn't feel that way. After all, he wasn't an orphan anymore. Not exactly.

"He headed back to Brooklyn?" Mariah looked confused. "Already?"

"No. He lives in Chicago now." Peter pushed the canned peas across his plate. This was beginning to feel like an interrogation.

"That's still a long drive," Hendrick said. "You should have asked him to stay with us."

"I—I think he's staying at Terchie's." At least Peter assumed he was at the boardinghouse.

Hendrick scowled. "Isn't our place good enough?"

Peter swallowed hard and stared at his plate of food. He wasn't hungry anymore, but he couldn't face his foster brother's reproach.

To his surprise, Mariah rescued him. "It was quite thoughtful of Mr. Galbini to take other lodging. Peter must have told him we were full."

Peter felt even worse. Why had he been so ashamed to tell Vince he was living at the orphanage? What would it matter to a guy who used to help out at one?

Mariah continued, "I may have to change my opinion of Mr. Galbini. It shows considerable integrity to keep a fleeting promise to a boy."

Peter squirmed. "Well, that wasn't the only reason he stopped by. He wanted to know if I could do some work for him."

That caught Hendrick's attention. "What kind of work?" Peter's foster brother was still in charge of the garage, though he'd handed over day-to-day management to Peter after his airplane-motor factory went into production.

Peter mashed the peas to pulp. "Nothing much. Just wants a luggage compartment for his car."

"Oh." Hendrick resumed eating. "You could make a rack like the one we built for Mariah's Overland."

Peter didn't point out that Vince wanted something entirely different.

"What make of car?" Hendrick asked.

"Pierce-Arrow."

Both Hendrick's and Mariah's eyebrows shot up.

Mariah picked up her fork. "Mr. Galbini must be doing very well in his new job to afford a Pierce-Arrow."

"Real well," Peter confirmed, "but the car isn't his. It belongs to his boss."

"Ah. That explains things." Still, Mariah looked concerned. "Just make sure everything is completely legitimate. I'm afraid that Mr. Galbini kept company with some pretty rough sorts."

"He did?" That came as a shock to Peter. Vince was nothing like Uncle Max. Vince kept his promises. He could turn a warped old board into a toy or a beautiful piece of furniture. Peter owed Vince a huge debt. "He was always good to me."

"I'm sure he was." She smiled weakly.

"And he's got money to pay. He gave me a deposit."

Hendrick looked up from his supper. "That's good thinking on your part."

Peter didn't want to explain that he hadn't asked for a deposit, but he appreciated Hendrick's confidence in him. "And there's plenty more to pay for the whole job. He showed me a money clip with a huge wad of bills. He's making his mark in the world."

Mariah cleared her throat. "A man's true worth isn't based on how much he earns."

"Tell that to Minnie Fox."

"Oh?" Mariah lifted an eyebrow. "Minnie, of all people, should understand that money does not make the man."

Peter wasn't so sure. He'd heard her comments in the drugstore and watched her chase after worthless guys just because they were swells.

"Speaking of Minnie," Mariah said softly, "why don't you invite her to the church supper tomorrow night?"

Peter smashed the last pea. "Maybe I will." If he got up the nerve. But if Minnie turned him down—which she probably would—he'd feel worse than he already did. "Maybe I won't," he added, just in case.

"If Mr. Galbini decides to stay longer, please invite him to stay here with us."

"That's not necessary, ma'am." Peter couldn't quite imagine Vince in a house full of orphans. But it was big of Mariah to offer the invitation. "Thank you, though."

"You're welcome," she said with a soft smile.

Still, the raw undercurrent of concern hung in the air. For some reason, she didn't trust Vince, but Peter did. He had to. Vince offered hope. If Peter did this job right, maybe Vince's boss would hire him to do more work. More work meant more income. He could help out Hendrick and Mariah. If there was enough work, maybe he could teach a couple of the older orphans to help out. And if the work included upholstery... The thought of working with Minnie made any risk worthwhile.

Today, she'd come to see him. In all the years he'd known Minnie, she'd never set foot in the garage. Nor had she come to Constance House. She barely acknowledged him at church. In school, she'd made faces at him, probably because he'd played tricks on her. She constantly pointed out that she was four months older than him—or at least she thought she was. He'd never told anyone that he'd lied about his age. But today she'd come to the garage to see him. And she'd complimented his woodworking. Maybe he stood a chance. Maybe she'd even agree to go to the church supper with him.

Winning over Minnie Fox would take effort. Asking her to help with the upholstery might be a good start. He'd find her first thing in the morning, before the dress shop opened. He fingered the hundred-dollar bill in his pocket. Maybe that would catch her attention.

"Cut it just like this." Minnie pointed to the picture on the cover of *Photoplay* and settled onto the chair in front of the cracked wall mirror. The silver beneath the glass had been scratched and tarnished years ago, so her reflection looked wavy.

Jen gathered a handful of Minnie's long hair and snapped open the shears. "Are you sure?"

The sound of the shears made Minnie hesitate. Her hair had always been long. This was a big step. She gripped the magazine and squeezed. After Ruth and Sam's devastating news that the clothing company hadn't bought her designs, this family could use a change. If short hair brought fame to moving-picture actresses, it could change her life, too. Maybe one day, she would step on the stage to grand applause. Wouldn't that make everyone take note?

She took a deep breath. "I'm ready, but make it quick."

Instead of snipping, Jen hesitated. "Mother will have a conniption. You know how she says that you have her hair."

"Which she always wears up so no one can see it."

"And that she thinks bobbed hair is boyish and a symbol of the 'degradation of our country's youth.'" Jen perfectly mimicked their mother's tone of voice.

In spite of her nerves, Minnie laughed. "I'd hate to become a symbol."

"Of the entire country," Jen snorted. "As if anyone in Pearlman has anything to do with the rest of the world.

We're so far removed from places like New York and Hollywood that it takes years for trends to reach us."

That brought a troubling thought. "Would a newcomer think I look silly?"

"A newcomer? Such as that man driving the Pierce-Arrow?"

"You know what kind of car it is?" Minnie marveled at her sister's knowledge of all things mechanical.

"Of course, but that's not the point. Was he handsome?"

Minnie hedged, "I didn't get a good look at him, but he sure had a nice suit. Did you see those gold cuff links?"

"Who could miss them?"

"Are you thinking what I am? Could he be another Mr. Cornelius?" A year ago, nurses at the Battle Creek Sanitarium had told them the story of a wealthy patient, Mr. Cornelius, who fell in love with a nurse and whisked her away to a life of ease. Ever since, the sisters had clung to the hope that just such a philanthropist would give their father the lifesaving treatment he needed.

"If not Mr. Cornelius," Jen said, "then surely Mr. Rothenburg."

After the sisters had hatched the idea to help each other marry wealthy men, their older sister, Ruth, had literally stumbled into department-store heir Sam Rothenburg and ended up marrying him.

"But Sam didn't turn out to be any help," Minnie pointed out. "Instead of owning a business empire, they run the dress shop and live across the hallway."

"They're in love. Ruthie says that's most important of all."

"I suppose so." Minnie folded up her hair so it was jaw length. "I just hope Vince likes short hair."

"Vince?"

"That's the man's name."

"Then you met him."

"No," Minnie had to admit. "Peter told me his name. They're friends."

"I didn't know that Peter had any friends from out of town. I mean, this Vince doesn't look like the kind of guy who would work at an orphanage."

"I think he did. Peter said something about Vince teaching him carpentry."

"Huh. Doesn't look like a carpenter, either, not with a suit like that."

"I know." Minnie sighed. "He's a mystery. Isn't that exciting?"

"Maybe for you." Jen snapped the shears again. "So, do you want to make sure he likes short hair before we do this?"

"Stop stalling." Minnie squared her shoulders and gripped the seat of the battered oak chair. "I'm ready. Do it now."

Jen grabbed a clump of Minnie's hair and hacked through it. Fourteen inches of dark blond hair dropped to the floor.

Minnie gasped at the jagged gap and instinctively clapped her hands to her head.

"Are you all right?" Jen asked.

Minnie nodded while trying to stifle the tears. "It's just that I've never had it cut before. Not really. Not like this. It looks so—" she searched for a word that wouldn't offend Jen "—peculiar."

"No turning back now, sis." Jen snapped the shears in front of Minnie's face. "Unless you want to walk around with a hunk of hair missing. I'll tell you right now that no guy is going to fall for you looking like this."

"Oh, no-o-o," Minnie wailed.

"You want me to stop?"

"No." Minnie moved her hands from her hair to her eyes. She couldn't watch. "Cut it all. Now."

Jen snipped and snipped until Minnie feared she wouldn't have any hair left at all. What had she been thinking? Jen had cut her own hair so short that Mother had dropped into a chair speechless when she saw it. Now Minnie would look just as bad, and Vince would never notice her. Not in a good way. She'd have to wear a hat until autumn.

"All right." Jen whisked the towel off Minnie's shoulders. "I'm done."

"Do I have anything left?"

"Just enough."

That didn't make Minnie feel any better. She peeked through her fingers. "Oh, Jen." She dropped her hands and jumped to her feet to get a better look. "It's gorgeous. Absolutely perfect."

Her head—indeed her whole body—felt lighter, as if she could float off the floor. She cupped the soft ends of her hair where it caressed her jaw. The waves in her hair had turned to loose curls, creating a soft bob. She looked just like the picture on the cover of *Photoplay*.

Jen tossed the shears onto the dresser. "Glad you like it. Hope your guy likes it, too."

Minnie grinned. "He's not my guy yet. But after he sees me, he might be."

"Oh? He's still in town?"

"He'll be back on Saturday."

"Then you have four days to get used to your new hairstyle," Jen said as she left the bedroom. "I'm getting a cup of tea. Want one?"

Minnie shook her head.

Four days. She had to wait four whole days. It might as well be an eternity. Between now and then, Minnie would have to clean houses and work her hands raw getting

Mrs. Neidecker's house ready for the Valentine's Day Ball. Everyone would stare at her at tomorrow night's church supper or even on the street. Kate would probably make a snide remark.

The waiting would be dreadful, but she could bear it if Vince liked her. Saturday! Between now and then, he might decide not to return at all. She couldn't wait. Peter said Vince was staying the night. There was only one place to stay in Pearlman—Terchie's boardinghouse. She could meet him there. But to do that, she would need an excuse. An unmarried girl simply did not go to a boardinghouse alone to talk to a man.

She tapped a finger against her lips and pondered the possibilities. Her gaze wandered over her dresser. Inside the top drawer she'd hidden the face powder and lipstick she'd bought earlier. On top sat the old bottles she'd collected as a child and the talcum powder Mother gave her for Christmas last year. On the wall she'd tacked a calendar that kept track of where she worked each day of the month. Of course! She cleaned houses. She could go to the boardinghouse at breakfast time and ask Mrs. Terchie if she needed help. If Peter's friend was still there, he'd see her.

She'd make sure of it.

Chapter Three

The next morning, Peter left Constance House before the sun rose. Mariah's reaction to Vince's appearance still puzzled him. Sleeping on it hadn't helped, but the icy predawn air cleared his mind. Vince had changed since Mariah knew him. He'd done well and wanted to spread the wealth. Why not accept his generosity? The income would help everyone. He might even be able to take the older boys off Mariah's hands after school and teach them carpentry. Best of all, Minnie's eyes would light up when he offered her the job.

The sun rose late this time of year. At seven o'clock, it barely grayed the horizon. Peter jammed his hands into his coat pockets and hunched his shoulders against the bone-deep cold. Each breath rose in a white cloud, illuminated by the lights brightening the windows of the houses and businesses he passed.

Smelled like snow.

Peter had always been able to sense bad weather. A storm was coming, sure enough. After talking to Minnie, he oughta warn Vince. That car of his might cost a fortune, but it could get just as stuck as a rusty old Model T.

By the time Peter passed the drugstore, he couldn't feel

his toes. He needed a new pair of work boots, but they would cost his entire savings. Some things were more important than cold feet. Minnie's pa, for example. He'd make do with this old pair as long as he could. A couple strips of rubber from an old tire would bolster the thin soles.

"Good morning, Peter," Pastor Gabe called out as he opened up the church.

"Morning." Pastor Gabe was Mariah's brother. That made him some sort of a relation by marriage. Peter liked Pastor Gabe. He wasn't like most preachers. A regular fellow could understand him, and he didn't traipse around in fancy robes or put on airs. Most times, he dressed no better than Peter, even though his folks had plenty of money. Gabe said God had blessed his family so they could help others. That was why he and Mariah had given so much time and money to the orphanage in New York. That was why she'd opened the one here in Pearlman. Peter remembered them stopping by the New York orphanage almost every day. That was how she'd met Vince. Maybe Pastor Gabe would remember him, too.

"Hey!" Peter hustled across the street. "Do you have a minute?" Even though he was anxious to catch Minnie, he figured he had a minute or two to spare.

"Sure, come on in." Gabe held open the door.

"No, thanks. I got a simple question. You remember Vince Galbini?"

"Sure. He helped out at the orphanage. Good with his hands, if I recall."

Peter was relieved that Pastor Gabe didn't look as concerned as his sister.

Gabe let the door swing shut and tucked his hands in his jacket. "Why do you ask?"

"He showed up yesterday."

"Here? Why would he come to Pearlman?"

"Back when he stopped working at the orphanage, he promised he'd look me up again."

"I remember that. You were disappointed when weeks passed and he didn't show up. I'm glad he finally kept his promise."

Peter wondered if he should tell Pastor Gabe about the job that Vince had offered him. That was what seemed to bother Mariah, but then she was a woman, and women had a way of worrying about things that could drive a man crazy.

"Anything else?" Pastor Gabe stomped his feet. He must be getting cold toes, too.

"Nope." Peter retreated down the church steps. Minnie would be leaving for the dress shop before too long. "I gotta get going. Have a good day."

"You, too."

Peter hustled back across the street, feeling better about his decision to take the job. He fingered the hundred in his pocket. This would impress Minnie. He grinned when he imagined her look of surprise. She'd probably never seen a hundred-dollar bill before. He hadn't, and he sure never dreamed he'd hold one.

After passing the mercantile, he rounded the corner onto the side street. On his right loomed the massive Hutton's Department Store. The Foxes lived across the alley from it. Second one in. Lights glowed warmly in the kitchen window. The curtains were still drawn, so he couldn't see who was up, but he figured the whole family would be eating breakfast about now.

He couldn't show up at the kitchen door. No, a man had to call on a woman at the front door. That meant crossing the street, going around the corner and navigating the short walkway in the dark. This wasn't the rich part of town. Most folks didn't have electricity, and a little town like Pearlman sure didn't have streetlamps like the big city. He hurried, his breath puffing like a steam locomotive. When he reached the walk, he noticed the front windows were dark. What if Minnie's pa was resting in the parlor? He paused, unsure whether to continue, wait a while or go to the kitchen door.

What he wouldn't give to take Minnie to the church supper tonight. She'd sure look fine on his arm. Maybe he could even convince her to wear her hair loose, instead of all pulled up like she wore it when she was cleaning houses. Peter liked long hair on a woman, and no one had prettier hair than Minnie. The color reminded him of toffee, all warm and sweet and inviting. In the summer, streaks of gold ran through it like shining ribbons. It floated in gentle waves, a little curlier near her temples. Perfect.

He looked up at the moonless sky and dreamed of taking her to the supper. Ma would smile. She liked Minnie and made little comments suggesting they were meant for each other. Peter liked to see his foster mother smile. She was the kindest woman he'd ever met.

While he daydreamed at the gate, the front door of the house opened and a slender female slipped out. Dawn's gray light only silhouetted her, but he'd recognize that figure anywhere. His pulse accelerated as he stepped forward to greet Minnie.

She bounced down the steps, and he halted in confusion.

This woman had bobbed hair. It couldn't be Minnie. Only Jen had short hair, and it wasn't bobbed. Ruth always wore her hair back in a bun, as did their mother. No other women lived there. Then who on earth was leaving their house so early in the morning?

Minnie almost died of fright when a towering man approached her out of the dark. Though thin, he was big enough to overcome her. Her shriek trumpeted through the still-morning air, but was it loud enough for her mother and sister to hear it all the way back in the kitchen?

"Keep away," she warned, raising her fists.

"It's me. Peter."

"Peter?" She dropped her hands, but her pulse still raced, fear turning to anger. "You frightened me out of my wits. Why are you skulking around in the dark?"

"Sorry." He toed the ground, suddenly getting all bashful. "Didn't mean to scare you. Just wanted to talk."

"Talk? At this hour? In the dark?" Oh, that guy could get on her nerves. Of all the rotten timing. Why did he have to show up now, when she was on her way to see Vince? She sure didn't want Peter following her to the boardinghouse. Neither could she wait. Vince might leave at first light. Maybe sooner. She tapped her toe. "Well, say what you came to say. I can't wait all day."

"What do you got going on that's so important?"

She crossed her arms. "It's none of your business."

"Maybe it is. A lady doesn't go sneaking out of her house in the dark."

"It's not exactly dark, in case you happened to notice." She tossed her head, delighting in the carefree swing of her new bob, and pushed past him. "Besides, it's my house. I'm hardly sneaking out of it. I have things to do."

He quickly caught up and matched her stride. "Are you going to work?"

Minnie didn't want to lie, but she couldn't have him following along after her, either. "Where I go and what I do is none of your business."

"Then you're not going to work." He kept pace with her. "If you're fetching something from the drugstore, I can help carry it."

Fiddlesticks. Was he going to follow her the whole way?

She couldn't very well impress Vince with Peter hanging on behind her. Minnie gritted her teeth and quickened her pace. "I'm not going to the drugstore."

That had to be obvious, since they'd already passed Terchie's boardinghouse. She'd have to double back once she shook Peter. If she could shake him. This street didn't have many businesses, just Terchie's and the cinema. The movie house wouldn't open for hours and hours. She could pretend to head for the parsonage, which she cleaned on Saturdays, except it was Wednesday. Moreover, Peter would know she wasn't supposed to go there, since he was some sort of relation to Pastor Gabe.

"So, where are you going?" Peter asked. "The flight school's not open."

"I know that." She halted and planted her hands on her hips. "Don't you have somewhere to go, Peter Simmons? Like the garage?"

He shrugged, hands in pockets. "Got some time yet." He shot her a glance. "Don't you have to open the shop?"

"Ruth and Sam do that." She pulled her coat closed at the neck and fastened the top button. Now that she was standing still, the frigid cold seeped into her bones. She had worn her Sunday gloves, and her fingers were starting to ache.

Back a block, the side windows of the boardinghouse reflected the crimson clouds on the horizon. That light also revealed the sleek Pierce-Arrow dusted with frost. Vince was still here. If Peter would just leave her alone, she could catch him before he left.

But Peter was staring at her as if she had a dab of egg yolk stuck on her face.

She glared back. "What's wrong?"

His Adam's apple bobbed. "Your hair. Don't like short hair. But it's all right."

"Oh. Is that all?" She didn't know why he talked all choppy around her, but it was getting annoying. "Is that why you were standing at our gate?" Impossible. Jen had cut her hair last night. Only the family had seen it. Mother had gasped and fanned herself, but at least she didn't faint. Ruth had shaken her head. Tears had risen in Daddy's eyes, but he'd still told her she looked beautiful.

"Uh, no," Peter muttered.

"Then why?"

He showed no inclination to answer, which only perturbed her more.

"I don't have all day," she snapped. "I need to get going." Unfortunately she couldn't walk to the boarding-house with Peter glued to her side. Maybe if she headed toward the dress shop, he'd go to the garage. Both businesses were located back in the direction from which they'd come.

Since he made no move to do anything, she trudged back through the ankle-deep snow, regretting that she'd decided to wear her good shoes rather than boots.

Naturally, he followed. "Me, too. I got to catch up with Vince before he leaves Terchie's."

Minnie growled with frustration. Now she'd never get to see Vince alone. She plodded forward, Vince's car in her sights. Smoke curled from the boardinghouse's chimney. Breakfast would be under way by now, with everyone gathered around the table. She supposed her chances of catching Vince alone were slim anyway. Maybe she ought to go there with Peter. It would ensure she actually saw Vince and not just Terchie.

"What a coincidence." She forced a laugh. "I was on my way to ask Terchie if she was hiring."

Peter's brow pinched in dismay. "You're looking for another job? Things not going well at the shop?"

Minnie wasn't about to tell him the troubles they faced.

He couldn't help. He didn't have any more money than they did. Maybe less. "Just looking for a little extra spending money. Why don't we go there together? You know, take care of two things with one visit."

He frowned. "I suppose."

But he didn't sound too happy about it.

What was Minnie up to? Whatever it was, she wasn't giving Peter a chance to ask the questions he needed to ask her. Why did it have to be so tough to talk to a gal? He wouldn't have a bit of trouble asking her older sister to sew up some seat upholstery, but around Minnie his tongue got all tied, probably because he'd been daydreaming about taking her to the church supper. He wanted to. So bad his gut knotted up tighter than an engine without oil. Was any gal worth this much agony?

He took a quick peek at her walking beside him up the boardinghouse walkway. My, she looked fine, even with short hair. He'd been pretty near shocked to death when he caught sight of what she'd done, but in the daylight, it didn't look so bad. The face powder and red lips, on the other hand, made her look cheap.

"Why'd you go putting that stuff on your face?"

Her jaw tensed, but he saw her blush under the powder. She jutted out her chin. "A girl has to look professional."

"I suppose." But the only profession he'd seen wearing that kind of stuff wasn't one that nice girls went into. "I thought you were just looking for a cleaning job."

"It's not like working in a private home. In the boardinghouse, people will see me."

That was when it dawned on him. She'd worn the powder to attract someone's attention. She hadn't stopped by the garage yesterday to see him. She wanted to know about Vince. Now he'd gone and committed to bringing the two of them face-to-face. Peter clenched his fists. If Vince looked at her wrong even once, he'd punch the man out, friend or not. That'd put an end to the job offer, but no money was worth a woman's honor.

He should turn around and let Vince head off into bad weather. With the sun peeking over the horizon, he'd have a tough time convincing the man that a storm was on its way anyhow. Minnie would think he was plumb crazy if he started talkin' about snowstorms. He couldn't let her go to the boardinghouse alone, though. It wasn't proper. So he trudged along, trying to think of something else to ask Vince.

They reached the porch. He'd better come up with another plan and quick.

Minnie climbed the steps ahead of him and stopped at the front door. "Are you coming? I thought you wanted to talk to your friend."

He dragged himself up the steps like an old man.

Minnie rolled her eyes, crossed her arms and tapped her toe. "I'm waiting."

When he finally got to the door, she stood aside. No door had ever looked so imposing. Peter licked his lips.

"Well, aren't you going to knock?" Minnie said.

He glanced at her. That was a mistake. His stomach lurched, and the last glimmer of thought exited his brain.

"Guess I'll have to do it," she huffed, reaching around him to rap the brass knocker three times.

The sound of the knocker against the wooden door gave Peter an idea. He could ask Vince if he wanted the lower compartment to hinge or lock. Better yet, he could then ask Minnie about doing the upholstery.

The door opened, and Terchie greeted them, her plump cheeks rosy and her portly figure topped with a flour-dusted apron.

"I'm looking for Vince," Peter said. At the woman's blank stare, he added, "Mr. Galbini."

"Oh, the Italian fellow. Most folks are eating breakfast," the cheerful proprietress responded. "Come on in. I'll see if he's in the dining room."

Only after Peter stepped into the warmth of the parlor did he realize how cold he'd gotten. While he waited, he held his hands over the steam radiator and noticed Minnie looking longingly at it.

He stepped to the side. "There's room for two."

She hurried over and tugged off her thin going-to-church gloves. No wonder her hands were cold. Those dainty things couldn't warm a mouse. Moreover, she'd worn shoes instead of boots. Her feet must be frozen.

When she thrust her hands over the radiator, her arm brushed his. Even through his thick coat, he shivered at her touch.

"Thank you," she murmured, eyes fixed firmly on her hands.

Had she felt it, too? Peter took a breath. Now was the perfect time to ask her to the church supper. "I was wondering—" he began.

"Peter!" Vince interrupted. "What you doin' here, old sport?" He clapped Peter's back so hard that he coughed. "See you brought a gal with ya. Howdy, miss."

Minnie blushed and ducked her head.

Peter felt sick. His suspicions were correct. She was sweet on Vince.

"You gonna make introductions, sport?" Vince gripped his shoulder so hard that Peter winced.

Peter supposed he didn't have a choice. "Miss Fox, this is an old, old friend of mine, Mr. Vincent Galbini. Mr. Galbini, this is Miss Fox."

"Buongiorno." Vince threw his arms wide and kissed Minnie on each cheek. "You have a first name, darlin'?"

"Minnie." Her blush deepened to red, and she patted her hair. Little beads of melted snow gleamed like diamonds in the electrical lighting.

"You can call me Vince."

Peter flexed his hands. He wanted to pound sense into Vincent Galbini. Minnie wasn't some floozy who frequented speakeasies and smoked cigarettes. She was a good Christian gal worth more than a hundred of that type of woman.

"You Peter's gal?" Vince asked.

"No!" The rapidity of her reply plunged an icy knife into Peter's gut, but then she darted a shy glance at him and twisted a lock of wavy hair around her index finger, and his pain eased. "We're friends. Good friends."

Good friends might have satisfied Peter a year ago, but now he wanted more. He wanted her to respect him, to want to be with him, maybe even to love him. He sure didn't want her to get tangled up with Vince. Visions of her leaving town in the Pierce-Arrow sucked the air from his lungs. He had to do something to keep her here, close enough to him that she'd forget all about Galbini.

"Minnie's a seamstress," he blurted out.

Galbini's brow lifted. "That so?" He clearly didn't understand what Peter was getting at.

"She can do the upholstery." There, he'd said it.

Vince grinned. "Good. I'm glad to have your gal on board."

His gal. Peter liked the sound of that. He dared to glance at Minnie.

Her brow was drawn in pure fury. Peter stared, speechless. She was supposed to be grateful. She was supposed to like him even more. He was giving her work. Why would that make her angry?

"I can do what?" she demanded, even though she'd heard every word.

"S-s-sew upholstery," Peter stammered, the confidence ebbing out quicker than oil into a drip pan. "For pay."

"You? Pay me? With what?" Her lips thinned as she crossed her arms.

Now he'd gone and done it. In that state, she'd never agree to go to the church supper with him. "Uh…" he croaked.

Vince roared with laughter. "Don't worry, darlin'. The boss is paying."

"The boss?" Minnie looked from Vince to Peter. "Whose boss?"

Vince answered, "Mine, darlin'."

Something like excitement lit her eyes. "Do you work for a motion-picture company?"

"Naw, but I wouldn't put it past Mr. Capone to give that a shot, too."

Capone. The name sounded vaguely familiar, but Peter couldn't quite place it. What he did know was that the bad feeling that'd been hounding him since Vince's arrival got a whole lot worse.

Chapter Four

Peter Simmons had some nerve. Minnie would give him a piece of her mind the moment they were out of Vincent Galbini's earshot. How dare he volunteer her to sew upholstery for some furniture he was making for Vince?

What was he thinking?

She had no idea how to upholster anything, least of all something for the man she was trying to impress. Her family ran a dress shop. They worked with voile and crepe de chine and georgette, not the thick fabrics used by upholsterers. She wasn't even sure their sewing machine could handle the heavier fabric, but she couldn't say that in front of Vince. She had to bite her tongue until she and Peter left the boardinghouse.

He closed the door behind her and followed her down the steps. The moment they reached the walkway, she punched him in the arm.

"Ow!" He rubbed his biceps. "What's that for?"

"For saying I would do something I don't know how to do."

He stared at her blankly.

She glared back. "Sewing."

"You don't know how to sew?"

"I don't know how to upholster furniture."

"Furniture? Who said anything about furniture?"

"You did." Minnie hugged her arms around her midsection to ward against the bitter cold. "Don't tell me you forgot already that you volunteered me to do some upholstery for your friend."

"No, uh—" his neck flushed red "—maybe I should have asked you first."

"Maybe?" She flung her hands into the air and headed back home. "I give up."

He ran to catch up. "Then you won't do it?"

She didn't stop. "Didn't you hear me? I can't upholster furniture."

"But it's not furniture. It's a car seat."

She halted. "A car? How is that any better?"

"You'd just have to fix what's already there. How hard can it be?"

"Much harder. Automobile seats are covered in mohair. It's thick. I don't know how to work with it. I don't think our machines would handle it."

"Uh, actually, they're leather."

"Even worse. Impossible."

"Oh." He cast his gaze down. "I thought maybe you could use the extra money for your pa."

She bit her lip. Her father ought to return to the Battle Creek Sanitarium for treatment, but they couldn't afford it. The family had banked on a ready-made clothing manufacturer buying Ruth's designs. Yesterday's failure set them back. "What car?"

Peter looked up hopefully. "The Pierce-Arrow."

"But Vin—" She caught herself. She oughtn't use his Christian name in public. "Mr. Galbini's car looks new. What would need fixing?"

"Actually, the Pierce-Arrow belongs to Vince's boss."

"Oh." Then Vince wasn't as well-off as he appeared.

"And I'd only need your help if I rip a seam or have to take the upholstery apart in order to make the luggage compartment he wants."

"Oh." This was getting less and less impressive, but if she just had to restitch something, it shouldn't be that difficult. She'd just have to use the existing holes and do it by hand. "That doesn't sound like much of a job. What does it pay?"

He shrugged. "I don't know. It'd depend on what needs to be done. Ten dollars?"

"Ten whole dollars for stitching up some leather?"

"It would have to look good," he added.

That was the problem. "I'm only an apprentice seamstress. You should hire Ruth." She tossed her head, feeling the swing of her short hair, and started back toward home.

Again he hurried after her. "I could ask your sister, but she's so busy with her designs and all that I figured you might have more time."

"Is that the only reason you asked me?" She tried hard to shove away the disappointment.

"No, uh...uh, that's not it." His Adam's apple bobbed above his coat collar. "I think you'd do the best job."

That was about the sweetest thing he'd ever said to her. "I wouldn't, you know. Ruthie is gifted and experienced. I muddle through."

His hazel eyes blazed with surprising intensity. "Don't cut yourself short, Minnie. You can do anything you set your mind to."

Her stomach did a crazy little flip-flop. "I suppose I could try." Then she remembered Ruth's tears last night. "But my sister would do a better job, and she's not too busy." She hesitated, unsure if Ruth would want her defeat known to anyone outside the family, and then decided that Peter was practically family in a convoluted way. His foster brother had married Pastor Gabe's sister. Minnie's oldest sister had married the brother of Pastor Gabe's wife.

She took a deep breath. "Ruth got bad news from New York last night. The company isn't going to buy her designs."

If anything, Peter looked more crestfallen. "Sorry."

Her fingers were getting numb again. "I'll ask Ruthie if she wants to do it."

"I suppose." But his shoulders drooped.

She wasn't waiting around to ask why. "'Bye, then."

After he echoed the farewell, she headed for home while he trudged toward the garage. For some reason, having her work on the car mattered to him. If not for Ruth's tears, Minnie might have snatched at the opportunity, but to keep Vince coming back, the work had to be done right, and Minnie was an amateur next to her sister. Besides, she could always come along whenever Vince was in town. Ruth might need her help. Minnie could carry something for her or hold the leather in place or something.

The kitchen was steamy hot when Minnie stepped inside. She wiped off the face powder and lipstick with a handkerchief and then tugged off her good gloves and shoved them into her coat pocket before her mother saw them.

Mother sat at the table mixing flour into milk and yeast to make bread dough. "You were out early this morning."

"I had something to do." Minnie held her numb fingers near the coal stove's firebox. "Do you want help?"

"I thought you were working in the shop this morning."

Minnie glanced at the clock. "It's not nine o'clock yet."

"You know your sister wants you there before the shop opens."

Minnie sighed. Go here. Do this. Take care of that.

The duties never seemed to end. Already the excitement of Vince's arrival had worn off. Though he'd greeted her in the romantic European fashion and called her *darling,* she didn't feel the flutter of excitement that she'd expected. It was more like…well, like greeting an uncle or older brother. How disappointing. Worse, the flutter had shown up when she least expected it. Why should Peter's statement that she could do anything send her stomach flip-flopping? Why then? Why Peter? He was just a friend, wasn't he?

"Go now." Mother motioned toward the door with flour-covered hands.

Minnie dragged her feet across the room.

"And put on boots," Mother chided. "Your good shoes are for Sunday only." She sighed. "Ask Ruth to trim up that dreadful mop of hair when you get there. It should at least look neat."

Minnie picked up her boots, stiff and dry from sitting near the stove overnight, and sat in the nearest chair. This day was going from bad to worse in a hurry.

She hadn't finished lacing the boots when Ruth pushed open the door, letting in a blast of icy-cold air. Ruth's face glowed pink from the cold, and she stomped the snow off her boots.

"I'm coming," Minnie said, tying off one lace, "as soon as I get my boots on."

Ruth didn't seem to hear her. "We've come to a decision, Mother." Her eyes shone bright.

Mother stopped working the dough. "A decision about what?"

"I promised Sam I'd tell you and Daddy at the same time, but I'll burst if I can't tell someone right away."

Mother rose on shaky legs, her face drawn in concern. "The baby?"

Ruth touched her abdomen. "Fine. Perfectly fine. Nothing's wrong, Mother. In fact, everything's right. We're going to New York!" She let out a squeak, which was about as excited as Ruth ever got.

Mother sank back into her chair. "New York City?"

"Yes. Sam thinks we have a better chance of selling my designs in person. He wants to show them to the clothing-line representatives. You know how persuasive he can be." She paced around the kitchen, more animated than Minnie had ever seen her. "Mariah's parents offered to let us stay with them. The train fare isn't too terribly much, and you and Minnie can run the shop while we're gone."

"Me?" It was Minnie's turn to squeak.

"You know how to do everything," Ruth said, "and Mother will help. Daddy is handling the orders and book-keeping. It'll be a breeze." She turned back to Mother. "Isn't it exciting?"

Mother frowned. "I understand Sam going. His business sense and contacts are essential, but are you sure you should travel, what with the baby and all?"

"Mother, I'm only three months along." Ruth sat down, still coiled with eager excitement. "Where Sam goes, so will I."

Mother pulled a hand away and tugged a handkerchief from her apron pocket. "Like Naomi and Ruth, going to a strange land."

"Don't worry," Ruth said. "We'll be back long before the baby is born. Why, we'll probably return before the end of winter."

Mother managed a feeble smile. "I'll miss you, dear."

"Me, too." Ruth hugged their mother. "There is one thing I need to ask."

Mother pulled away. "What is that?"

Ruth ducked her head. "The fare. We don't quite have enough saved. I wondered if you might loan us the rest."

"You'll have to ask your father."

Ruth hurried off to do just that, but Minnie knew what the answer would be. Daddy would never deny his most talented daughter a chance at her dream. That left Minnie at home and in charge of the shop. The responsibility was enormous.

Mother must have realized that, too, because she gave her a very stern look. "Are you ready to take charge, Miss Wilhelmina?"

Minnie cringed at her full name. Mother only used it when angry or extremely serious. "I guess so."

"Humph," Mother grunted, returning to the bread dough. "We'll see what your father says. This will be an added burden on him." She looked up. "And you'll have to quit your cleaning jobs in order to manage the shop."

Minnie hadn't thought of that. Though she'd longed to stop cleaning houses, quitting those jobs meant less money coming in. They would have to get even more frugal. No more cherry sodas or magazines. No frivolous purchases at all, unless she took the job that Peter had offered. Ruth couldn't do it. Ten dollars would buy a lot of food. She would have to accept the offer—and pray that Vince found her so enchanting that he overlooked the poor workmanship.

Peter stepped away from Mr. Kensington's Packard and scratched his head. His plan had gone wrong somehow. Now he was stuck working with Ruth instead of Minnie. Worse, Minnie had tittered and giggled at everything Vince said. It was disgusting. What could she see in Vince? He must be ten years older than her. Then again, she'd been fascinated by Reggie Landers, and he was years older than her, too. After that crush ended, he thought she would come to her senses. Apparently not. It seemed that anyone with a fancy suit caught her eye, but not a hardworking man.

He tossed the wrench into his toolbox and wiped his forehead with a rag. Kensington wanted his car by the end of the day, but he couldn't seem to concentrate. The morning's efforts had amounted to removing two valves and picking up the wrong-size wrenches time after time. At this rate, he'd never finish the job on time.

Concentrate. By fixing his attention on the tools, he managed to pick out the proper wrench this time. It slipped from his damp, greasy fingers and clattered to the floor. He wiped his hands on the rag and picked up the wrench.

Just thinking about Minnie made him sweat. She'd twisted things around so much this morning that he'd plumb forgot he wanted to ask her to the church supper tonight. Now he'd have to sit alone with the rest of the family. Hendrick had Mariah. Anna had Brandon. Even Ma Simmons had memories of her beloved late husband. He could only dream of having a gal to love, but he wanted just one. Minnie. He'd fallen for her the moment he set eyes on her, but she'd never given him the time of day. One chance. That was all he wanted. Just one chance.

"Peter?"

The most precious voice in the whole world yanked him out of misery and into a firestorm of hope. "Minnie. What are you doing here?"

She stood in the doorway between the office and the shop, looking so pretty he couldn't rip his gaze from her. From the red plaid skirt to the matching hat, she could warm up the coldest heart. The snow dusting her shoulders and hat made her even more beautiful. He wiped his brow again.

"You busy?" Her gaze dropped to the floor, her boots dripping with melting snow.

"Not at all."

She looked up hopefully. "I was wondering if you might reconsider."

Peter quickly thought through what she might mean and came up empty. "Reconsider?"

"Hiring me." She shrugged and tilted her head in that way of hers that drove him crazy. "Instead of Ruth. She's going to New York, you see, and can't do the upholstering that you wanted. But, if you'd give me a chance, I'd like to try."

Peter's heart nearly stopped. She wanted to work with him. His plan wasn't dead at all.

She dropped her gaze. "I understand. You want someone experienced to help out your friend. Here I went and said I didn't know how to do it and would do a horrible job and all—"

"All right." He had to cut her off before she dug a bigger hole.

Her wide-eyed wonder shot an arrow straight into his heart. "You mean it? I can help?"

"Yeah." Then a thought occurred to him. If she was willing to work with him, maybe she would agree to a little more. "Maybe you can come to the church supper with me."

She blinked. "Tonight?"

"Yeah. We can, you know, talk things over."

"Oh. We can't do that now?"

Peter examined the wrench in his hands. "I suppose, but I'm pretty busy."

"Oh. But it's Ruth's last night home, and we all want to be together. Daddy can't go out, especially not in this heavy snow."

Peter could have kicked himself. "I forgot."

"You couldn't know." Her quick smile dazzled him. "I'll stop by later, then. Your friend is bringing the car on Saturday?"

He nodded, unable to think of a word to say.

"Saturday, then." She gave him a little wave before waltzing through the office and out of the building.

Peter watched her go, unable to move a muscle and not entirely sure what had just happened except that she wanted to work with him.

He finally had a chance.

Chapter Five

The rest of the week flew by in a flurry of activity. Between Ruth and Sam leaving Thursday morning and two clients wanting last-minute alterations on their ball gowns for Friday night's Valentine's Day Ball, Minnie didn't have time to think. She also forgot to notify Mrs. Neidecker that she was giving up her job while Ruth was gone and thus had to serve punch at the ball.

By Saturday morning, she was exhausted.

"Get up, get up," an annoyingly cheerful Jen called out. "It's another gorgeous day."

Minnie pulled the covers over her head. "It's dark out."

"I can see the moon and the stars. That means sunshine. Mr. Hunter says that sunny days and cold nights make the airfield perfect for flying. He wants to test out the new cold-weather engine they've been designing over at the factory. It's got a special cowling—"

"Sorry I asked." Minnie hadn't understood a word her sister just said. Honestly, she couldn't fathom how any woman could be the slightest bit interested in mechanical things. She had to practically hold her breath inside the motor garage.

"Better get moving. You have to open the shop this morning."

"You can do it," Minnie moaned. "Please?"

"Not a chance. I want to be at the airfield at first light. That's when the Hunters are testing the motor. If it works, they're going to start planning for the run to the North Pole." Jen whistled "Ain't We Got Fun?" as she headed out of the room and downstairs to the kitchen.

Peace at last. Minnie breathed in the quiet and relaxed. Just a few more minutes. She reveled in the warm blanket cocoon. If only she could stay here all day. If only she could rest a little bit longer.

"Minnie!"

At Mother's command, Minnie shot up. "I'm coming." She rubbed her eyes.

Mother set a lit lamp on her dresser. "The Saturday after the ball is often busy, what with the guests and all the revelry the night before. Someone always needs a repair. Hems torn out, underarms ripped and who knows what. It's different every year. And now that Ruth and Sam have added cleaning, it's sure to be busy. Guests could come pouring in."

"Guests." That woke her up. Saturday meant Vince would return. "What time is it?"

"Eight o'clock. I let you sleep as late as I could."

"Eight o'clock?" Minnie scurried out of bed. She had less than an hour to dress and do her hair and eat breakfast. How could she ever look presentable in that amount of time, especially when she couldn't put on the face powder and lipstick until she reached the shop?

"The oatmeal is ready," Mother said as she headed downstairs.

Minnie squinted at her reflection in the wall mirror. She

looked dreadful. Hair stuck out every which way, and blue half-moons circled under her puffy eyes.

She splashed cold water on her face and pressed a damp cloth to her eyes.

Though Vince Galbini hadn't exactly excited her at their first meeting, maybe this time would go better. He was older than she'd imagined, and that crooked, flattened nose made him look more like a prizefighter than a movie star, but he was definitely on his way up, and that had to be worth something. Though he didn't wear a wedding band, she couldn't be certain he was unmarried. Today, she'd unearth the truth on that subject.

As she dressed, her energy returned. With Vince's return came the start of her new job. She hadn't exactly told Mother or Daddy yet, but they'd understand. They both liked Peter. They might not care that she would have to work evenings at the garage.

She tugged a brush through her wavy hair. Maybe she wouldn't have to tell Mother or Daddy about the job. She could simply present them with her wages after she finished. Wouldn't that be a wonderful surprise? She tucked the face powder and lip color into her handbag and headed for the stairs.

"Minnie?" Daddy's soft voice drew her to a halt. He leaned on a cane in the doorway to his bedroom.

"Daddy, you shouldn't be up."

After the seizure last summer, which Doc Stevens attributed to his weak heart, he spent most of his time in his room. Mother brought his meals there, and Ruthie gave him the receipts at the end of each day so he could do the bookwork.

He waved off her concern. "I'm fine." But he leaned against the door frame.

"Let me help you back to bed."

He managed a grin. "I'm not an invalid quite yet."

"Oh, Daddy. I didn't mean that."

"I just wanted you to know how proud I am of you." His blue eyes misted. "How quickly the years pass. I remember holding you shortly after you were born, and now you've grown into a fine, responsible woman."

Minnie clutched her handbag to her midsection and averted her gaze. The cosmetics secreted inside burned like hot coals.

"How pretty you are," he said softly. "I like your hair. It reminds me of the style worn by Mariah Simmons."

She pushed the unruly locks behind her left ear. "I suppose it is similar."

"She's a fine woman. You could do worse than to emulate her."

Minnie kept her head down so he didn't see the guilt. She wasn't emulating Mariah or anyone else that Daddy would consider respectable.

"Give me a hug before you go to work," he said.

She set down her handbag and held on to his thin shoulders as he squeezed her tight.

He tapped a finger to her chin. "Do good work, my little princess, and don't be in too much of a hurry to grow up."

"All right, Daddy." He'd meant to encourage her, yet as she picked up her handbag, she felt terrible.

"I could use some advice," Peter admitted to Hendrick once they were alone at the breakfast table.

Mariah had left to get the children ready for a toboggan outing at the hill in the park. Ordinarily, Hendrick would help, but he was headed to the airfield for the test of the new engine. Instead, Pastor Gabe and his wife were joining Mariah for the sledding expedition. Judging from the disputes and shrieking already under way, the three adults would have their hands full, especially when Pastor Gabe's two children were added to the mix.

Hendrick eyed him solemnly. "Advice on what?"

Peter squirmed. "Women."

"Ah, women." Hendrick dug into his eggs with more fervor. "Mariah might be a better person to ask. Or Anna."

"No. I want a guy's perspective." Even though Peter had gotten closer to his foster brother over the years, he still felt awkward asking such a personal question.

"All right, but I warn you I don't have a lot of experience."

"You caught Mariah's attention."

Hendrick shrugged. "That was more than likely God's doing. I said a lot of dumb things around her."

"You did?" Peter was feeling better already.

"Afraid so. I even left her."

"I remember that. You went to New York, right?"

"Long Island. Dumbest thing I ever done." Every once in a while Hendrick got his grammar wrong, just like Peter. "By the time I realized how much I missed her, I figured I'd blown my chances."

"But you didn't."

Hendrick grinned. "She's a forgiving woman. But enough of me. What's your question?"

Peter looked at his cold scrambled eggs and half-eaten slice of bread. "Just wondering how a guy can impress a gal."

"Anyone in particular?"

That was the part that made Peter squirm. "Minnie Fox."

"I see." Hendrick scooped up the last of his eggs, and Peter had to wait for him to finish. "She's pretty young. What? Eighteen?"

"Almost nineteen."

"Humph. Same age as you. Don't worry. You've got plenty of time. I didn't get married until I was twenty-eight. Wait it out."

That didn't help, especially since Peter was a bit older than he'd claimed to be. "But she's looking at every other guy."

Hendrick quirked an eyebrow. "Anyone in particular?"

"Vince." Peter's shoulders drooped. "He's your age at least. Why would she think he's so great?"

"Because he's new. Give her time. The newness will wear off. Then you mosey up and show her who she really should be looking at."

Peter frowned. "How?"

"Like I said, you should probably ask a lady." He must have spotted Mariah, because he called out to her.

She ducked a head into the kitchen, looking rather frazzled. "What is it?"

"What do women want from a guy?" Hendrick said.

Peter slumped down in his chair and shoveled the cold eggs into his mouth as fast as he could.

"Hendrick," she said, "what a time to ask something like that. I have children running around everywhere."

"Just thought you might shed a little light on the subject for Peter."

Why did Hendrick have to go and name him?

"Peter? Oh," Mariah said, "be yourself. You're already a special young man. Any girl with half her wits can see that." Then she hurried off to break up a row over mittens.

"I see what you mean," Hendrick said. "She wasn't much help."

Peter shook his head, seeing as his mouth was jammed so full of eggs that he couldn't even figure out how to swallow them. He reached for his cup of tea, now cooled to lukewarm.

Hendrick leaned back and folded his hands across his chest, like a sage elder. "If you ask me, a woman likes a man to make her feel special. Tell her she's beautiful."

Already tried it. With the tea, Peter managed to choke down part of the eggs.

"You could dress nice," Hendrick added.

Peter gave him a look of disgust. How could he dress nice when his hands and arms were covered with grease most of the time? Today, Vince was going to show up. Knowing him, he'd have on that nice suit of his. Next to Vince, Peter looked like nothing, especially to a girl who dreamed of meeting a moving-picture actor. With his last swig of tea, he swallowed the rest of the eggs.

It was hopeless. He'd never dazzle Minnie. Not in a million years.

Though Minnie kept a lookout from the dress shop all day, she never saw the Pierce-Arrow cruise through town. She had intended to walk down to the motor garage as soon as Jen showed up, but her sister never did arrive. Instead, the post-ball customers kept her busy with requests for repairs and cleaning.

When she finally closed the shop at five o'clock, she headed directly for the garage with the envelope containing the day's receipts and orders tucked in her coat pocket. Soon enough she saw the Pierce-Arrow in the first bay. Vince and Peter hovered near the front end, discussing something.

Minnie pinched her cheeks for color and pressed her lips together, hoping the lipstick hadn't bled. Her pulse thrummed as she crossed the street and stepped into the garage office.

"Got one that'll fit?" Vince asked from the work area.

Minnie wrinkled her nose at the pungent combination

of grease and cigarette smoke. She instinctively opened her handbag to fetch a handkerchief to place over her nose and then changed her mind. It might muss her face powder, and it certainly wouldn't impress anyone.

So instead she forced a smile and stepped boldly through the door into the work area. "I'm here."

Both men stopped talking to look at her.

Her jaw dropped. "What happened?" Their trousers were wet and muddy.

"Flat tire," Peter said.

The front passenger's side was balanced on a jack, and the punctured tire lay on the floor.

"I see." She couldn't think of anything else to say.

Vince's lips curved into a smile. "Well, hello, darlin'. You're shore a sight for sore eyes."

For some reason, his attention made her feel awkward and, well, vulnerable. She looked to Peter. "I thought maybe you'd want to go over what I need to do."

His hazel eyes looked black in the low light. "Don't know yet if I'll need your help. If I do, I'll talk to you later. You might as well go home."

She couldn't leave now, not before she knew for certain that Vince wasn't married. She looked around for an excuse to stay.

"But I wanted to look at the car. I haven't had a good chance to see it yet."

"Nice one, ain't it?" Vince said. "Why don't I show you around?" He tossed his cigarette butt to the floor and ground it out with the heel of his shoe.

Everything about him made her cringe, and she clutched the handbag to her chest, uncertain if she should accept the offer or not.

"I can do it." Peter stepped in front of his friend and opened the rear door.

What a relief! Minnie gave him a smile of gratitude and tried to listen as he explained what he planned to do with the rear seat.

"It'll have to come out while I make the compartment," Peter said.

"What are you going to use?" Minnie asked. "Metal?"

"Wood," Vince interjected. "Wood is quieter than metal."

Minnie stuck her head in the car and looked around the spacious rear area until she could visualize the project. The seat cushion was covered in leather, just like Peter said.

"How does the cushion come out?" she asked.

Peter crawled in the other side and showed her how to lift it off the wooden pegs securing it in place. His hands brushed hers, and that crazy flip-flop happened again in her stomach. She looked at him, and his gaze met hers.

"You sure look pretty tonight," he said, kind of low, as if he didn't want his friend to hear. "Want to sit with me at church tomorrow?"

Sit with him? Why did he always have to turn friendship into something more? She jerked away from him and hit her head on the door frame. "Ouch!"

"Careful there, darlin'," Vince said.

His hands gripped her shoulders, but his touch didn't have the same effect as Peter's. It felt wrong. Just plain wrong.

"I'm fine." She shook him off and stuck her head back in the car. Everything was spinning a little, and she had to hold on to the seat to get her balance.

"You sure you're all right?" Peter looked concerned.

"I said I'm fine." She ran her hands over the leather upholstery. Anything to not think about what had just happened. The plan was to find a beau who could help out her family. Peter Simmons didn't fit that plan, so why was she reacting like this? That was what made her head spin, not clunking into the door frame. She took a deep breath and concentrated on the seat.

An idea had started to wiggle into her head until Peter mucked it up by asking her to sit with him at church. It had to do with the seat. She stared at it until the idea returned. "That's it."

"That's what?" Peter asked.

She gave him a grin of triumph. "If Mr. Galbini's boss doesn't want the luggage to make noise, we need to cushion the compartment."

"How?"

She got out of the car, her mind racing over the details. "We could pad it, like the seats. That would make it extra quiet."

"But you'd lose space," Peter countered.

"Not if I keep the padding thin, like a layer of felt."

Galbini nodded. "Good idea, doll."

The endearments grated on her nerves, but extra work would mean extra pay. She could start at once, if Galbini agreed to the proposal and Peter went along with it. She didn't dare look at Peter, though, or her emotions would overtake sense again. This was a business deal she didn't want to lose. "It would cost more."

Galbini laughed. "Cost ain't a problem. Quality's what the boss wants."

"Your boss must be rich," she said, impressed.

Galbini grinned. "Rich don't come close ta the truth."

"Really?" Maybe if Mr. Galbini wasn't the one for her, his boss was. She closed her eyes and imagined the celebrities and posh nightclubs she'd read about in the magazines.

"Honest." Galbini put a hand over his heart.

"Wow. Wonder if I'll ever meet him."

"Why would you meet him?" Peter snapped. "I'm sure

he's too busy with his business and family to come to Pearlman."

"True," Galbini said.

Oh, dear. Naturally Mr. Galbini's boss was married and had children. What had she been thinking?

Peter wasn't done. "Besides, money doesn't make the man. Look at Hendrick. Your pa. They're the best."

The joy of the moment vanished as Minnie remembered her father's words to her this morning and how heavily he'd leaned on his cane. She bit her lip to stop any tears, but nothing could prevent the lump from forming in her throat. Daddy. He'd asked her to act her age, yet she'd gone and put cosmetics on her face and pursued an older man that she didn't even like. What would Daddy think of her if he knew? He'd be so disappointed. So terribly disappointed.

"Minnie?" Peter was looking at her strangely. "Is something wrong?"

She backed away, unable to bring a word to her lips.

"Don't get shy on me, doll." Galbini's grin mocked her.

In that moment, she felt small and weak and foolish. Nothing like a motion-picture star. She turned and ran. Tears blurred her vision before she'd cleared the office.

The icy air slapped her. Snow drifted down from the deep blue sky. Not wanting to meet up with anyone, she headed down the alley. A trash can stood behind the department store. Already, two inches of snow blanketed its cover. Minnie brushed off the fluffy snow and lifted the lid. She then opened her handbag and threw the face powder and lipstick away. Taking her handkerchief from her coat pocket, she rubbed the cosmetics off her face. She'd made such a fool of herself. Such a fool.

She let the cold air calm her. Melting snowflakes blended with the tears, washing her cheeks clean. Already the kitchen window glowed, illuminating the swirling snow. Mother would have supper ready. Minnie blew her nose and took a deep breath, finally ready to go home.

The snow crunched underfoot as she crossed the alley and navigated the backyard in the near darkness. As she stepped inside, her mother raced toward her and enveloped her in a hug.

"I'm so relieved you're all right."

"Of course I'm all right." Minnie extricated herself from the hug. "Why wouldn't I be?"

"When Jen went to help you close the shop and found you gone, we thought you'd be here any minute. Do you realize how late it is?"

Minnie looked at the clock. "After six? How could it be that late?"

"At first we wondered if you forgot it was Saturday and tried to take the receipts to the bank. When you still didn't return, I sent Jen to the drugstore, in case you went for a soda...."

Minnie didn't hear anything past *receipts*. She patted her coat pocket. The envelope wasn't there. "The receipts!"

Her mind tumbled over all the places she'd been. Main Street, the garage, the alley. Had she accidentally lost the envelope when she got out her handkerchief?

"What about the receipts, dear?"

Minnie couldn't explain. Bad enough she'd gone against her parents' wishes by wearing cosmetics, but to lose the day's orders and receipts? That was unforgivable. Her first week on the job, and she'd failed. There must have been fifty dollars in that envelope. The family needed that money badly. Daddy needed it.

Her throat swelled nearly shut. "I need to go back."

"Did you forget them? It'll wait until morning."

Mother didn't understand. Minnie had failed. Failed. And the whole family would suffer.

"No, it won't."

Choking back a sob, Minnie flung open the door and raced outside, but darkness had fallen and the snow fell even thicker. It now reached to her ankles. How on earth would she ever find the envelope now?

Chapter Six

❧

Once Minnie's eye adjusted to the dark, she searched around the trash can and looked inside. She retraced her steps to the garage, which was now closed, and along Main Street. She kicked aside the snow in key areas. No envelope. By the time she returned to the house, she'd gone numb—but not from the cold.

What would she tell Daddy? What would Mother say? They had trusted her. Ruth trusted her. She'd let them down. Once again, she'd failed in the crucial moment.

Past failures replayed in her mind. From dropping the coffee service in the parsonage on Christmas Eve to declaring her affection to an uninterested Reggie Landers, each defeat had chipped away at her confidence. Those gaffes, embarrassing as they were, hadn't impacted her family. Pastor Gabe and Felicity didn't fire her for spilling coffee all over their parlor floor. The hopeless crush on Reggie had only inspired eye-rolling and warnings from her sisters. This was entirely different. For the first time, she'd let her family down.

Minnie sat on the back stoop, letting the snow gather on her hat and coat. Oh, that it could bury her. If only she could run off to a place where money didn't matter and where others didn't suffer for your mistakes, but even storybook characters faced consequences.

She sighed and propped her head in her hands, elbows on knees.

The door cracked open.

"Why are you sitting out in the cold, dearest?" Mother asked.

Minnie couldn't look her mother in the eye. "I'm sorry." Fear strangled her words. This was the moment of judgment. She whispered, "I—I lost the receipts."

"What did you say, dear? I can't hear you. Do come inside." Mother opened the door wide.

Minnie couldn't keep mumbling at the ground. She looked at her mother—dear, loving Mother—and her throat swelled shut. "I—" It came out in a croak.

"Come now," Mother insisted. "We're letting the warm air out."

Minnie had to spit this out. A grown woman admitted her mistakes. She took responsibility, no matter the outcome. Minnie squared her shoulders, though she didn't feel brave at all. "I lost the receipts. I put them in an envelope with the orders and stuck it in my coat pocket, but now it's not there. I retraced my steps, but with the snow I can't find it. Oh, Mother." She started to cry.

Mother stood there a moment before stepping outside and descending the steps.

Minnie braced for the punishment she deserved.

Instead, Mother wrapped her arms around her. "My poor child. My poor, poor baby. These things happen."

The sobs came. Slow at first and then harder and faster.

Mother rubbed her back. "Come inside, dear. You need to get warmed up."

Minnie let her mother guide her up the steps and into the kitchen, where the snow slid off her shoulders.

Jen stopped halfway across the kitchen, plates in hand. "You're making a mess."

"Hush, now, Genevieve," Mother said. "Finish setting the table while your sister dries off and goes to see your father."

"Daddy?" Minnie gasped. "Do I have to?" Mother was bad enough, but the memory of Daddy's confidence in her this morning was still fresh. She couldn't bear to see his disappointment.

"Yes, dear. He is not only your father—he also owns the business. You must tell him what you told me."

"Will he…? That is, what if this upsets him? He's not supposed to have any stress."

Mother could not be swayed. "Your father is stronger than you think. Go."

Minnie numbly removed her coat and boots. As the youngest, she'd watched her sisters shoulder a heavy load of responsibility while she daydreamed. Years ago, her oldest sister, Beatrice, had married. Now Ruthie was married, too. Minnie had wanted that. She'd longed to grow older, but with age came responsibility. Responsibility wasn't fun, as she was about to find out.

The staircase never seemed so steep, the hallway so long. At the end, the door to Daddy's room stood ajar. Light streamed onto the hallway floor.

This news could kill him. Or her.

Minnie dragged her feet. Her room beckoned. She could slip inside until things calmed down. No, eventually Mother would come upstairs. Then she'd learn that Minnie hadn't confessed. If Mother told Daddy what had happened, the punishment would be far worse. Better to get it over with now.

Her legs threatened to collapse as she drew near. She paused outside his bedroom, lifted her hand to knock and let it drop. What would he say? What could she say? There was no excuse. Her heart pounded in her ears. She couldn't hear anything else. Maybe he was sleeping.

The bed creaked.

Not sleeping. She lifted her hand again, but it shook so badly that she let it fall again.

"Come in, Minnie."

"How did you know it was me?" Now that she'd been discovered, she edged into the doorway.

He wore his spectacles and, judging from the papers spread over the rolling table Peter had made, was working on the bookkeeping. "Your footsteps give you away, little princess."

"Oh." She stood in the doorway, feeling like a four-year-old who had to tell her daddy what she'd done wrong while he was away at work. Her knees trembled. How could she admit she'd lost the day's receipts?

He took off the spectacles and set them aside. "What happened?" His grim expression didn't make this any easier.

She took a deep breath. "Oh, Daddy, I'm so sorry. I should have come straight home. I shouldn't have gone to the garage after work."

He frowned. "Why would you go to the garage?"

There was no sense holding anything back now. "Peter offered me some work repairing upholstery. I thought it would help out the family, but I ended up making things worse."

He patted the bed. "Sit down here and tell me everything."

Something about his expression told her it would be all right. She hurried across the room and threw herself upon his mercy. "Oh, Daddy."

He patted her back before holding her an arm's length away. "Now, then, let's have the whole story."

She spilled everything, from her foolish hopes that Mr. Galbini would be rich and important, to losing the money and searching everywhere for the envelope. "I even looked in the trash can, but it wasn't there. It must be lost under the snow. We'll never find it."

He leaned against the pillows and scratched his chin. "Well, now, there's no use crying after spilled milk. Look again in the morning, but if you can't find it, the money's gone."

"I'm so sorry," she sobbed, blotting her tears on her sleeve.

"Now, now. Not all is lost. Can you remember the orders?"

"I—I can't remember anything."

"Calm down, now. Take a deep breath. The mind is a wondrous thing. Even when we think we can't remember, it has cataloged every moment of the day."

After two or three deep breaths, which did nothing to settle her nerves, she blurted out her greatest fear, "You're not going to punish me?"

"I think you realize how much losing that money will hurt your family. How do you propose to repay it?"

Minnie could think of only one possibility. "From the wages I earn elsewhere. Once Ruth returns, I'll go back to work cleaning houses, and I'll give you everything I earn from the upholstery job." The little bit of regret that she couldn't buy magazines or sodas vanished under the peace of knowing she would help her family.

"That sounds reasonable," Daddy said. "Now to the day's customers. Try to recall who came into the shop and why."

Now that Minnie had calmed down, she found it easy

to picture each customer who'd arrived that day. Soon they had a list of every order placed.

"Leave me now, princess. I need to rest."

Minnie hugged her father and rejoined her mother and sister downstairs. Jen glared at her from the kitchen table, where she was eating supper, but didn't say anything.

"Did you settle everything?" Mother asked.

"Daddy and I worked out a way for me to repay the money," Minnie replied.

Mother nodded, as if she'd expected nothing less, but Jen's expression didn't change. The loss of that much money meant no meat and less to eat at mealtime. The peace Minnie had felt upstairs departed. There would be no forgiveness until she earned back the lost money. That would take months. Five months, to be precise, if she could get five upholstering jobs that paid ten dollars each.

"Maybe I'll find the envelope in the morning," she said hopefully.

Jen communicated her doubt without words.

Snowfall meant getting up early to shovel out the orphanage and Ma Simmons's cottage so everyone could get to church. Peter accomplished the first task before Hendrick and Mariah arose. After a cup of coffee, he went to Ma's place. She would have breakfast ready and insist he join her. Ma was the finest woman he'd ever met outside his real ma, who'd died when he was eight. Ma Simmons loved him like her own. She also understood things.

After scraping her short walkway free of snow and ice, he rapped on the cottage door. Ma lived in the guesthouse on her son-in-law's estate. The cozy stone building had only two rooms—compared to the dozens in the large house—but Ma preferred having her own place. Anna and

Brandon had installed a little oil cookstove for her over the summer, giving her independence.

She opened the door before he'd finished knocking. "Come, now, son, and give your old ma a hug."

He had to bend way over to embrace her, but it was worth the effort. Her wide arms took him in like the grandmother he'd never known.

"Now get out of your coat and sit a spell. I'll fry you up some eggs and bacon. How does that sound?"

"Better'n oatmeal." He grinned as he settled on one of the two chairs at the little table.

Ma bustled at the stove, humming hymns as she laid bacon in the frying pan. Once finished, she wiped her hands. "How are things going for you, Peter?"

He shrugged. "Fine, I suppose."

"Hendrick said you have a new customer."

"Yeah." He didn't want to talk about Vince. For some reason, the man had attracted Minnie's attention. Maybe he should return Vince's money and refuse the job. His friend was still in town until the morning train. Maybe then things would go back to normal. Vince would leave town, and Minnie wouldn't have any swells to chase after. Leastways not until some other man showed up. He sighed.

"Is that a problem?" she asked.

Peter shrugged. He wasn't about to admit that he was a little jealous. The meat had started to sizzle and pop. "Bacon smells good."

"Yes, it does." She walked slowly across the room and settled into the other chair. "It'll take a few minutes to cook. Time enough for you to tell me what's bothering you."

"How do you know something's bothering me?"

"You've never been good at hiding your feelings."

Peter had never thought about that, but he supposed she was right.

"So what is it?" she asked again. "Let's lay it at the Lord's feet and ask His help."

"I don't think He's going to care if I get a gal or not."

Ma smiled ever so slightly. "Of course He does. He has already chosen someone for you."

"He has?" Peter found Ma's faith shocking at times. She was so certain. Even now she affirmed her statement with a confident nod. He couldn't quite get past the doubts. "But how do I know who it is?"

"You'll know, deep inside." She pressed a hand to her heart.

Peter sighed. "That doesn't help. I thought I knew, but she's not interested."

"Ah, so that's the trouble. Sometimes two people don't realize at the same time that they're meant for each other." She patted his hand. "You need to be patient."

"Don't know if I can. She turns me down every time. She won't even sit with me in church."

"Would this happen to be Minnie Fox?"

Peter ducked his head. "Hendrick said I should dress nice and compliment her."

"That always helps, but the ways to a woman's heart are unique to her. She must also be ready. Have you considered that Minnie might not want a beau quite yet?"

"She carries on after every swell that shows up in town." That was the part that stung.

"Do any of them show interest in return?"

"I don't know." Vince called her *darling,* but then Vince said that to every pretty gal. "I'm not sure. Besides, if she liked me, it wouldn't matter."

Ma patted his hand. "Don't give up, son. If she's the one for you, God will make sure you have the opportunity you need. Pray and wait for that chance to win her trust and affection."

Peter had tried to be patient. He had. Most guys wouldn't wait half as long as he had, but it was the last part of her statement that got to him. "I gotta win her trust?" He hadn't heard that one. The fact that he'd fibbed about his real age years ago, not to mention the bad things he'd done while living on the streets, didn't give him much hope he'd ever succeed in that area.

"Of course. Trust is essential. You're building a life together. Love isn't about the heady early days of getting to know each other. It's about working through life's ups and downs."

"Oh." Peter studied his fingernails, but Ma seemed to see right through him.

"Is there something you want to tell me?"

Peter shook his head. If he could ever tell anyone, it would probably be Ma Simmons. She was the most understanding person he'd ever known. She might forgive him, but a little doubt crept in. Ma held firm to God's commands. She wouldn't look kindly on what he'd done, especially since he hadn't seen fit to confess in the pretty near four years since she took him in. Peter couldn't bear to lose her and the only family he had left in this world.

So instead of telling her the truth, he said, "I think the bacon's burning."

She hurried over to the stove, and, just as he'd anticipated, the subject was soon forgotten.

Minnie didn't hear a word of the sermon that morning. She spent the entire service calculating how to scoot across the church after the closing hymn so she could reach Peter before he dashed out into the snow and cold.

At first light she had retraced her steps. Jen had even

joined her. They'd ransacked the department store's trash can and shoveled aside a mountain of snow. They'd even checked all over the dress shop. No envelope. Her last hope was the garage. It had been closed last night by the time she began searching, and it was closed today. She'd pressed her face to the office window, hoping to spot it, but the frost was so thick on the inside that she couldn't make out a thing.

The envelope had to be there. It just had to. Maybe it was lying on the office floor. Or maybe inside the car. Or underneath it on the dirty garage floor. She wouldn't even mind a little grease if she could just have the envelope back. Maybe Peter had already found it. That was probably wishful thinking. If he had, he would have sought her out right away. He might even have come to her house. Neither had happened. Nor did he so much as look her way. No, he couldn't have found it.

What if Mr. Galbini picked it up? That thought made her nauseous. Something told her that despite his fine suits and willingness to spend his boss's funds, he wouldn't hesitate to keep any money he happened to find. She would never get it back.

She tried to concentrate on the sermon. Daddy would want a full report. But before she could figure out the theme, her mind had drifted back to the missing envelope.

Dear Lord, if You care at all for this family... Minnie couldn't quite bring herself to finish the plea. She wasn't supposed to bargain with God, but couldn't He fix things just this once?

Beside her, Mother sat ramrod straight, her gloved hands folded atop her handbag and her gaze riveted on Pastor Gabe, who was finishing up. Jen sat on the other side, her expression unreadable. Minnie tried to recall something from the sermon so she could discuss it with Daddy.

Jen glared at her. Oh, dear, she was still angry. After this financial setback, Jen would have to give all of her wages to the family instead of saving for flight lessons.

Yet another dream lost, and it was all Minnie's fault. Why did she always bungle things?

The congregation rose for the closing hymn. As Minnie stood, a thought came to mind. Maybe she should give up the upholstery job entirely. Though it paid well, since she had to manage the dress shop, she would lose housecleaning clients. Housekeeping was safe. It guaranteed a small income. It wouldn't hurt anyone.

But it was dull.

For almost nineteen years Minnie had done the safe thing. Others stretched and grew. Beattie had married into the most prominent family in Pearlman. Ruthie was following her dream in New York City. If she and Sam found a buyer for her dress designs, hundreds—no, thousands—of women would be wearing her dresses. Even Jen dreamed big. She worked at the airfield, where the Hunters planned to try for a world-record flight. Jen intended to be part of it. That was exciting.

Minnie, on the other hand, was still cleaning houses and filling in at the dress shop. Mr. Galbini had brought the first excitement into her life in a long time. Never mind that he hadn't proven a romantic option. He knew people. Celebrities, no doubt. This was her one chance. Another might never appear.

As the last strains of the closing hymn faded away, Jen edged out of the pew. Minnie followed, doing her best to keep Peter in sight. Thankfully, he was tall. Though Minnie was the shortest of the Fox sisters, she could spot his shock of brown hair, combed into submission for church.

He was heading for the far aisle.

Mrs. Grattan stepped in front of her, blocking her view and her path.

"He's getting away," Minnie cried with frustration.

"Who?" Jen whipped her head around, and her brown felt hat slipped off.

"Peter." Minnie bent to pick up Jen's hat. By the time she stood, he was gone. "I need to ask if he found the envelope in the garage."

Jen caught her meaning at once. "Follow me."

She darted behind Mrs. Grattan and ahead of Mrs. Evans. The women took offense to the sudden interruption, and Minnie murmured an apology before dashing after her sister. Once through the crush, Jen slipped into an empty pew, and they crossed the remainder of the sanctuary unhindered.

Peter waited behind his foster mother, who was greeting everyone with either a hug or a handshake. Each person had something to tell her, and she listened intently. Peter, on the other hand, fidgeted, turning his hat around and around in his hands.

"Peter!" Jen bellowed as they drew near.

Several heads turned. A few shushes and fingers to the lips communicated the unwritten rule that they were supposed to be quiet in church, despite the fact that nearly everyone was chattering away.

Minnie shrank under the withering glares. Why did she say anything to her sister? She should have known Jen would act like this.

"He's waiting for us." Jen grabbed her arm and tugged her forward.

Seconds later, Jen pushed her into the pew next to Peter. That crazy stomach dance started again and wouldn't go away, even when she looked elsewhere or bit her lip.

"What is it?" He looked from Jen to Minnie and back again.

Minnie noticed Hendrick was looking at them while Mariah talked to her brother and his wife.

Jen elbowed her. "Go ahead. You explain."

Minnie swallowed. The back of her throat was dry. Peter was looking at her, and she couldn't bring herself to meet his gaze. Those hazel eyes would steal every thought from her head. So she looked at her hands, her boots, the pew, anything but him. "Wondered if you found an envelope."

"What's that?" Peter asked. "I can't hear you over everyone else."

She inwardly growled. Now she'd have to repeat herself loud enough for the whole congregation to hear. "Did you find an envelope at the garage?"

His brow pinched. "What kind of envelope?"

"A regular one. Full of papers and such." She didn't exactly want to admit that she'd lost actual money, not when some of their customers were standing within hearing distance.

"No."

Her hopes died. "Oh. I'd hoped…" Her voice trembled, so she stopped.

His expression softened. "I didn't look around, though. Wanna go check?"

"Can we?" In her excitement, she made the deadly mistake of looking into his eyes.

They twinkled. "Sure." He held out an arm. "Let's go now."

Warmth came back to her fingers and toes. She told herself it must be due to her renewed hope that they'd find the money, but deep down she knew it was something else. Or rather *someone* who just so happened to have twinkling hazel eyes.

Chapter Seven

Peter never set foot in the garage on Sundays. When he'd lived on the streets, he'd lost respect for the Sabbath. The orphanage and Ma Simmons had revived moral stability. Now he wouldn't dream of working on a Sunday. The dinners hosted by Hendrick or Anna were the highlight of the week. For the first time since his parents died, he felt part of a family.

Today, he would arrive a little late. Ma and Anna understood. His foster sister, Anna, who wasn't all that much older than him, had even pushed him toward Minnie with a smile.

Now, as he unlocked the door to the garage, Minnie and Jen stomped their feet and complained about the icy wind.

"Wish I was wearing trousers," Jen grumbled.

Minnie had pulled her coat collar up to shield her ears. "I just hope we find the envelope."

Peter would have preferred that only Minnie had come with him, even though that wouldn't be proper.

"Ladies first." Peter pulled open the door, scraping aside the fluffy snow.

Minnie hurried in with Jen right behind her.

"I'll search the office," Jen said. "You two check the work area."

Peter opened the door to the work bay. "Let's look around the car first. You crawled in and out of it so much that it's the most logical place for the envelope to fall out." He turned on the electrical lights that Hendrick had installed last fall. They hummed something fierce but lit the place up like daylight.

Minnie looked up as the lights warmed and brightened. "I wish we had these in the dress shop."

"Why don't you?"

At her crestfallen expression, Peter bit his tongue. They didn't have the money.

"Sorry," he murmured. "Stupid thing to say. Why don't you look inside the car? I'll check underneath. But be careful. The car is still up on a jack. I don't want to get crushed." At her horrified expression, he laughed. "Just don't crawl inside, and we'll all be safe."

"All right." She peeked into the car, taking care not to touch it.

He stifled a grin. At least she liked him enough not to want him dead. Meanwhile, he scanned the floor from the office to the car and then knelt to look under the car. No envelope. Hopefully, she'd find it. Any money lost would hurt the family. The image of the hundred dollars flashed through his head. Maybe he could help.

"I oughta give you something to buy the felt and stuff you need for the project."

She pulled her head out of the car. "What did you say?"

He repeated the offer.

A strange expression crossed her face. "We already have what I need. Did you find anything?"

"No." He stuck his hands into his coat pockets and

looked around the floor near the workbench, even though she'd never gone there.

She stuck her head back into the car and rummaged around. "Where is it?"

Her anguished cry hit him hard. "We'll find it." He hoped.

"No, we won't. I can't find it anywhere." She stood up and buried her face in her hands. "It's hopeless."

"No, it's not."

Her shoulders heaved, and he struggled with wanting to hold her yet knowing he shouldn't. "We'll keep searching until we find it."

"Where?" she cried.

"Let's think back to everywhere you went."

"I already did that. It's nowhere."

"And everything you did." Peter wasn't about to give up. He strode to the office doorway. Jen shot down to look under the desk, but he suspected she'd been watching and listening to him and Minnie. He refocused. "You came in through the office and walked to the car." He retraced her steps.

She looked up, her eyes a little teary.

"Vince and I were talking over here." He stood on the spot. "You were standing there." He pointed a little to her right.

"I don't see how this is going to help. You already checked the floor. I checked the car. It's not here."

Peter continued as if she hadn't said a thing. "I opened the door for you on this side and then went to the other side of the car." He rounded the vehicle and opened the door on the other side. "You crawled into the car."

She didn't move.

He could see the floorboards were empty. "Then you asked me if the seat cushion lifted up."

Her eyes lit with hope, and she ducked into the car. "I did. And you opened it for me."

Together they lifted the seat cushion.

She squealed. "There it is." She snatched it up and then, before he quite knew what was happening, raced around the car and threw her arms around him. "You found it. You found it."

Peter instinctively wrapped his arms around her waist. Touching her made him feel jittery and happy and worried all at once. He'd dreamed of holding her for so long, but she'd always pushed him away. Now she'd come to him, and he didn't quite know what to do.

She pressed her face into his shoulder and...what was that? A sob?

"Why are you crying? We found the envelope."

"I know." Pulling back, she swiped at her eyes. "I'm just so happy."

"Oh." He didn't understand any of this except that the moment she stepped away, his head stopped spinning. "You cry when you're happy?"

"When I'm really, really happy. You can't know how much this means to me." She clutched the envelope to her chest. "To my whole family."

He looked at his feet, unsure what to say. The girl he'd liked for ages was smiling at him as if he was some kinda hero.

"Thank you," she breathed, placing her small, gloved hand atop his large, callused one.

How pretty and dainty and perfect it was. He turned his hand over and grasped hers, raising it to his lips like he'd seen Hendrick do with Mariah. After kissing it, he murmured, "You're so pretty."

Her eyes widened, and she yanked her hand away. Before he could think of a thing to say, she ran to the office, where she told her sister that she'd found the envelope. They squealed and hugged and danced. They were happy. Ecstatic.

Then why did Peter feel as if he'd just been hit with a sledgehammer?

Minnie waited several days before returning to the motor garage. Every time she got near Peter, he acted peculiar. Kissing her hand? He wasn't some English noble. He was an orphan. A mechanic. A carpenter. Four months younger than her. Just friends. She shouldn't have felt a thing. Trouble was, she couldn't stop thinking about him. What did he think when she threw her arms around him? Was he mad at her for pulling her hand away? Would he take back the job offer?

That was the real problem. Minnie stared out the dress-shop window instead of basting the hem on Mrs. Evans's dress. Dull work, but even Minnie could handle it.

The car, on the other hand, would present challenges. She'd never worked with leather. That idea of hers to pad the luggage compartment had seemed brilliant at the time. Now she wasn't sure how to attach the felt or even if Peter would want her to help out anymore.

"You're going to have to talk to him," Jen said from behind her.

Minnie jumped. She hadn't heard Jen enter the shop. She must have come in through the rear entrance. "Stop sneaking up on me." She rethreaded the needle.

"I made enough noise to wake up the dead." Jen plunked onto the stool across from her, blocking the view out the window. "So? Are you going to go see him?"

"I don't know who you're talking about."

"You've been moping around the shop all week, all because of—"

"No, I'm not," Minnie said before Jen actually named Peter. Somehow saying she was attracted to him was worse than thinking it. "Maybe I'm moping around, as you say, because I'm sick of snow and cold. Spring can't come fast enough."

"Uh-huh. You've never hated snow before. Could you be dreaming of moonlit walks with a certain young man?"

"No. Absolutely not." She gathered the nerve to stare her sister in the eyes. "Besides, there's not a bachelor in town who meets our criteria."

Jen's eyebrows shot up. "Criteria?"

"Well-off enough to help out the family."

"Oh, that. I wish you'd forget that foolish idea."

Minnie picked up the pincushion. "We all put our hands on this and vowed to help each other, remember?"

"It's not a Bible. It doesn't count. Besides, you should marry for love. Look at how happy Ruthie is."

Minnie sighed at the memory of her older sister looking into her husband's eyes. The rest of them might not have been there for all Ruth noticed. Her world only included Sam. "I wish I could feel that way."

Jen spun the pincushion like a top. "Maybe you will one day."

"One day seems like forever. It's fine for someone like you, who doesn't want to get married, but that's all I've ever wanted. How am I supposed to sit around and wait? I haven't got Ruthie's patience. If I have to wait another seven years until I'm her age, I'll die."

Jen chuckled. "Then stay busy. Do things. Find out when you can start that job that Peter offered."

Minnie's stomach bottomed out. "I don't know. He hasn't said anything since we found the lost envelope."

"Have you gone to see him?"

Minnie shook her head.

"Then do it now. I'll watch the shop."

"Now?" Minnie gulped. "What will I say? What if he's not there? What if I make a fool of myself?"

"That you want to start the job. Come back here. You won't."

"What?" Minnie was lost.

"I'm answering your questions in order." Jen counted off the answers on her fingers. "Tell him that you want to start the job. If he's not there, come back here and try again later. And you won't make a fool of yourself."

"Oh."

Jen lifted Minnie's coat and hat off the peg in the back. "Now go."

Minnie reluctantly donned her outerwear. She hated to face Peter in front of anyone else. The way he looked at her sent shivers up and down her spine. What if she blushed? What if she stammered or said something foolish? She had acted the fool in front of Reggie Landers, and he'd laughed at her. Emotions weren't to be trusted. No, sir. She'd have to keep her head. This was a business venture. Nothing more.

Yet the moment she entered the motor garage and discovered Peter was alone, all those intentions vanished.

Peter hadn't heard Minnie come into the garage. He didn't notice her until he pulled his head out from under the hood of the Pierce-Arrow in search of the right-size wrench to unhook the battery cable.

"How long you been standing there?" he asked.

She tipped her head to the side, which only made her prettier. "Awhile."

Peter swallowed and repeated the question Hendrick insisted he use with every customer. "What can I do for you?"

Her smile faltered, and she lowered her gaze. "Just wondering." A shrug. "Do you still want me to help with the car?"

"Of course." He didn't have to think that answer through. "I thought we'd already settled that."

She gave him the most dazzling smile. "When?"

His pulse accelerated even though he didn't know what she was asking. "When what?"

"When should I start?"

The answer would send her away, but Peter wasn't ready to let her go yet. "Why don't you come over here and take a look? It wouldn't hurt for you to learn a little about motors."

Her smile faded, but she did as he asked. She settled in at the front of the car, rather than at his side. "What are you doing?"

"Disconnecting the battery so we don't get any unwelcome shocks."

Her eyebrows lifted. "That could happen?"

"It's possible. Plus the connections need to be cleaned. Take a look."

That drew her closer. He felt a jolt that had nothing to do with the battery.

"First I need the right wrench." He reached around her to grab the elusive tool from his toolbox. "Then I loosen the nut on this cable." He showed her which one.

"Is it safe?" Her hands gripped the edge of the engine compartment.

Her concern felt better than good. It warmed him more than Ma's hugs. "If you don't let any metal make a connection between the positive and negative terminals."

She looked horrified, so he explained how to disconnect the battery safely. Then he loosened the first cable and pulled it off. "See? No shock."

She looked up at him with awe, as if he'd done something amazing, like scale a mountain or win a race. "You know so much."

"It's nothing. You could do it, too. Wanna try?"

"Oh, no." She backed away. "I'd bungle it."

"No, you wouldn't. Here, I'll loosen the bolt. All you need to do is pull off the cable."

She drew near again and watched him work. He liked the feel of that, the way she smelled, the way she looked at him, her surprise over the smallest things.

"All right." Having loosened the bolt, he set aside the wrench. "Now you pull off the cable."

She tugged off her gloves and pushed her coat sleeve up to her elbow. Her dainty fingers reached ever so hesitantly into the compartment. "Just pull?"

"Straight off the terminal." He itched to steady her shaking hand, but that wouldn't give her confidence.

Her pale fingers wrapped around the cable. "You're right. There's no shock." She tightened her grip and pulled. "It's not moving."

"Maybe I didn't loosen the bolt enough. Let me check."

"No, I can get it." She tucked her lower lip between her teeth and put her weight into pulling off the cable.

It didn't budge at first, and he motioned for her to let him help. She shook him off. Then all of a sudden the cable came off. Her hand struck the metal housing, and she yelped. Dropping the cable, she yanked her hand out. To his horror, a bright red line formed on the back of her hand.

She was bleeding!

Minnie stared at her hand as if she couldn't believe she'd cut it. Peter leaped into action. He whipped a clean handkerchief from his pocket and applied pressure to the cut.

"I'm sorry." He swallowed hard. This was all his fault.

He should never have urged her to pull off the cable. What had he been thinking?

The initial shock over, tears pooled in her eyes. That made him feel even worse.

"Does it hurt?" He hoped the wound wasn't deep, but they'd have to get it cleaned either way. "Let's go into the office. Hendrick keeps some hydrogen peroxide in there. We can clean and bandage it."

He didn't let go of her hand as he led her to the office.

Darkness had settled over the town. Lights twinkled here and there, but the office was dark. He turned on the electric light, keenly aware that anyone could see inside but more concerned about Minnie's hand than idle gossip. The peroxide and bandages were on the shelf behind the desk. He sat Minnie down, had her maintain pressure on her hand and fetched the medical supplies. If the cut was deep, he'd take her to Doc Stevens for stitches.

Please, Lord, don't let it be serious.

He'd never forgive himself.

Chapter Eight

"All right." Peter knelt before Minnie, a pained expression on his face, and unstopped the bottle of hydrogen peroxide. "You need to remove the handkerchief now."

A whimper snuck out before she caught it. She lifted the handkerchief and tensed in preparation for the medicine. A bead of blood formed on the thin line of the cut.

He bent over it and then relaxed. "It doesn't look very deep, but I still need to put peroxide on it. Hold your hand out. I'm going to pour it over the cut, and I don't want anything getting on your dress or coat."

Her hand shook a little as she extended it, but she was not going to let him know that she was even a little bit afraid. "I'm ready."

"This might sting."

She tossed her head, as if this was a common occurrence. "I know. I've had cuts before."

He looked skeptical.

When the peroxide first hit the wound, she jerked her hand a little, but through sheer determination, she held it perfectly still. If Peter noticed, he didn't say anything. Instead, he kept his focus on the job at hand.

"Now I'll bandage it." He picked up the soft cotton

gauze and wrapped it around and around her hand, keeping her fingers and thumb visible.

His touch was gentle. He took such care that she almost wished he wouldn't finish.

"You could be a doctor," she said.

"I'd rather be a carpenter or furniture-maker."

"Not a mechanic?"

"This is all right, but I like making things."

She recalled the shelving and counter in the bookstore. "Your furniture is beautiful."

He'd stopped wrapping, but he still held her hand. The comfort of his touch somehow outweighed the stinging pain. "Vince taught me."

"Oh. Right." She didn't want to think about him. "Back in New York?"

Peter nodded. "When he helped out at the orphanage. He gave me hope. I'd like to give that to other kids, teach them how to work with their hands. Before he taught me how to build things and fix things, I didn't have any skills or much education. I wasn't good about attending and stopped going completely when my aunt died."

"Your aunt?" Minnie hadn't heard anything about an aunt. "Did she die at the same time as your parents?"

"No. My folks died when I was eight. My aunt died a year or so before I came here. She got influenza." He rushed the words, as if he didn't want to talk about it.

"During the epidemic?"

He nodded.

"Were you living with her?" This story got sadder by the moment.

"Yeah." He squared his shoulders. "Let's finish that hand."

She didn't care about a silly old cut anymore. Peter had lost everyone close to him. "And then you had no one."

Peter didn't look up from the bandage. "I got by, but that's not my point. If God hadn't been looking out for me, I could have ended up in a bad spot. There aren't many things an unskilled, uneducated guy can do."

"You're not uneducated. You graduated from high school."

"Yeah. After I got here. But it's what Vince taught me that helped me get this job."

"So that's why you want to teach other kids the same things he taught you."

His hands stilled. "I suppose."

Minnie felt for him. "Living in an orphanage must have been awful."

He shrugged. "Not so much. They were all kind. Could have been worse."

"I can't imagine not having a family. We're all so close—my sisters and my parents. When Daddy was in the hospital and when he had that seizure last summer..." Her throat closed, and she was unable to finish. It was easier not to admit the fear that she'd end up fatherless. And if Daddy could die, so could Mother. Then what? Minnie would be an orphan, too.

He seemed to understand what she was thinking. "Don't worry. People here watch out for each other. It's not like the city."

Minnie eagerly grasped the chance to change the subject. "The city can't be all bad. Look at the fancy clubs and big department stores."

"Who cares about stores when you can't buy anything?" Peter bent over her hand again. "And the clubs? They're the worst of it. Trust me, you want to stay away from them. Promise you'll never go near one."

"I'll do no such thing. That's where the celebrities go."

"You don't know what you're saying. Fame and fancy

clothes only hide the real person. The glitter and glamour of the club is the same way. You can't find God in a place like that."

What an odd thing to say. Minnie puzzled over it as Peter finished bandaging her hand.

After tucking the end of the gauze under at the palm, he sat back on his heels. "I'm sorry I asked you to help with the motor."

He looked sad, like he had when he'd arrived on the train with the other orphans four years ago. He'd been much taller than the rest of them. His trousers were so short that she and her friends had snickered at him. He must have heard, because his shoulders had drooped. But when people said mean things about one of the other orphan boys because he was Italian, Peter tried to protect the boy. She'd gained a lot of respect for Peter that day. She'd even liked him a little, but once he got comfortable with his new family, he starting acting like every other boy in school, pestering her until she couldn't stand him.

At this moment, he was more like the boy who'd first arrived, unsure and fiercely protective of those less fortunate than him. He wanted to help other kids. He wanted to give them a chance at a good life. He wanted to teach them skills. That meant a lot.

"I'm glad you asked me to help. You're a good teacher." She grinned. "Besides, why should Jen be the only one in the family who knows mechanical things?"

His hopeful smile sent her stomach flip-flopping again. Was this what love felt like—the crazy up-and-down emotions? The wondering what he thought of her and the worry that she'd said something stupid? Or was she just lightheaded because of the injury?

That must be it. Love was something else entirely, according to the stories she read. Someone in love fell madly, passionately in love with the other person. He became the center of her thoughts and dreams. She didn't feel that way about Peter. He was a friend. That was all.

The glare of automobile headlamps through the windows sent Peter to his feet and wiped away her confusing thoughts.

Peter crossed the office and pushed open the door. "We're closed for the night."

The car didn't budge. In fact, the passenger door opened, and a woman got out. Minnie recognized that woman. It was her oldest sister.

Beatrice pushed past Peter into the office. "What are you doing here?" When she saw Minnie's bandaged hand, she gasped. "What happened? Did he hurt you?" She turned on Peter. "How dare you touch her."

Minnie hurried around the desk. "No, Beattie. Peter didn't do a thing. In fact, he helped me. I cut my hand, and he bandaged it." She tugged her sister away from him.

Beatrice calmed down a little, even if her frown didn't ease. "You stay here," she said to Peter. "I want a word with my sister." She pulled Minnie into the work area, still bright under the electric lighting, and closed the door behind them. "Do you have any idea how this looks?"

"Looks?" Minnie had never seen Beatrice so upset. Other than the dots of color on her cheeks, her face was pale as snow.

"You. Alone with Peter after dark. In the motor garage." Beatrice wrinkled her nose.

"Nothing is going on. I'm working with Peter on a project."

"At night?" Beattie's horrified expression nearly made Minnie laugh.

"It's not night. It's before supper and after closing the dress shop. When else can I do it?"

"But it's not proper. People will talk."

Minnie crossed her arms, more determined than ever to complete this job. "I don't care what people say. The job pays well, and Daddy needs the money."

Beatrice's indignation wavered. "That may be—" her gaze darted toward the office "—but you cannot work with him unsupervised. Get Jen to join you. Ask Hendrick to stop by."

"Impossible and impossible." Minnie was not going to be governed by her sister's prudish sensibilities.

"What's impossible is this situation. You'll ruin your reputation if you continue this way. If you were courting with a promise of marriage, it might be acceptable. Might."

"Courting?" Minnie choked on the word. "Certainly not."

"Then I suggest you find a chaperone."

"And I suggest you keep your nose out of my affairs."

Beatrice glared at her. "I can't believe Mother and Daddy approved this."

Minnie examined her bandaged hand.

"You haven't told them, have you?" Beatrice demanded. "Well, we'll remedy that right now. Come along." She grabbed Minnie's arm. "Blake and I will take you home. It's on our way, and we can have a little discussion with Mother and Daddy."

Minnie resisted. "Don't you think they have enough to worry about already? Tell me how this is any different from anyone else."

"I don't have to tell you anything. This is up to our parents. Moreover, you do not have to do things like everyone else. Come along, now."

"I'll go when I want to." Minnie was not going to be treated like a baby.

"Stubborn girl! Don't you care about your father?"

That hurt, but Minnie wasn't quite ready to give in. Most people weren't as old-fashioned in their thinking as Beattie. After all, hadn't Beattie's friend Darcy done practically the same thing with her future husband? "What about Darcy and Jack? They worked together on his airplane."

"That's different."

"Is it?" Minnie shot her sister a look of defiance.

"Yes. They got married."

Minnie started to protest that Jack Hunter and Darcy Shea didn't marry until after they'd built the plane and took it on the disastrous test flight, but then she saw Peter through the office windows. It must have been the way the light hit him, for he looked older and more handsome than ever before. His face was sculpted, his posture commanding, as if he could take on the world and win.

In that moment, every lucid thought disappeared.

Peter had heard enough of Beatrice Kensington's scolding to know he'd gone too far with Minnie. Guys and gals got together all the time to go to the movies and ball games and whatnot, but the Foxes were pretty strict about things. He should have sent Minnie home right away instead of showing her the Pierce-Arrow's engine. If he had any hope of a future with her, he'd have to do things the right way.

That meant asking Mr. Fox's permission.

As Peter walked home, he glanced at the dark windows of the dress shop, the shades drawn for the night. Next door loomed the massive Hutton's Department Store, its windows lit into the evening hours to tantalize shoppers. Minnie's house was behind both buildings. He should walk around the block and ask to speak to Mr. Fox. Maybe he could clear up any worries about Minnie and him working together. His intentions were honorable and all, but she didn't seem to feel the same way about him as he did about her.

He paused on the street corner, teetering between the two options. Go to her house and convince her father, or return home and hope for the best. If he asked to talk to Minnie's father, she might get mad at him. Probably would, considering how much she resisted his invitations. He blew out his breath, and the air turned to a cloud of steam.

Sally Neidecker and Reggie Landers exited the department store arm in arm. She laughed and laid her head on his shoulder. He grinned and led her past Peter as if he was invisible. The two moved as one, their chatter pure nonsense to outsiders but perfectly understandable to each other. Peter wanted that kind of closeness. He wanted a real family, one that would laugh with him and be glad to see him. He'd had that with the Simmonses. Then Hendrick married, Ma lost the house and Anna married. Now everyone except him had a new life.

Why not me? he wondered.

Drawing up courage, he walked up the side street and looked down the alley between the department store and the Fox house. The kitchen window still glowed dimly, but Blake Kensington's auto wasn't there. He must have parked in front of the house. The family could be in the front parlor.

Peter shuffled down the snowy street to the next cross street. There sat Blake's Cadillac. The house's front windows were all lit, casting enough light across the yard to reveal a man pacing near the car. A second man hurried down the street toward the first.

"Ready?" the second man asked.

Voices must carry in cold, calm air.

"Still waiting on the wife." Kensington's voice was

tinged with the sort of anxiety Peter hadn't heard since his street days in New York.

Peter backed away. He didn't want to overhear a private conversation, especially if it revealed anything that would harm Minnie's sister or family. Something about Kensington had always sat wrong with him. Maybe it was the money. As heir to the Kensington empire, Blake liked to throw his weight around. Fancy clothes, big talk and overindulgence were traits Peter recognized from the seedier elements he'd come in contact with in New York. Too bad Blake didn't spend that money on his wife's family. Maybe that was what got to Peter most of all. Family had to come first.

As he slipped out of sight, Kensington's next words sent prickles up his spine. "Is the rumor true? Are they looking to run out of here?"

Peter slowed to listen for the response.

"That's what I hear. They'll be looking for deliverymen."

Peter raced away, not wanting to hear another word. The men could be talking about anything. The Kensingtons owned the mercantile. Maybe Blake was looking to bring in something new to replace the ready-made clothing business lost to the new department store. Maybe he was opening a new store in another town.

Yet as Peter hurried home, he knew deep down that was only wishful thinking.

"Now, Beattie," Daddy said, "things aren't the same today as they were when you were courting."

"That was only six years ago. Six." Beatrice, her face flushed above the fox-fur collar of her fashionable wool coat, practically quivered. "Propriety never goes out of style."

Jen rolled her eyes and made a face from the kitchen doorway. She'd either finished washing dishes or had abandoned the task Mother gave her in favor of better entertainment.

Minnie clasped her hands around her knees, wishing she'd chosen to sit next to Daddy rather than all alone opposite him and Mother, whose frown deepened with every word.

"Now, Hugh, Beatrice has a point. We don't want people to talk."

Minnie groaned and buried her face in her hands. "It's a job. With Peter. Peter! We're just friends. We've never even gone to anything together." She stopped short of saying she never would. "This is ridiculous."

"What's ridiculous is taking on that sort of job when you're already busy," Mother said. "Who did you expect to run the dress shop?"

"Ruthie will be back soon."

"I'm afraid she won't. I received a letter today saying they are staying in the city until April."

"Until April?" That dealt Minnie's hopes a fateful blow. "Why so long?"

"Apparently they have an opportunity to display your sister's designs at a fashion exhibition." Daddy beamed. "It's an incredible honor. Our little Ruthie. In front of the biggest names in the industry."

Minnie drooped. There was no hope Ruth and Sam would return early.

"So you see," Mother added, "you will need to manage the shop for at least another five weeks and likely more. There's no time for another job."

"You can't expect me to spend every waking hour at the dress shop. You might help," Minnie pleaded with Mother.

"And I can help out until the snow melts," Jen added,

forgetting that she was supposed to be in the kitchen and not listening to the conversation.

"See?" Minnie leaped on the offer before Jen changed her mind. "There's plenty of time for me to work in another job. And it's business for the shop. It might be just the start. Maybe if we do this job right, Mr. Galbini will send us more work."

"How many automobiles could one man have?" Mother responded. "One is plenty for even the wealthiest family."

Minnie leaped on the first possibility that came to mind. "Maybe he has friends?"

"Exactly." Daddy took up her cause. "He'll want to show off the excellent workmanship. Once they see it, they'll want the same thing in their automobiles. If you ask me, it's a brilliant proposition. Not only is it good for the dress shop, it's a whole new line of business. If Minnie proves she can upholster automobile seats, why not expand into home furnishings? Ever since the Baumgartners closed their shop, there's been a void in Pearlman. Reupholstering tired, worn chairs and sofas could be a big boost to business."

"As long as it takes place at the dress shop," Beatrice declared. "Not in a motor garage alone with a bachelor."

Minnie rolled her eyes. "How am I supposed to get an automobile into the dress shop?"

Jen snickered.

Beatrice frowned at Jen before answering, "You have Peter remove the seats and bring them to the shop."

"That makes sense," Daddy said.

Mother added her approval with a nod.

"But I can't do that with the luggage compartment," Minnie protested.

"Why not?" Mother leveled her gaze at her. "Peter can install the compartment after you've finished."

"Yes, but…" What could Minnie say? Their argument made perfect sense, but she felt chained to the dress shop. Unhooking the battery cable had demonstrated that she could do something that few women could do. She liked that feeling and wanted to learn more.

"It's not the same." Jen came to her rescue. "You always do fittings for your customers, right?"

Mother and Daddy nodded.

"I think what Minnie's trying to say is that she needs to do a fitting or two for the automobile."

Minnie could have hugged her sister.

Unfortunately Beatrice wasn't done. "That doesn't solve the problem. Minnie must guard her reputation."

Jen appeared unfazed. "Then I'll chaperone them. I don't have much to do at the flight school for a while."

Though Beatrice looked skeptical, Daddy put an end to the discussion. "That settles it, then."

Minnie shot her next-oldest sister a look of gratitude.

We promised, Jen mouthed.

Their vow! Minnie felt her cheeks heat, but she couldn't explain that this job had nothing to do with pursuing Peter Simmons as a suitor. Nor did it have to do with any affection for Mr. Galbini. She couldn't exactly articulate what it did mean, except that she'd never wanted something so badly. The glamour that Galbini represented certainly played a part in it, but this was more. This job represented a chance to both shed the commonplace and help her family. She could try her hand at something new. Minnie wasn't going to let the opportunity slip away.

Chapter Nine

Peter was glad Minnie didn't show up at the garage the rest of the week. He had a decision to make and didn't need her presence distracting him.

When he had to think things through, he turned to wood. Feeling the grain beneath his fingertips always gave him peace. He'd think on how every ring measured a year's growth. Good years and lean ones showed in the grain. Through it all, the tree endured. Strong as the oak. That was how he'd managed to live his life lately. It helped him get by.

Now he could only think how a single man could fell that mighty oak. Was Vince that man? Would this job send Minnie's family crashing to earth? The thought kept him up at night, staring at the darkened window of his tiny attic room. He could turn down the job, but he'd given his word. A man's word must not be broken. Moreover, Minnie's family could use the money. But what if this wasn't a luggage compartment? What if the deliveries he'd overheard Kensington mentioning were of liquor, not dry goods? But the luggage compartment was so small and the hidden portion barely tall enough for a bottle lying flat. A man couldn't store enough bootleg liquor in there to make it worth the risk.

No, it must be exactly what Vince said—for luggage and personal valuables.

Still, Peter found no peace. He pressed his hand to the frosted window, melting a clear spot through which to see. Outside, the tree branches rattled in the breeze, lifeless fingers reaching for the hope of spring. The waning moon offered no comfort. Countless prayers gave him no answer.

So he turned to wood. Hendrick let him keep a little workshop in the back corner of the garage. He retreated there after closing the garage each day. Maybe if he could finish up this job before Minnie's hand healed, he could talk her into showing him how to fit the felt to the inside of the compartment. If she had no part in the actual construction, she couldn't be considered an accomplice. He'd still pay her. That should solve everything.

Then why didn't he feel better?

"Peter?"

He jumped at the sound of Minnie's voice and dropped the planer. It clattered against the concrete floor. He must be hearing things. The doors were locked. No one could be in the garage. He picked up the planer and slid it over the surface of the wood, peeling off the rough outer layer.

Someone pounded on the doors to the work bay. "Peter! Let us in."

Us? The voice was Minnie's, but she must have brought someone with her. He set down the planer and worked his way out of the back of the garage until he reached the big doors. He lifted the board used to secure the doors and pushed one open a little. Minnie and Jen Fox stood just outside.

"I'm here to work." Minnie looked rather pleased with herself.

"Can't." Peter had to stand firm.

"What do you mean I can't? You hired me."

"I'm alone. It's not proper."

Minnie rolled her eyes. "That's why Jen is chaperoning us." Her cheeks were rosy from the cold evening air. "So, are you going to let us in?"

"Don't suppose I have much choice." Peter reluctantly opened the door, and Minnie traipsed in with Jen following.

Minnie went straight to his woodworking area. "Is this it?"

"Yeah." Peter glanced at Jen, who perched on the edge of a workbench and pulled a magazine from her coat pocket.

"Don't mind me," she said.

Some chaperone. He supposed he should be grateful. He walked back to the wood shop, where Minnie was inspecting the boards. "This board forms the back of the compartment. I had to shape it so the seat cushion will fit."

"Does it fit flush? Will I need to cut the felt lower to accommodate it?"

Peter was impressed with Minnie's questions. They showed a surprisingly mechanical mind for a girl. By the time he'd finished explaining every construction and design detail, he figured she'd be bored to tears.

Instead, her expression got more and more animated. "I can see exactly how it will look. And these smaller pieces will work perfectly with the restrictions my parents put in place."

Her statement made no sense. "What restrictions?"

"They want me to do most of the work in the dress shop. Whenever I'm here, I need a chaperone."

"Oh." That pretty much killed his hopes for time alone

with her. Jen might pretend to read a magazine, but her ears were undoubtedly wide-open.

Minnie sighed. "I told them there was nothing to worry about, but my oldest sister is such a stick in the mud. I said we were just friends, but she insisted."

Peter struggled against a tide of disappointment. Not only had he lost time with Minnie, but she also still thought of him as a friend. Why couldn't she see him for who he was? Why was she always chasing after swells? Would she have agreed to such restrictions if she was working with Vince? No. She'd battle to the death. But not for him.

"I don't think I'll need you," he blurted out.

"What?" Her eyes widened, the blue so dazzling in the electrical lights that he couldn't look away. "What do you mean you don't need me?" Her gaze narrowed.

"Uh." He gulped and tried to gather his thoughts.

"Well?" She planted her hands on her hips. "We made an agreement. In front of Mr. Galbini."

"Yes, well, if you remember, I told him you could do the upholstery *if* I needed any done."

"You also agreed to my plan to line the compartment."

"It's not difficult—"

"It's my job." She jabbed her finger into her chest. "Mine. You promised." She blinked rapidly.

Not tears. Why did women always resort to tears? "I'll still pay you."

Her pout didn't ease. "For doing nothing? Never. And what if we get more work based on this? Maybe I want to do this. Maybe I need to do this."

This was going badly. One careless statement fueled by jealousy, and everything he'd hoped to build between them came crashing down. Peter raked a hand through his hair, and his cap tumbled to the floor. He stooped to pick it up while he tried to figure out how to get out of this mess. "I'm sorry."

"Sorry isn't good enough. A promise is a promise, Mr. Simmons."

Her formality kicked him in the stomach. "All right."

She glared at him. "All right what?"

Peter mopped his brow. Vince wouldn't lie to him. The Pierce-Arrow was a personal car. Bootleggers used trucks, not cars. He must be reading too much into what he'd heard. This was Pearlman, after all, and two men talking loudly in the open could not mean anything sinister. He took a deep breath. Those months living on the street had made him too suspicious. That was over now. Peter had asked Jesus into his life. The slate was wiped clean. Pastor Gabe said so. The past would not resurface. It was gone forever.

He swallowed. "All right. You can do the work."

He hoped he hadn't made a huge mistake.

Minnie wanted to start that night, but Peter made her wait, saying he had work to do first. The following week, he brought the first board to the dress shop.

Minnie stared at the flat, varnished board he set on her worktable. "Just one?"

Peter shrugged and shuffled his feet, the way he always did when nervous. "When you finish it, I'll bring the next one."

"But how am I supposed to know where I can attach the felt and where I can't?"

He pointed to the board. "I marked it."

She leaned close, trying to make out what he was pointing at. "I don't see anything."

"Can't you see the pencil mark?" He leaned over the worktable until the top of his head nearly touched hers.

She moved back a little. "No, I can't."

He rubbed his finger over the glistening finish. "It's right there."

"Well, I don't see it. You'd need a microscope to make out anything under that finish."

Instead of being offended, he puffed up like a turkey. "Here." He guided her finger to the spot.

At last she made it out. "Why'd you make it so light?"

"I guess it's easier to see in electric lighting." He pointed to the top two marks. "Don't go any higher than this, or I won't be able to get the seat to settle right."

"What about this side?" She pointed to the bottom, where he hadn't marked anything.

"Bring the fabric around the bottom and attach it on the back." He lifted the board on its side. "See how I shaved off a little so you could tack the fabric to the wood here? Be sure to use flat-headed tacks. Nothing with any depth."

"All right." Minnie didn't want to admit she didn't have any tacks, least of all flat-headed ones. The mercantile should have them. They had a lot of hardware supplies. If they didn't, the feed store might, assuming farmers had need of flat-headed tacks. At least she now knew how to attach the stuff. She smiled with relief. "Thank you for showing me."

Peter smiled back at her. "You're welcome."

Minnie sucked in her breath. Up close, the flecks of green and gold in his eyes shimmered like gems. It must be getting dark, because his pupils grew larger and larger, and in the center was her reflection. She ought to look away but couldn't seem to do so. The floor tilted, and she had to grip the table to keep her balance.

Breathe. Just breathe. It's only Peter.

He broke eye contact first. "Oh, I almost forgot." He

reached into his pocket and pulled out a handful of tacks—flat-headed tacks. "Thought you might need these."

She tried to thank him, honest she did, but nothing came out until after he left. Then the only thing she could manage was "Where do I get a hammer?"

Minnie did good work. Real good. Every day Peter brought a new board and carried the completed one back to the garage. She reveled in his praise, which made him hum and whistle the rest of the day. Each time she talked more. Today, she'd chattered on and on about how to pound in the tacks. He didn't care what she said. Every word and every movement was beautiful.

Mr. Evans pulled up to the fueling pump, and Peter strode out to fill his automobile. March had dawned cold and windy, but he barely noticed. Why should he when later that day he'd see Minnie?

Those long eyelashes of hers made her the prettiest girl he'd ever seen. Add in the big blue eyes and tender smile, and he couldn't get her out of his mind. Sleep and concentration vanished, but he didn't care. Minnie was warming up to him. She'd even talked to him after the church service on Sunday.

Tonight the varnish on the last board would be dry. He would take it to her as soon as he closed the garage. Then what? He'd pick it up tomorrow or the next day, but after that he wouldn't have any reason to stop by the dress shop.

"You planning to pump the fuel anytime soon?" Mr. Evans chirped from the driver's seat.

Peter jerked to attention. "Yes, sir."

Mr. Evans chuckled. "Looks like you're falling for a girl."

Peter fought embarrassment as he pumped gasoline into the pump's glass cylinder. Then he began to release the fuel into the Model T's tank. Mr. Evans attended the same church. He'd probably seen Minnie talking to him last Sunday.

"It's a fine time of life." Mr. Evans then launched into the story of courting Mrs. Evans in a horse and buggy.

Peter's thoughts drifted back to Minnie. If he owned an automobile and got her father's permission to court her, he'd take her on a Sunday drive to this pretty spot down-river where the water flowed deep and clear and the willows drooped so low their leaves dipped into the river.

"That's enough, Peter! I only wanted two gallons."

Peter stopped the flow of fuel and checked the glass cylinder atop the pump. He'd put in two and a half gallons. "Sorry, sir. I'll only charge you for the two gallons."

"Nonsense. I can spare the extra." Mr. Evans held out a dollar bill. "Happens to all of us, son. I hope she likes you, too."

Peter felt the heat crawl up his neck. "I'll be back with your change."

"Keep it. Buy your gal something nice."

Peter fingered the dollar bill as Mr. Evans drove away. That was the difference between Pearlman and the big city. Vince had a money clip full of hundred-dollar bills. Peter had an extra fifty cents.

After padding the last board, Minnie wasn't ready for the project to end. She smoothed her hands over the thick felt instead of pushing the board toward Peter. "Are you sure there isn't anything else you need me to do? I can help you put the compartment together."

He didn't take his hands out of his pockets. "Not necessary." He glanced around the empty shop. "But I could use your help if...well, your sister..."

Minnie gritted her teeth. She was sick of being treated

like a baby. "I'm nineteen years old now. An adult. I ought to be able to do as I please."

He flinched. "Your birthday! I should have remembered. Buy you a soda?"

Why did he always manage to turn everything into a reason to ask her out? "No, thank you. I can't." He looked so downcast that she added, "Maybe after we finish. Is Mr. Galbini still coming to pick up the automobile on Saturday? There's a lot to get done between now and then. I can help. Maybe hold the boards in place while you nail them together."

He gave her a strange look, as if she'd made the dumbest suggestion ever.

"What?" she challenged. "You don't need anyone to hold them? Or are you still worried about a chaperone?"

"I'm using screws, not nails."

"Oh." She had no idea what he was talking about.

"But I could use your help, if..."

Minnie groaned. "You still insist on having Jen watch us?"

The red started to seep up his neck. "Don't your parents want that?"

"You're as much of a stick in the mud as Beattie. All right. I'll get Jen to come with me." Somehow. Her sister was busy at the airfield again, with the flight school gearing up for another season.

He shot her a shy smile that almost made up for the inconvenience. "You need to bring a strong needle and heavy thread."

Now he'd lost her. "To assemble a wooden box?"

He shrugged. "Actually, most of the compartment is already together. I just need to add the last board, but I accidentally ripped open a seam in the seat back."

"Is it just the seam?" Her pulse beat a little faster. This would put her sewing skills to the test.

"I think so."

"I hope we don't need more leather. We don't have anything like that here. Since the carriage factory closed and Mr. Jones retired, no one carries leather. I'd have to order some. It could take days to get here. Then I'd have to stitch a whole new seat cover. That would take forever. I'd never get it done by Saturday."

Every thought made her more and more frantic. Worse, Peter stood there grinning, as if her panic was the funniest thing he'd ever seen.

"Stop laughing," she demanded.

"Now calm down. Don't you think you should see it before you go making another cover?"

"This is a Pierce-Arrow. A fancy new automobile. Do you really think the owner wants a patched-up backseat?" She threw her hands into the air. "What are you thinking?"

"I'm thinking you can do it."

The way he stood there brimming with confidence gave her pause. He thought she could work miracles. Her. Minnie Fox. Apprentice dressmaker. Sewer of hems and straight seams.

"I can't."

"It wouldn't hurt to give it a try," he urged.

"Except I need to order the leather today, if I'm going to get it before the end of the week."

Still, he grinned at her. "In case you haven't noticed, it's past closing time."

Minnie blew out her pent-up frustration as Jen burst through the door.

"Let's close this place and go home," her sister said.

Minnie looked at Peter, who nodded encouragingly. Somehow, his calm confidence bolstered her own. Maybe she could do it. And he was right. She couldn't order material at this late hour.

She turned to Jen. "After we close, we need to go to the garage. Where does Ruthie keep her heaviest thread and sturdiest needles?"

Chapter Ten

When Minnie saw the gash in the leather, she gasped. "I can't fix that. It's not just the seam. Some of the leather ripped, too."

"Are you sure you can't do something?" Peter looked stricken. "The torn part is real low. The seat cushion will hide it." He scrubbed a hand through his shock of hair. "New leather will cost a lot. It'd take most of our profits. And we'd never get the job done on time."

Put that way, Minnie had to give it a try. "But I can't promise anything."

"You can do it." Peter gave her a winsome smile that sent her stomach fluttering.

She tamped down the unwelcome feeling with a stern warning. "I'll have to take the seat back apart in order to work on the material. It'll be tough to get it repaired and back together by Saturday. Will Mr. Galbini wait if it takes longer?"

Peter shook his head. "I don't know how to contact him by telephone. A letter won't get there in time."

Minnie nibbled on her fingernail. "I suppose we don't have any choice. We'd better get the seat back apart to-night."

They set to work. Jen even pitched in. Within twenty minutes, Minnie held the folded leather seat covering in her arms. Unlike the envelope, she couldn't possibly lose this between the garage and home. Once there, she'd enlist her parents' advice. One of them must know how to repair leather.

It took every spare minute the rest of the week to fix the tear. When neither parent could advise her, Minnie visited old Mrs. Baumgartner. The retired upholsterer showed her how to painstakingly repair the tear. The stitching fell to Minnie. Lacking a machine capable of handling leather, she had to sew by hand. Each stitch took both strength and patience. Her fingers ached. Her hands cramped. Her eyes burned.

"What a foolish idea," she muttered Thursday night after toiling on the project for hours. "He'd better appreciate this."

"Who, dear?" Mother looked up from her embroidery. "Your father always appreciates your work."

"I know he does." Minnie bit her lip, sorry she had ever complained. Daddy had taken a turn for the worse today and hadn't come downstairs. "How is he?"

"Sleeping peacefully." Mother slipped the needle effortlessly through the cotton fabric. "He just caught a cold. Nothing a little rest won't cure."

Minnie returned to the dreadful leather. "This is the last time I tackle upholstery. No wonder Mrs. Baumgartner retired."

Mother's lips curved ever so slightly. "I'm sure her seventy-year-old hands were tiring from the work."

Minnie refrained from expressing her frustration with the material in front of her mother, but she couldn't hold back a sigh of relief when she finished early Friday morning. Peter would be pleased. Hopefully, Mr. Galbini wouldn't notice that the material had been repaired. His boss, either. All they had to do was put it together that night, in time for Mr. Galbini's arrival tomorrow.

"I can't go to the garage," Jen stated as they closed the dress shop for the day. "The Hunters are hosting a welcome supper for the new students, and I'm helping out."

"You? You can't cook."

"I can carry plates and fill water glasses and teacups."

"Why did you agree to do this? You knew all week that I'd need you tonight. What am I supposed to do? The car has to be ready before morning. Mr. Galbini is due on the early train."

Jen shrugged as she locked the back door to the shop. "Do what you have to. I won't tell Mother and Daddy if you don't." After pocketing the key, Jen took off toward the Hunters' house at her usual rapid pace.

Minnie looked first toward home and then down the alley where it ended near Simmons Motor Garage. What choice did she have? The work must be done, and her parents' silly restrictions made no sense now that she was nineteen. Besides, who would know? Jen had promised not to say a word. She walked straight to the garage.

Peter balked at first. "Where's your sister?"

"Busy." Minnie laid the leather seat covering on the workbench.

"But she has to be here. Someone has to be here."

Minnie put her hands on her hips and rolled her eyes in her best impression of Kate Vanderloo. "Peter Simmons, we have work to do—unless you plan on re-covering the seat back all by yourself."

Peter looked first at the folded leather and then at the frame of the seat back. "Maybe Hendrick would help." His shoulders drooped. "No, he can't."

"He and Mariah are at the Hunters' supper, aren't they?" Minnie asked.

Peter nodded glumly.

Minnie squared her shoulders. "Well, then, by my calculation, we only have a couple hours to get this together. I suggest we stop talking and start working."

Though Peter hesitated a moment longer, at last he capitulated. Good thing, because stretching the leather proved torturous. Oh, the first side slipped on with no problem, and the second wasn't bad, but then the struggle began.

Minnie panted as she strained to pull the material over the frame. "It's as if it shrank. How is that possible? It never got wet."

"I don't think leather is like wool. Why don't you hold on to this end and let me pull that one in place?"

"Then what? Are you going to attach it?"

"Let's get it over the frame first and figure out the rest later."

Minnie did as Peter suggested, but again the material slipped from her fingers. "It's hopeless. Maybe I somehow made the cover smaller when I repaired it. But how? I was so careful."

"I can tell you were." The softness of his comment calmed her growing frustration. He ran an appreciative hand over the repair. "I've never seen such beautiful work."

"You can't mean that." She felt suddenly self-conscious.

"Yes, I do." He looked at her then, his hazel eyes soft.

Her stomach tumbled again, this time in a pleasurable way. She took a shaky breath. Really she ought to say something, anything, to break this crazy connection before it went too far. "I'm only an apprentice."

"You're much more than that, Minnie. Can't you see? You're talented."

No one had ever said that to her before. Ruthie was the talented one. Compared to her, she was a bumbling beginner. "No, I'm not."

Peter lifted her chin. "Believe in yourself."

His touch sent electricity shooting through her to the tips of her fingers. His gaze drew her like iron to a magnet. No! This could not happen. This was the very reason why Mother and Daddy insisted on a chaperone. If she succumbed, she'd betray their trust.

She drew back and stared at the unyielding material. "It won't much matter how good the repair is if we can't get the cover on the frame."

That effectively ruined the moment. Peter cast his gaze down and stared at the material. He took off his cap and pursed his lips, deep in thought. "Maybe it's too cold. Maybe if we warmed up the leather, it would stretch better."

"Let's try it."

Together, they moved the frame in front of the potbellied stove and then held the leather near the radiant heat. Then they attempted to stretch it again. Minnie struggled to hold the material at one end while Peter tugged it over the frame at the other. It still took effort, but it worked.

An hour later, they finished the seat back. After Peter installed it in the automobile, they lifted the seat cushion into place atop the new luggage compartment.

Minnie drew in her breath. "It's beautiful."

"And your repair doesn't show at all." Peter pointed to the spot.

Minnie circled the auto to check. "You're right." After all the struggle and worry of the week, this was such a relief that her spirits soared. She impulsively threw her arms around Peter. "We did it!"

He hugged her back, and they spun around like kids.

Laughter bubbled up, and soon they were both giggling. It felt good. Too good.

Minnie stepped away and wiped her eyes. "Silly, isn't it?"

"No, it's not. You do beautiful work."

She caught her breath. "You, too. Maybe it's only the start. With work like this, we might get more work. We could make a success of this." Maybe she had put too much emphasis on glamour in the past, but tonight she wasn't thinking about fancy clothes and jewelry. "Maybe I can make enough so Daddy can go back to Battle Creek for treatment."

Until Minnie said she wanted to earn enough to help her sick pa, Peter was going to tell Vince that this was the last job he'd do for Mr. Capone. Now he couldn't. His only hope was that Vince would get mad over the repaired seat back and refuse to give Peter future work.

The rumor he'd overheard still had him on edge. What if Blake Kensington wasn't talking about legitimate business? Even if he wasn't, nothing connected the conversation to Vince except the odd timing. Why did Vince seek him out now? More than four years had passed.

It didn't make sense.

Maybe he was making a fuss out of nothing. Maybe Vince's boss did get his money from furniture and antiques. Maybe this job was a onetime project that would put a little extra cash in the Fox family's coffers.

By the time Peter arrived at the garage the next morning, the only thing he knew for sure was that he had to protect Minnie at all costs. She was an innocent. He couldn't risk bringing her anywhere close to the seedy underworld he'd witnessed in New York.

Vince arrived early. Peter had just gotten into the Pierce-

Arrow to drive it to the train depot when his friend strolled in the open work-bay doors.

"A little late, Stringbean."

Peter stuck his head out the window. "You're already here? The train's not due for ten minutes."

"Came in early." Vince tossed his cigarette butt on the floor and squashed it with heel of his shoe. "Hop out, and let's have a look."

Peter slipped out of the driver's seat and opened the rear door. "There it is." He hoped his nerves didn't show.

Vince got inside and tested the seat. "Feels good," he said while getting out. "Looks good, too. Let's look at the compartment."

Peter circled around to the other side of the car and with a shaking hand opened the opposite rear door. This was the moment of truth. Once they pulled aside the seat cushion, Vince would see the repaired rip in the seat back. Together they pulled the cushion up and set it on the floorboards, revealing the cushioned luggage compartment.

Vince checked the padding and whistled. "Better'n I imagined, kid. You and that gal of yours really know what you're doing." He ran his hand along the back wall of the compartment, mere inches from the repaired seat back.

Peter waited for Vince to comment. When he didn't, Peter showed how to access the hidden compartment by pushing on the front panel, which was spring-loaded.

Vince whistled. "Nice job, kid. The boss'll be impressed." He stepped away, lit a cigarette and blew a cloud of smoke overhead. Then he dug in his pocket and pulled out the money clip. "What did we agree on? A couple hundred?"

Peter's stomach felt like squirrels were racing around inside it. He had to say something. *Please, God, let Vince be disappointed enough to drive away and never come back*. He swallowed the acid taste of the morning's cup of coffee. "There's something you gotta know."

The dark slash of Vince's eyebrow lifted. "What's that?"

"We hadta make a repair." Peter pointed out the repaired seat back.

Vince stared at the spot for a moment and then straightened up and laughed. "That? Can't see it at all." He sobered for a moment. "That gal of yours fix it?"

"She did. She's an expert with needle and thread."

"Ya don't hafta convince me." He peeled three hundred-dollar bills off the wad and held them out to Peter across the roof of the car. "Give her the extra. Say it's from Vince."

Peter would have tossed the cash back at his former friend if Minnie's father didn't need it so badly. "She wants to help her pa. He's got heart trouble."

"Sorry ta hear that. What d'ya say we make it an even four?" He peeled off another bill.

"No." Peter backed away. "It's too much."

"Not for you, kid—for your lady. And her pa. Think o' him."

Peter could only think of the huge amount of money. "It's not worth this much."

"It is to my boss. Like I said, he's generous. Likes ta reward good effort." Vince grabbed the hundred, rounded the car and slapped it against Peter's chest. "If ya want some advice, take the cash. The boss don't like people refusin' his generosity."

That was what had Peter worried, what had his gut churning like an electrified washtub.

"Thank him," he mumbled, but the bill felt like a lead weight in his hand.

Back in New York, he'd seen what happened to people who fell in with the wrong crowd. Mariah's warning rang in his ears. *Mr. Galbini kept company with some pretty rough sorts.* What if he still did? What if accepting this money positioned Peter at the top of an icy slope from which there was no escape?

"Tell you what, kid." Vince leaned against the side of the car puffing a cigarette. "With work like this, the boss will definitely want more. In fact, I can pretty much guarantee I'll have another job for you next Saturday."

Peter felt sick. "Your boss has more than one automobile?"

Vince laughed. "He's got friends. When they see this, they'll want the same."

"Oh." He supposed that made sense in a way, but it was also a pretty big coincidence. "They all like to travel?"

"Sure, kid." Vince seemed oblivious to Peter's discomfort. "I tell you, if you play your cards right, you'll be givin' that gal of yours all the furs and diamonds she wants." Vince tipped his fedora to a jaunty angle and grinned. "Know what I mean?" He punched Peter in the shoulder. "It'll make a man outta you."

This was wrong. All wrong. Vince made Minnie sound like some cheap floozy.

"She's not that kinda gal!" Peter's voice came out louder than he'd intended, but this was Minnie, not some ordinary girl.

Vince backed away, hands up. "Hey, kid, I didn't mean nothing by it."

Peter couldn't stop. Vince's comments fueled an anger Peter had thought dead and gone the moment he'd asked Jesus into his life. Behind that white heat lurked the memory of a friend sprawled dead on the concrete sidewalk, his head lying in a pool of blood, and the taunt of a rival. All over nothing.

Only this wasn't *nothing.* Minnie mattered. She was sweet and innocent, too good for the likes of Vince.

"Don't ever say that about Minnie again."

Vince held up his hands. "Aw right, kid."

That should have soothed him, but Peter couldn't forget how he'd failed his friend. He wouldn't fail Minnie. "You don't deserve someone like her. She's not like you or me. She's good, and I don't want her mixed up in your kinda business. Don't think I can't see what's goin' on here. This ain't no luggage compartment and your boss ain't no furniture dealer. I don't know exactly what you're mixed up in, but it stinks something rotten. Women, gambling or bootlegging? I don't care what, but I don't want any part in it. Hear me? Take your car and get outta here. And never come back."

Vince's jovial expression vanished, replaced with a hardness Peter had never witnessed in his friend before. His brow drew low, his jaw set, and a menacing smile curled his lips. "Ya better watch what ya say." He poked a finger into Peter's chest. "I'm tryin' ta help ya, set ya up so you can get a cozy little house with your lady."

Peter stepped back, repulsed by the idea that Vince would have anything to do with his future. "I don't want it. I don't want anything to do with it. And I don't think anyone else in this town would want this kinda business here, either."

In a flash, Vince grabbed Peter by the collar. Beads of sweat glistened on his brow. "Listen to me, kid. Ya got everything wrong. Your old chum would never steer you into trouble."

The violence from years ago replayed in Peter's mind. The gang jumping out at them. Peter running. His friend caught and pummeled to a bloody pulp. He raised his hands to push Vince away.

At that moment, a woman screamed, "Stop! Stop this minute!"

Minnie! Peter jerked his head toward her. Vince released him and grunted out some nonsense about joking around. But Peter's ears buzzed. He gulped for air and coughed.

"Peter! What are you doing?"

She was blaming him? Incredulous, he stared at her. She stood at the front of the car, so pretty and freshly scrubbed that he couldn't stand it.

Her attention whipped to Vince. "Why were you choking him like that?" She walked straight to Peter's side.

His. Not Vince's. The light-headedness from the fight was replaced with another kind of dizziness. She liked him. She cared. She actually cared for him.

"Choking?" Vince laughed, pulling Peter back to the cold edge of reality. "We were just discussing things." He clapped Peter on the back. "I would never hurt Stringbean."

Why did Vince have to go and use that old nickname in front of Minnie? Peter set his jaw. It wasn't a joke, no matter how much Vince laughed.

Go, he mouthed, but no sound came out.

Minnie still stood by his side, her wide eyes taking in everything Vince said as gospel truth. "Do you apologize, then?"

"Sure thing." Vince extended a hand toward Peter. "Promise it won't happen again, kid."

"There." Minnie beamed as if she had just brokered peace in Europe. "Everyone deserves a second chance."

Not Vince. Not after what he said about Minnie.

"Peter," she chided. "Everyone makes a mistake now and then. Didn't I hear you yelling, too?"

He could have kicked himself. Why hadn't he realized she would come to the garage this morning?

"Aw, that was nothing," Vince said. "Like I said. A little discussion."

That wasn't true, but Minnie was looking at Vince as if he was a hero. By default, that made Peter the bad guy.

If he hoped to claim Minnie's affection, he had to concede. Reluctantly, he shook Vince's hand. "Apology accepted." Even though Vince hadn't exactly apologized.

"Glad that's cleared up." Vince grinned. "Why don't you show your gal what I brought for her?" Without waiting for Peter to speak, he turned to Minnie. "Peter told me about your pa. I was mighty sorry to hear that and want you to have a little extra to help out."

Peter balled his fists. Now Vince was taking credit for helping out Minnie's pa. He gave Peter no choice but to pull the cash from his pocket. Peter had wanted to do this in private, where he could explain to Minnie that they wouldn't be doing any more customizing work. Instead, he had to do it in front of Vince, where he couldn't offer any explanation.

Peter shoved the bills into Minnie's hand. "I want you to have this."

Her eyes widened at the sight of the four hundred-dollar bills. "All of it?"

Peter nodded. Hendrick would be furious, but this was the only way he could best Vince.

His former friend didn't give up easily. "There's more where that came from. I'll be bringing more cars to outfit, right, Peter?"

Peter could clock Vince for working him over this way.

"You will?" Minnie's eyes shone—but not for Peter. "Thank you, Mr. Galbini. And thank your boss, too. Oh, Peter!" At last she turned to him, tears pooling in her eyes as she clutched the bills to her chest. "Now Daddy can get the treatment he needs."

Peter's protest stuck in his throat. When she threw her arms around his neck, it completely died.

Chapter Eleven

It wasn't until later that Minnie realized Peter hadn't seemed very happy about the additional work. Mr. Galbini drove off with his customary wave, but Peter hadn't waved back. She'd thought they were friends.

At the time, all she could think about was the unexpected windfall. She had four hundred dollars in her handbag. Four hundred! Surely that was enough for Daddy to go back to the sanitarium for treatment.

Minnie clutched the handbag to her chest, pausing only a moment to look at the pretty spring gowns in the window of Hutton's Department Store. The blue georgette gown with the fashionable cape effect at the shoulders cost far too much, but a crepe version without the cape cost half that. One little dress wouldn't make much of a dent in four hundred dollars.

She squeezed her handbag tight. The bills crackled beneath her fingers. Why not? She had done the work, after all. Didn't she deserve a little reward? She started toward the door. Then Mrs. Highbottom stepped into the display and removed the caped georgette gown for a delighted Mrs. Vanderloo. Minnie choked, all desire for the gown gone. She hurried past and went straight home.

Minutes later, she was glad she had.

Mother gasped at the sight of the four hundred-dollar bills. "All that for upholstering an automobile?"

"Actually, I only had to fix the tear and pad the new luggage compartment."

Mother looked from the money to Minnie and back again. "It's too much." She pushed the money across the kitchen table. "Peter did the bulk of the work. This belongs to him."

"But…"

Mother was right, of course. Peter had probably worked every night for weeks, whereas she had spent no more than a couple hours on the padding and a few evenings on the seat cover. On the other hand, this money was supposed to help her father get treatment.

"But he gave it to me. And Mr. Galbini wanted to help Daddy."

Mother frowned. "You're telling perfect strangers about private matters?" Her stern tone left no doubt she disapproved.

"I—I—" she stammered. "It slipped out. But if I hadn't mentioned it, Mr. Galbini would never have given me extra."

"This is extra?" Mother looked even more upset. "How much did Peter get?"

"I don't know. I wasn't there when Mr. Galbini paid him."

"Well, I insist you take it back. Make sure Peter received all that was due to him."

"But Daddy needs it," Minnie protested.

"Your father would never take ill-gotten money."

"It's not ill-gotten. Mr. Galbini is Peter's friend."

Mother would not budge. "It's ill-gotten if it is not the

amount agreed upon or earned." Mother stood, signaling the end of the conversation.

No wonder they were poor, if her parents wouldn't even accept a gift. Minnie slid the money back into her handbag. Wealth was fleeting indeed.

Peter had been backed into a corner, and he didn't like it. The only thing about this deal that felt right was helping out Minnie's family. If not for that, he would have kicked Vince and his fancy car out of the garage with an order never to return. Instead, he'd choked.

After closing the garage, he automatically headed for Constance House, but what he really wanted was to talk this over with someone. Not Hendrick or Mariah. They gave good advice and all, but they'd warned him about Vince, and he didn't much want to hear an *I told you so.*

Ma gave good advice, too, but this was completely outside her experience. She'd never been to the city, least of all lived in the rough areas where gangs ruled with their fists and whatever weapons they could get their hands on. Same for Anna, though he'd never much thought of her as someone to give sound advice. She was only a little older than him.

The church bells rang the five-o'clock hour. As the last peal drifted away on the breeze, Peter realized he knew someone who both gave good advice and understood the streets. Pastor Gabe. He hadn't lived on the streets like Peter, but he'd helped round up street urchins like him. Urchins. Vandals. Criminals. He'd been called that and more. Some of it deserved. But Pastor Gabe never once brought up the past. Not once. The pastor acted as if Peter's life had started the day he entered the orphanage. Good thing. If he knew what Peter had done…

No. That was past. Over. Dead and gone.

Except it had come back today as vividly as the day it happened.

Peter looked at the church door a good five minutes, debating whether or not to call on the preacher. When Pastor Gabe left the building, Peter wove his way across the street between motorcars, trucks and the wagons that some of the farmers still used.

"Hello, Peter!" Pastor Gabe, in an old mackinaw and no hat, closed the church door. "You look like a man with a mission. Anything I can do for you?"

Peter buried his hands in his coat pockets and glanced up at the graying sky. The sun stayed up a little longer now, but twilight still started to set in around closing time. "Just wanted to talk."

"All right." Gabe glanced toward the stepping-stone path that led to the parsonage behind the church. "We won't get any privacy there with little Branford and Tillie visiting Genie and Luke. What do you say we get a cup of coffee at Lily's? Or is this confidential?"

"No." Peter didn't want to put Pastor Gabe out more than he already was. The restaurant would be busy on a Saturday. Even if people wanted to listen, they'd have a tough time hearing anything in that din. He dug around in his pocket and found sufficient change. "Coffee's all right."

"Good. I could use the boost before going over my sermon tonight."

"With all the children running around?" Peter matched the pastor's gait. "I can't concentrate at all after supper at the orphanage."

Gabe laughed. "You have a point. Maybe I'll go back to the church after supper."

The restaurant was only a block away on the opposite side of the street. It occupied the lower level of a two-story building topped with a squared-off facade in front of the pitched roof. Other than the name painted on the windows, little marked it as a restaurant. Locals knew it as a first-rate bakery and the only place in town to dine out. By supper, the rolls, pies and cakes were usually snatched up. Peter was surprised to see a pecan pie in the bakery case.

"Looks like I'll have to have a slice of pecan pie with that coffee," Gabe said. "You want one, too?"

If Peter had kept any of the money Vince shoved at him, he would have said yes. "Nope. Just coffee."

"Saving room for Mariah's cooking?" Pastor Gabe said as the waitress led them past several open tables to one at the far end of the room. Its location gave them automatic privacy, especially since none of the surrounding tables were filled.

Peter sat down. "She makes a great caramel cake."

They chatted about favorite foods until the waitress served the pie and coffee. Then Gabe asked what was on his mind.

Peter stirred milk and sugar into his cup. He took a cautious sip and considered how to approach the problem. "You ever have trouble figuring out the right thing to do?"

Pastor Gabe leaned back. "We all do at one time or another."

"How do you do it?"

"Well, let's see." Gabe ran the edge of his thumb along his lower lip. "Personally, I pray. Read the Bible. See where God wants me to go."

"What if He doesn't answer?"

Surprisingly, Pastor Gabe nodded with understanding. "Sometimes it seems like He doesn't, but that's usually when we already know what we want and are more or less asking God for confirmation."

"Oh." Peter frowned. "I didn't think that's what I wanted."

"The mind is a fickle thing. Sometimes we get so lost thinking that we forget what we really wanted in the first place. It feels like we're going around and around in circles."

"That's it! I want to do what's right, but doing that will hurt someone else. Then I start wondering if what I think is right is actually wrong."

Pastor Gabe looked lost for only a moment. "Why don't you give me some details?"

Peter blanched.

"This is strictly between us, Peter. Not a word goes beyond this conversation."

Peter felt a little better. "Remember when I asked you about Vince?"

"Vince?"

"Vincent Galbini. He helped out at the orphanage in New York."

"Right. Vince." Pastor Gabe focused in on Peter. "You said he stopped by to fulfill his promise."

"Yeah." Peter shifted in his chair, suddenly uncomfortable. Gabe was a minister, after all, a man of God. He might not understand. "Do you remember him much from New York?"

Gabe sat back and looked off into the distance. "Stocky build? Boxer's nose?"

"Yep. He taught me carpentry."

"Right. He fixed a lot of things around the place, too. Good with his hands, but I never worked with him directly. Why do you ask?"

Peter toyed with the handle of his coffee cup. "Mariah seems to think he had the wrong kind of friends."

Pastor Gabe planted his elbows on the table and leaned forward. "Go on," he said in a low voice.

Peter looked around, afraid someone was listening in,

but they were alone. He licked his lips. "Well…" Peter cleared his throat. This was tough to admit. "I think she might be right."

"When did you come to this conclusion? Before or after she suggested he kept the wrong company?"

"After."

"Do you think it's possibly her opinion affected yours?"

Peter had never considered that. "Do you think so?" He felt a little relieved.

"It's possible. But tell me why this is bothering you."

"He offered me work."

Now Pastor Gabe looked surprised. "He wants you to leave Pearlman?"

Peter shook his head. "I didn't say that right. I can do the work here. He had me put a luggage compartment in his boss's car."

"I don't see the problem."

Now that he'd said it aloud, Peter wondered if he'd blown this all out of proportion. After all, he did the job. He got paid. The money! Maybe that was it. "He paid a lot, more than it's worth."

"Did he give you a reason?"

Peter stared into his milky brown coffee. "Wanted to help out Minnie's folks."

"All right. You lost me. How did he even know Minnie's family needed help?"

"Well, she helped me with the job, and I kinda told him about her parents and how much she wants her pa to see special doctors but they don't have the money."

"So Mr. Galbini was generous. That's a good thing, Peter. A man who gives willingly to someone he doesn't even know has a good heart."

"I'm not so sure about that."

"Why?"

The thoughts tumbled around in Peter's head. He remembered the way Minnie had looked at Vince, the eager anticipation, the adulation. Was he simply jealous of Vince? Was that why he thought his friend wasn't telling him the whole story about that luggage compartment? He squeezed the coffee cup between his hands. "I think maybe I have some confessing to do to God."

"We all do. Every day. He'll listen, Peter. Have no doubt."

Peter recalled overhearing the conversation between Blake Kensington and the unknown man. The way they talked led him to think they expected bootleg liquor to come out of Pearlman, but Peter had no proof that was even what they meant. He sighed with frustration. "Do you know there's a speakeasy out back of the drugstore?"

Pastor Gabe sat a little straighter. "I do. What of it? Have you been in there, Peter?"

He shook his head.

"Has Mr. Galbini?"

"I don't think so, but I got to wondering how they get the liquor."

Pastor Gabe sighed. "Home brew and bootlegging, I'm afraid. Back when I first came to town—the same summer you arrived on the train—I got caught up trying to stop a bootlegging ring. It nearly got Felicity killed." He sobered. "I came to the wrong conclusions and took matters into my own hands instead of relying on the law." He looked Peter squarely in the eyes. "If you think Mr. Galbini is involved with that business, steer clear of him and anything to do with it. I was fortunate. No one got hurt from my mistakes, but someone easily could have."

Peter swallowed hard. This was the same conclusion he'd come to, except... "But what if steering clear means hurting someone you love?"

Gabe sat back. "Then, my friend, you have to take this to the only one who can help—God."

Minnie didn't catch up to Peter at church the next day. He arrived late and hurried off with Mrs. Simmons before she could get to him. He didn't even look her way once.

"Why the frown?" Mother asked after they buttoned up their coats and hurried out into the chilly March morning.

Minnie stomped her feet to bring a little warmth into them as they waited for Jen, who was chatting with the Hunters. "Nothing."

"Hmm. Then you're pouting for no reason."

Minnie scrunched her shoulders against the stiff breeze. "I don't see why it has to be so cold when the snow is almost gone."

"Something tells me that's not what's troubling you."

Her mother could be relentless. "Peter didn't look at me once."

"I see." Mother pulled a handkerchief from her handbag and dabbed at her nose. "Are you serious about him?"

"No!" Minnie pulled up her coat collar. "You said I had to give him back the money."

"You brought that to church?"

"No. But I figured I could arrange a time to meet him."

Mother wrapped her arm around Minnie's shoulders. "Don't fret, dear. You can stop by the garage tomorrow."

That was true, but tomorrow came and went without an opportunity to walk down to the motor garage. Jen was busy at the airfield and couldn't spell Minnie at the shop. Daddy's coughing got so bad that Mother called in Doc Stevens and wouldn't leave Daddy's side. That meant Minnie had to run the dress shop by herself. By the time she closed, the garage was also shut down for the day.

The next day and the next turned out the same. The

shop had never been busier. It seemed half the women who bought a dress at the department store wanted alterations. Minnie took measurements, made notes and carefully labeled each gown. The work orders piled up, and she only had time to work on them after supper. Ruthie could not get home soon enough.

By Friday, Minnie had completely forgotten about the money. At five o'clock, she ushered out the last customer and flipped the sign to indicate they were closed before turning the lock.

"Whew." She leaned her back against the door, exhausted.

What a week. Dresses hung everywhere. Work orders littered the table. Thread and pencils and pins and tape measures were strewn across every surface. Tonight she wouldn't work. Tonight she would put her feet in a tub of warm water and Epsom salts.

Rap, rap, rap.

The knocking from behind startled her. Not another customer! Well, the woman could wait until morning. Minnie spun around and came face-to-face with Peter.

"You!"

"Can we talk?" he called through the glass and motioned to the door handle.

This was the last thing she needed tonight. Her feet ached. Her back ached. Her mind could barely process a thought, except that she still needed to return the four hundred dollars. Which she did not have at the shop. Still, he was giving her such a sorry look that she had to let him in.

"Thank you." He stepped just inside the door and tugged off his cap while she locked the door again. "I won't take much of your time."

"Wait right here." Minnie hurried to the back room and grabbed her coat. "I'll be right back."

"Where are you going?"

"Home. I need to bring back the money you gave me. Mother says it's too much and belongs to you."

He flushed. "No, it's not. I got paid up front."

"You did?" She stopped buttoning the coat. "You mean all that is just for me?"

He nodded.

"Will you tell my mother that? She doesn't believe me."

He smiled. "Sure."

Her spirits soared. "Thank you, thank you." But he didn't look happy. "What's wrong?"

He wouldn't look at her.

"Did you hear something from Mr. Galbini? Was there a problem?"

He licked his lips and shrugged. "No, but I don't think he'll bring us any more jobs."

"Why? I don't understand. I thought he was pleased with our work. He promised to bring more work."

He still wouldn't look at her. Something was definitely wrong. "He said maybe."

That wasn't what she remembered, but then Mr. Galbini might not have noticed her repair until he got home. "He was angry about the tear, wasn't he? I did my best, but it wasn't good enough."

"It was wonderful." Peter lifted her chin and swiped away the tear that had dropped onto her cheek. "You did great. It's just over. Take the money. Use it for your pa. Be grateful for that." He glanced at the worktable. "You look plenty busy anyway."

She tried her best to smile, but she could only think of Daddy and how he wasn't getting any better. Peter didn't need to know that, though. He'd done his best by asking her to do the upholstery. "I'm being silly."

"No, you're not." If anything, he looked more distressed than her. "You're worried about your pa. I would be, too, if…"

If he had a pa. In all her concern about Daddy, she'd forgotten that Peter had been orphaned. "Do you remember your father?"

"A little." He tucked his hands into his coat pockets. "I remember Ma more, even though they died at the same time."

She gasped. "Both at once? What happened?"

"They got sick. People said influenza, just like Aunt Ursula. I just know that one day Ma died, and the next Pa was gone."

"I can't imagine losing every living relative."

He hesitated while a mix of emotions played across his face. "There's still Aunt Ursula's brother, but he's a bad sort. A criminal. I don't want anything to do with him." Again he looked down at his feet. "Listen, Minnie. I seen some terrible stuff during that time, things no kid should see. There are bad people out there. You don't see them much in a nice town like this, but they're everywhere in the city."

His stricken expression drove a pang of sympathy deep into her heart. What had he been through? Whatever it was, it still hurt. She reached up and cupped his cheek. "At least you're here now and with a good family."

"The best." He took her hand and held it, as if she was his lifeline. "Thank you for understanding."

She didn't know what to say. He'd uncovered something deeply painful, something she couldn't understand. Embarrassed by her deficiencies, she looked over his shoulder and out the window to the darkening street and was surprised to see a man in a dark overcoat approaching the shop.

"We're closed," she called out as the man lifted his hand to knock.

The man tipped up his hat to reveal his face. It was Mr. Galbini.

"Hey, kid." Galbini pointed toward the street, where a black sedan was parked. "Brought you the next job."

Minnie stared at Peter. "I thought you said there wouldn't be any more work."

Peter looked distressed.

Mr. Galbini pounded on the door. "You gonna let me in?"

Minnie hurried over and unlocked the door.

Galbini strode in with a rush of icy air. "There you are, kid. Looked all over until some guy said you'd headed here." He looked around the shop. "Nice place, doll. Can see why you did such a good job. Keep it up, and there'll be another good payday for ya."

"Do you mean it?" Minnie reveled in the turn of events. "Peter, we have more work! Isn't it wonderful?"

His shoulders drooped. "Sure."

Why didn't he look happy? This was the answer to prayer. If Mr. Galbini paid like the last time, Daddy could get all the treatments he needed. Peter knew that. The extra work would help him, too. He could help out the orphanage. Maybe he could put together that apprenticeship program for the older kids. He should be thrilled. Instead he looked as if someone had died.

She would never understand him. Ever.

Chapter Twelve

Trapped.

Vince and Minnie had sandwiched Peter between dazzling promise and desperate need. He couldn't back out now.

Even though he'd wired Vince earlier in the week and cut off future business, the man showed up anyway. If Peter had been alone, he would have sent Vince back, but Minnie's desperate hope sealed the unhappy deal.

She didn't know Peter's suspicions, and he didn't dare tell her. If Blake Kensington was involved, so was her oldest sister. If Minnie knew, she'd be an accomplice. Peter could take the consequences, but not Minnie. No, he must protect her at all costs.

He raked a hand through his hair, trying to figure a way out of this.

Then Vince invited them to supper at the local restaurant. Minnie looked to Peter with such excitement that he couldn't refuse. He sure couldn't let her go with Vince unescorted. So the three of them walked down the block to Lily's.

The meal was miserable. They sat around a small table in the middle of the room, Minnie between the two men.

Peter might not have been there for all the attention she gave him. Minnie focused completely on Vince, who went on and on about fancy nightclubs. Peter tried to point out their seamy underside, but Minnie was so caught up in Vince's description that she didn't hear a word he said.

"We had one swell little songbird in the joint last weekend." Vince sighed. "Pretty as a peach and no older'n you."

Minnie blushed. "I sang in the school choir. Second soprano. I would have been first, but the teacher thought Kate Vanderloo had the best voice."

"That so?" Vince's gaze drifted to the other diners, mostly couples and families, until it landed on the pretty, young waitress who had taken their order. "That gal there, is she a friend of yours?" He nodded toward the counter, where Lucy Billingsley was getting direction from Lillian Mattheson, middle-aged owner of the restaurant, on the proper way to carry the meals to their table.

Minnie wrinkled her nose. "Lucy? She's still in high school. Kate is in college."

Peter didn't like the way Vince was looking at the girl, so he changed the subject while Lucy served their meals. "Minnie, is your pa doing better?"

Minnie blinked at him, as if just realizing he was there, and her excitement deflated. "We had to call in Doc Stevens."

"I'm sorry." Peter glanced across the table. Vince looked uncomfortable with the change of topic. Now that Lucy had vanished into the kitchen, he focused on shoveling the food into his mouth at a rapid rate. Peter turned back to Minnie. "I hope Doc was able to help."

Minnie shrugged. "He says Daddy needs to get a little better before he can make the train trip to the sanitarium."

Peter swallowed a gulp of coffee. "I don't understand. The train should be the most comfortable way to travel."

"Daddy would have to change trains in Grand Rapids and again in Kalamazoo. It's too taxing." She sighed. "I wish there was a direct route."

"I could drive him there."

"You could?" Her face lit with eager expectation.

"Sure."

Doubt creased her brow. "In what? I didn't know you had an automobile."

"I'm sure Mariah would loan me hers." At least he hoped she would. Mariah could usually be talked into any charitable cause.

Vince interjected, "Take the Lincoln. On me."

That drew Minnie's attention—and appreciation—back to Vince. "The car you drove here? You'd let us use it?"

"Of course." Vince grinned smugly. "Just don't let nothin' happen to her." That warning was meant for Peter, even though Vince said it to Minnie.

"Oh, we wouldn't, would we, Peter?" She barely glanced at him, her attention entirely focused on Vince. "Peter's a good driver. I know most people his age can't drive, but he's an expert."

Peter ought to feel better than he did about the compliment.

"His age?" Vince laughed. "A man of twenty oughta be able ta drive, especially when he's a mechanic."

Peter sucked in his breath, regretting that he'd shared his true age with Vince years ago. He hoped Minnie hadn't noticed.

She had. Her gaze whipped around to meet his. "Twenty?" She turned back to Vince. "Peter's only eighteen. He doesn't turn nineteen until summer. I'm four months older than him."

Peter put a finger to his lips, but his friend ignored him.

"Eighteen?" Vince snorted. "That what he told you? He's twenty if he's a day."

Minnie turned back to Peter. "Is that true?"

Peter considered the options. Lie. That was what someone like Vince would do. Explain. That was what Ma Simmons would tell him to do, but Minnie might not understand. He licked his lips. "Well, now..."

"It is true, isn't it?" she demanded. "Why would you lie about your age?"

Vince took that opportunity to excuse himself to use the facilities.

Peter was glad to have Vince out of the way for this painful admission.

"Well? Why did you say you were younger than you were?" Minnie demanded.

When Peter turned his back on the past, he hadn't counted on the price he'd have to pay. The bill had now come due. "I did it because I heard no one wanted kids over fourteen. I thought the orphanage would send me back on the street if they knew I was sixteen." He stared into his coffee and waited for her reproach.

"How dreadful." Instead of anger, she offered sympathy. "Why didn't you tell me?"

He swallowed hard. "I couldn't tell anyone. Once a kid turns seventeen, the orphan society considers him an adult. I would have been cut loose with nowhere to go."

Her lip quivered. "Oh, Peter. Mrs. Simmons would never send you away."

"I know that now, but I didn't know that then."

"But it's been four years."

"I know, but how do you tell someone you love that you lied to them? I didn't want to hurt her. I didn't want to hurt anyone. So, what's a couple years?"

"I suppose you're right, but I would have kept your secret." She quickly squeezed his hand, and a jolt of electricity shot through him. "I'll keep it now, if you want."

Her understanding pretty near overwhelmed him. "Thanks, but I suppose there's no point now. Let me tell Ma first, though, will you?"

"Of course."

His heart swelled with compassion. "You're the best, Minnie Fox. You always were."

She cast him a tentative smile. "You're just saying that."

He wanted so badly to hold her hand, but he didn't dare. "No, I'm not. You're the smartest gal I know. And the prettiest."

This time her smile didn't waver.

She made him feel about ten feet tall.

Peter's admission about his real age changed the whole way Minnie thought about him. She'd always considered him a kid. Those little tugs of attraction meant nothing. He just had a crush on her, like she'd had on Reggie Landers.

So she'd kept Peter at arm's length and called him a friend. Now she noticed the pleasant curve of his lips and the way his hazel eyes shone when he looked at her. Over the years, his shoulders had broadened, while his waist stayed nice and trim. Best of all, she enjoyed spending time with him and looked forward to the day he would bring the first board of the new luggage compartment to the dress shop.

At church on Sunday, he glanced her way at least a dozen times. She smiled back and was thrilled to see his neck redden. Unfortunately, other girls looked his way, too. Some even hurried over to intercept him before he left the sanctuary. He treated each one with kindness and respect, which only made them hang around. Minnie couldn't say anything personal, so she settled for telling him that Doc

Stevens had shot down the idea of taking Daddy to Battle
Creek by automobile.

"I'm sorry," he said before Lucy Billingsley pressed in
to ask if he could sing.

Frustrated, Minnie left. No use trying to have a private
conversation with those girls hanging around.

When over a week passed without word from Peter,
Minnie headed for the garage after closing the dress shop.
She would simply ask how the car was coming along. It
was a perfectly understandable question. To her surprise,
three girls were peering in the garage windows and giggling. They hopped from one window to another until one
shrieked that she'd seen Peter.

"He's too old for you," Minnie called out.

They shot her a look of disgust before hurrying off in
a chorus of giggles.

When she stepped into the office, no one was there. The
work bays were empty, too. "Peter?"

He stepped out from behind a tall set of shelves. "I'm
glad it's you. I was afraid they were coming after me."

She burst out laughing. "You're so afraid of high-school
girls that you had to hide?"

A sheepish grin split his face. "I guess that sounds
pretty silly. Anyway, I'm glad you're here."

The admission made her all warm and mushy inside.

"Is everything all right?" he asked.

She knew he meant her family, but she felt a little awkward now saying why she'd come over, as if she was ques-
tioning his ability to do the job. On the other hand, she did
need some idea when to expect the work. She examined
her shoes, which needed shining. "Daddy's still too weak
to travel, but that's not why I stopped in. I wondered if you
can tell me when to expect the first board."

"Soon. I haven't rushed, since Vince said he wouldn't

pick up the car until the beginning of next month." He looked out the window. "It's too nice a day to work. Want a soda? I'm buying."

Minnie hadn't had a soda in ages. "At the drugstore?" Companies were selling them in bottles now, but she preferred the ones at the soda fountain.

"Sure thing. Let me close up, and we'll head right there."

Minnie waited outside, glorying in the first warmth of the season. Crocuses peeked out of the half-frozen earth and waved their lavender petals in the light breeze. Daffodils and hyacinths would come along next, followed by the showy tulips. How she loved the colors of spring. From bleak grays to a vibrant rainbow. That would lift anyone's spirits.

When Peter finished locking up the garage, they strolled along Main Street, looking at the window displays in the department store and the mercantile.

"Look at that!" Minnie pointed to a cube-shaped wooden box with black Bakelite dials. She pressed close to the glass to read the manufacturer's label. "RCA Radiola. What's that?"

"A radio. You can listen to music broadcast through the air. Wouldn't it be wonderful to have one?"

"It looks complicated to operate and costs a fortune. Thirty-five dollars. I'll never own one."

"Maybe someday." He wrapped an arm around her shoulders, and they strolled on.

"I suppose." But it seemed hopeless.

When they reached the drugstore, Peter grasped the door handle, but something caught Minnie's eye. A handwritten notice on plain white paper announced that a new community theater group had formed and was conducting auditions for a musical revue.

"Look!" Minnie pointed at the notice, her pulse accelerating. "Imagine that. A musical revue right here in Pearlman. And they're holding auditions in two weeks."

Peter joined her. "A musical revue?"

"You know, like the *Ziegfeld Follies*."

His eyebrows shot up. "Aren't those a little risqué? Are you sure your parents would approve?"

Minnie was tired of everyone telling her what she could and couldn't do. "I'm nineteen now. I don't see why I have to have their approval for everything. Besides, I'm sure this revue won't be the slightest bit risqué. It says here that Mrs. Kensington is the director. She's president of the Ladies' Aid Society and as proper as they come. Oh, Peter. This could be my big chance. Maybe one day I'll be famous. They could even play my songs on that machine."

"Maybe." He squinted at the sign. "It says rehearsals will be every evening in April and May. That would mean no more working on automobiles."

For some reason, he looked pleased, which completely mystified her. Didn't he like spending time with her? Hadn't he just put his arm around her shoulders? Well, he couldn't get rid of her that easily. "Don't worry. Ruth and Sam will be back in April to manage the dress shop. Then I can work on cars in the daytime."

He didn't look relieved. "First you have to audition and get a part. Have you ever sung solo?"

"Well, no," she admitted. "But it shouldn't be much different than singing in choir."

"If you think so."

"You're always telling me I can do whatever I put my mind to."

"Yeah." But his brow refused to release a frown. "But I didn't mean you should put your mind to any old thing. You gotta be choosy."

"I am choosy." Sometimes that man could drive her to

distraction. "Quit being such a stick in the mud and buy me that soda you promised."

Finally, he smiled.

Though Peter prayed Mr. and Mrs. Fox would refuse to let Minnie audition for the musical revue, they gave their permission. Didn't they know this would only fuel her daydreams about singing in a nightclub?

She got more and more excited each day and could talk of nothing else. She finished the boards Peter brought her, but he deliberately dragged his feet while he figured out a way to wriggle out of this agreement with Vince. Now, with her auditions for the musical revue coming up the first week of April, one more thing hounded his thoughts day and night.

Minnie didn't know that those fancy nightclubs she idolized often used the musical acts as a cover for the real moneymaking activities taking place behind closed doors. The thought of Minnie anywhere near that scene made him sick.

"Will you go with me Tuesday?" Minnie asked as the audition date approached.

While finishing the luggage compartment, they'd become closer as friends, though she still gave no indication she wanted anything more than that. Mariah had advised him to be there for Minnie, not to pressure her and to wait for her to let him know she was ready for more. He supposed going to the auditions fit into that, but he couldn't pull up much enthusiasm, even when they stood in the school auditorium waiting for the director to call her to the stage.

Girl after girl tried out for a spot. Each brought some applause, but the loudest applause came after Sally Neidecker, dressed in a shocking flapper dress, belted out "Second

Hand Rose." Sally, with her sleek bob and painted face, looked artificial to Peter, but Minnie oohed and aahed with the rest of the crowd.

"Do you think I look all right?" she asked, fussing with her hair.

"You look pretty."

She rolled her eyes. "You always say that."

"I mean it." He didn't know how else he could say it. "You'll do great."

"Are you sure?" She nibbled her lip.

"Don't worry." He squeezed her cold hands in his warmer ones. "You can do anything you put your mind to."

For a second, her confidence buoyed, but then Mrs. Kensington called Minnie's name, and the nerves came back full force.

"I can't," she whispered. "Tell her I don't feel well."

Peter wanted to do just that, but if he let her walk away now, she'd consider it failure. So, against better judgment, he pushed her forward. "You can do it. I'll be right here. Just watch me when you're singing and forget everyone else."

She looked terrified but managed to walk to the front of the auditorium and climbed the stairs to the stage.

How small and pale and vulnerable she looked! He wanted to hold her, to hug her and tell her she didn't need to do this to prove herself to anyone. But then the pianist played the opening notes, and Minnie started to sing. Her sweet soprano began in a whisper before the words to "Amazing Grace" gathered steam. He'd never heard her sing solo before. In the choir, her voice blended with the others. She was good. Real good.

By the second verse, he had tears in his eyes. She couldn't possibly know how much that song meant to him, for he'd been headed down the wrong path, doing the wrong things, until God, through Mr. Isaacs and the orphan society, gave him a second chance.

When she finished, the previously raucous auditorium was dead silent. For long seconds, no one said a thing or applauded. He looked around and saw the same stunned expression on each face. In that moment, he knew she would win a spot in the revue. Minnie, on the other hand, paled. She ran from the stage and up the aisle past him, trying her best to cover sobs.

"Minnie, wait." He went after her.

She left the auditorium and stumbled onto the barren lawn. Her sobs came more audibly now.

"You did wonderful." He reached for her, but she pushed him away. He caught her arm. "It was beautiful."

"They hated it," she choked out. "I should have done a popular song, like the other girls, but Mother wanted me to do a hymn. Why did I listen?"

"It was the right song."

She pulled away. "Leave me alone. You never wanted me to do this. You've fought me from the start. Well, you won. Are you happy now?" She backed away, tears streaming down her cheeks.

"But don't you want to see the results?"

"No!" she shouted. "Leave. Me. Alone."

She ran, and he let her go. Her despair would turn to ecstasy when she learned she'd made the revue. Nothing he could say before then would convince her of the truth.

He shuffled toward Main Street, hands in his jacket pockets. At the corner, a newsboy hawked the evening edition of the newspaper. Peter could use something to take his mind off the events of today. He paid the nickel and tucked the newspaper under his arm. He didn't want to go back to the hubbub of the orphanage. Tonight, he needed some time alone, so he stopped at Lily's for a cup of coffee.

After settling at the back table, he opened the newspaper and sipped on his coffee.

"May I join you?"

Peter pulled down the paper to see Pastor Gabe. Anyone else he'd ask to leave, but he couldn't say that to his pastor. "All right."

Gabe sat. "I see you got today's newspaper."

"Yeah." Peter lifted it back up. "I'm reading"

"I see that. I was wondering about something, though. What's the name of the town that Vince is living in these days?"

"Cicero, Illinois." Peter dropped the paper. "Why?"

"Page five." Gabe stood. "I'll be at the parsonage if you need to talk."

"Why would I need to talk?"

"Page five," Gabe repeated before leaving.

Peter leafed to the spot and nearly knocked his cup of coffee over when he saw the headline: Cicero Police Shoot Capone.

In minutes he'd scanned the short article and discovered policemen had shot and killed Frank Capone after a day and a half of brutality surrounding the local elections. Vince said his boss was named Al, not Frank. Could they be the same? Peter read more carefully and discovered Frank was a brother to Al. Apparently three men had been accosting citizens outside the polls, trying to force them to cast their vote for the Republican ticket. Chicago police approached, and Frank Capone fired at them. A firefight ensued, and Capone got shot. The police captured and arrested a second man, but the third—described as dark, short and stocky—vanished into the night.

The air left Peter's lungs in a whoosh. Short, dark and stocky. Vince. What if the man who'd escaped, the man who'd terrorized citizens trying to vote, was his old friend?

Chapter Thirteen

Minnie hurried home from the auditions, wishing she'd never gone. Why did every risk she took end in disaster? Before entering the house, she wiped her eyes and took a few deep breaths. Then she forced a smile. Mother had refused to let her audition until Minnie agreed to sing a hymn. If only she'd been able to sing a popular song, like Sally. Then she would have gotten lots of applause and won a spot in the revue. Mother *knew* that singing a hymn would ruin her chances. Minnie would not let her mother know that she'd failed the audition.

She opened the door and stepped inside. The kitchen was still warm from the day's cooking. Minnie peeled off her coat and removed her hat and gloves. The house sounded unusually quiet. The kitchen was empty, as it often was at this time of day, but so was the living room. How odd. None of her family had come to the auditions. Where would they be? Father hadn't left the house since Ruthie's wedding last October.

A note of panic chased away Minnie's despair. "Mother?"

No answer.

She crossed to the front door. Maybe her mother was

outside pulling last year's flowers from the beds lining
the front of the porch. Minnie shivered as she opened the
door. It had been a fine day, warm for early April, but the
setting sun took the heat with it. She wouldn't choose to
work outdoors after dusk.

Neither did Mother. Then where…? There wasn't anyone outside, just an automobile. Minnie turned back to the
living room when she realized that was Doc Stevens's car
parked in front of the house. The doctor! She raced through
the house and up the stairs, reaching the landing just as
Mother and the doctor left Daddy's room.

"Daddy?" she gasped, out of breath.

Mother's eyes were red and her complexion pale.

"Is he…?" She couldn't ask the rest.

"He's resting now," Doc Stevens said. He looked to
Mother. "I don't see any other choice."

Minnie's heart nearly pounded from her chest. "Other
choice? What's going on? What happened?"

"Hush now, child," Mother said, her tone brooking no
discussion. "Let me see the doctor out, and then we will
talk."

Minnie trailed her mother and the doctor down the
stairs. While Mother talked quietly with Doc Stevens on
the porch, Minnie stood in the doorway to the kitchen,
watching the conversation that Mother clearly did not want
her to hear. The doctor's shoulders were rounded, as if
he carried the burden of every painful diagnosis. Mother
nodded, calm and businesslike. Mother never broke down
in front of others.

After Doc Stevens drove away, Mother stood on the
porch a long while. Minnie didn't dare interrupt. Mother
would not speak until she was ready. Minnie waited at the
kitchen table that seemed so small yet had once seated
six at every meal. Minute after minute ticked by. She

drummed her fingers and then checked the clock. She straightened the salt and pepper shakers and then checked the clock. She made sure the hot-water tank was full and then checked the clock.

Jen burst in, coatless and hatless. She halted the instant she saw Minnie. "What happened?"

"I don't know. Doc Stevens was here. Mother hasn't left the porch yet."

"She didn't tell you anything?"

Minnie shook her head. "Doc said there was no other choice, but I don't know what he meant."

Jen blew out her breath and sank into one of the kitchen chairs. The scene felt just like the one they'd gone through last summer except this time Ruthie wasn't there. "Did he have another stroke of apoplexy?"

"I don't know, but what else could it be? Doc said Daddy was resting now."

"Well, at least there's that." Jen gnawed on her knuckles. "Maybe he's just weaker."

Minnie heard the front door creak. She touched a finger to her lips and pointed toward the living room to make Jen stop talking.

Mother walked into the room. "Well, girls, we have work to do."

She sank into the chair that Jen kicked out for her without even correcting Jen's manners. This must be very bad news indeed.

Mother sighed and folded her hands. "Your father needs to go to the hospital in Grand Rapids."

"Grand Rapids?" Jen exclaimed. "Why there when his doctors are in Battle Creek?"

Minnie noticed the blotchiness of Mother's cheeks and kicked her sister's shin under the table.

"Ouch!" Jen glared at her.

Minnie glared back.

Mother seemed not to notice. She stared off into space, unnaturally calm. "Doctor Stevens doesn't believe your father is strong enough to make the trip to Battle Creek. Grand Rapids is closer. The hospital has fine doctors, and your father would only have to transfer once from the train to a taxicab."

"Peter said he'd drive Daddy to Battle Creek," Minnie repeated.

This time Mother noticed that Minnie had spoken. She laid her hand on Minnie's, but it shook so much that the gesture did nothing to comfort. "I know, dear, but we can't ask Peter to leave work for the entire day. Your father was adamant. The train will do. But I will need you to watch the shop and both of you to take care of things around the house. I will wire Ruth in the morning, but it'll be a few days before she can get here. Until then, I'm looking to both of you to manage."

Mother and Daddy were leaving them again. Minnie looked at Jen, whose stricken expression made Minnie feel even worse.

"Will you stay there?" Minnie choked out.

"As long as necessary." Mother gave Minnie a soft smile. "How did the audition go, dearest?"

A lump grew in her throat. She had completely forgotten her misery of the past hour, but not Mother. "How can you think of something so unimportant at a time like this?"

"It's important to you," Mother said, "so it's important to me."

"It went all right." Minnie wouldn't say more. She wouldn't reveal the dead silence and shocked expressions in the audience. She couldn't add to Mother's burden.

"That's good, dear." Mother patted her hand. "I'm sure

you did your best. The Lord might have touched hearts through your singing tonight."

Minnie hung her head. How selfish she'd been! The entire audition, she'd thought only of what she wanted, instead of how her singing might reach others. No wonder Mother wanted her to sing a hymn. She hadn't wanted Minnie to fail. Her focus was on higher goals, while Minnie dreamed of lesser, unimportant things. A sob rose in her throat.

"I'm sorry, Mother."

"Oh, dearest. I know." Mother enveloped her in an embrace and kissed the top of her head. "I know. This is hard on all of us, but remember that your father is in the Lord's hands." She wiped a tear from Minnie's cheek. "There's no better place to be."

A loud rapping on the front door startled them all.

Jen hopped up. "I'll get it."

Mother handed Minnie a clean handkerchief. "Now wipe your eyes, child. You don't want company to find you out of sorts."

"Yes, ma'am." When it came to public appearance, Mother was a stickler for putting on a good face. Minnie blotted the tears from her eyes and blew her nose.

By the time she'd tucked away the handkerchief, Jen led their oldest sister, Beatrice, into the kitchen.

"Minnie! There you are!" Beattie bubbled with excitement. "Eugenia was looking for you everywhere."

Minnie stared blankly before remembering that Eugenia was Mrs. Kensington's first name. "Oh. The audition. I'm sorry I wasn't more gracious. I should have thanked her like the others did."

"Don't be silly," Beattie said. "That's not why I'm here. You made the show!"

Half an hour ago, that news would have sent Minnie into fits of excitement. Now it meant nothing.

Beatrice looked from Minnie to Jen to Mother. "What's wrong? Why the glum expressions? This is good news."

Jen's lip quivered for a second before she reined it in. "Daddy has to go to the hospital."

"What?" Beatrice sank into a chair. "What happened? When? What can I do?"

"Your father felt worse this evening," Mother replied. "I went to the mercantile and called Doc Stevens. He said there's nothing more he can do for your father, that he needs to go to the hospital. Jen and Minnie will handle things here while your father and I take the train to Grand Rapids."

"The train! You'll do no such thing. Blake and I will drive you there."

"Your father insisted on the train. He wouldn't want Blake to miss a day of work."

Beattie's face blanched, and she looked down at her fingernails for a second before coming back up with an expression of fierce determination. "We will take you in the automobile. It will be faster, and the road is relatively good between here and there."

"Your father—" Mother began.

Beatrice held up a hand. "I won't listen to any objections. We are taking you, and that's all there is to it." She stood. "I'd better tell Blake." That odd expression returned for a moment before Beattie wiped it away. "What time do you want to leave?"

While Beatrice and Mother made arrangements for Friday morning, Minnie's thoughts drifted back to the startling news that she'd gotten a spot in the musical revue. It was an enormous opportunity, but she would have to turn it down. There would be no time for frivolous pursuits. She must run the dress shop and help keep up the house. Her family needed her.

Once again Peter had intended to tell Vince that this was the last car he would customize when his friend arrived on Saturday. After learning that Mr. Fox had suffered another attack and needed to go to the hospital, he was torn. The family would need the extra money. Badly.

Recalling Pastor Gabe's offer to talk things through, Peter headed for the church after closing the garage for the day. The minister was just leaving when Peter arrived, out of breath.

"You have a minute?" Peter asked between gulps of air.

"Sure." Pastor Gabe pushed open the door. "Felicity can hold supper."

Now Peter felt badly. "I don't want to keep you from your family."

Gabe chuckled. "It happens four out of five days. She's used to it."

"All right." Peter followed the minister to his office. The late-afternoon light cast a warm glow on the room.

"Have a seat." Gabe motioned to a comfortable-looking stuffed chair tucked into a little nook with another chair and a little round table.

Peter sat down. He'd never been in here. No reason to. His ma and pa had made sure he was baptized, and Aunt Ursula took care of getting him confirmed. He'd never caused trouble in Sunday school. Until today, he'd had no reason to consult the minister. He looked around while Pastor Gabe riffled through his desk drawers for something.

Two desks occupied opposite ends of the office. One was neat as a pin, without a single paper out of the place.

Pastor Gabe's overflowed with open books, notebooks and papers.

"It's in here somewhere." Pastor Gabe scratched his head. "Aha!" Turning around, he looked through a pile of folders until he found the one he wanted. "Here we go."

"What were you looking for?" Peter asked. "I didn't say why I wanted to talk to you."

Gabe sat down in the other stuffed chair and leaned slightly forward, as if eager to chat. "You're right. I'm probably jumping to conclusions. I thought you might want to know a little more about your friend."

"Yeah, I suppose, but I don't think he's my friend anymore."

"Why do you say that?"

Peter explained how Vince had ignored Peter's decision not to customize any more automobiles. "You can't tell me he didn't get the wire. I sent it days before."

"I see." Pastor Gabe sat back and set the folder on the little round table. "So he just assumed you would do the job. You told him no, of course."

Peter threaded his fingers together, pulled them apart and knit them again. "I couldn't refuse. Minnie needs the money for her pa and all. And that was before he had another attack. Anyway, I figured one more job wouldn't hurt." He waited for Gabe to criticize that decision, but the minister said nothing.

Peter took that as a signal to go on. "Now I'm not so sure. I want to keep helping out Minnie's family, but Vince said he was working for Mr. Al Capone. What if the compartment isn't for luggage? What if they're hauling something illegal, like bootleg liquor?"

Pastor Gabe stroked his clean-shaven chin. "I see the dilemma."

"I was hoping you'd have an answer."

"Why don't you tell me what you've done so far?"

"Well, I did pray on it." Peter figured that was what the minister would want to hear.

"Good. Anything else?"

"I tried the Bible, but I can't find anything in it on boot-legging." Peter propped his elbows on his knees and hung his head. "I might have missed it. It's such a big book, and I didn't have time to look through it all."

"The Bible can be pretty intimidating for a newcomer. I'm glad you accepted my invitation to talk. Maybe we can think of something together."

Peter felt better already. "Isn't there something in the Bible about sharing the burden?"

Pastor Gabe grinned. "You know more of the Bible than you think. Both Solomon and Jesus talked about sharing the load."

"They did?" Pastor Gabe's approval filled him with confidence to ask what he really wanted to know. "You said you know more about Vince?"

"Not exactly." Pastor Gabe leaned back and lifted the folder. "Mr. Galbini is a bit of a mystery to me. I did call Mr. Isaacs, the former director of the Orphaned Children's Society."

Peter squirmed in the chair, unsure he wanted to hear this.

"He couldn't shed much more light on the man than you already know." Pastor Gabe flipped open the folder. "Mr. Galbini worked part-time at the orphanage for two years. He quit the job to take a better one in Brooklyn. Mr. Isaacs didn't know what type of job it was or Mr. Galbini's new employer. Mr. Capone's name certainly didn't come up. Vince might not have met him yet."

"Maybe, but Mariah said Vince ran with a rough crowd back then. Did Mr. Isaacs say anything about that?"

"No, but my brothers were aware of Mr. Galbini's friends. Charlie said he once suggested to Mr. Isaacs that he shouldn't hire someone with those kinds of connections, but Mr. Isaacs stressed the need to give everyone a chance. That's a good principle to keep in mind, Peter. Rumor and innuendo can doom a man."

"I suppose so." Peter mulled that over. "But what if it's true? What if a guy falls in with a bad lot? Does that mean we shouldn't protect the people we care about?"

"Of course we need to protect those in our care. On the other hand, we shouldn't condemn a man based on rumor. Even if those rumors prove true, he still deserves a chance to change his ways. Sometimes those are the people who need our witness most."

Peter heaved a sigh. "That doesn't really help me decide what to do."

Pastor Gabe's gaze met Peter's. "Let me tell you the mistakes I made a few years ago. I think it might help you."

Peter had a feeling this was serious stuff, the kind of thing a man like Pastor Gabe didn't tell just anyone. "Yes, sir."

Pastor Gabe sat back, gazing off into the past. "I arrived in Pearlman in the summer of 1920, a little before you did. It wasn't long before I noticed strange goings-on behind the drugstore."

"The speakeasy."

Pastor Gabe nodded. "They called it a blind pig back then. Seems it had been open for years. You see, Michigan was dry long before national prohibition. I found that refreshing and didn't expect to find a saloon operating without drawing any interest from the police. Some of the town's prime citizens visited it."

"Still do."

Pastor Gabe ignored that observation. "One day early

on, I happened to stumble across a shipment of bootleg whiskey and took it upon myself to stop the ringleader, whom I mistakenly thought was my future father-in-law."

Peter sucked in his breath at this revelation.

Pastor Gabe chuckled. "That's right. I could have lost Felicity right then, thanks to jumping to the wrong conclusion. I thought the police were corrupt and that I was the only one who could save Pearlman. Now, that's a pretty sorry display of pride, and the Lord wasted no time showing me just how arrogant I'd become. I was so busy trying to root out evil that I didn't notice Felicity's anguish. She ran off and got tangled up with the real bootleggers while I was trying to accuse the wrong person. It turned out that her father was working with the police, and my interference nearly cost Felicity her life."

"I don't want to hurt Minnie! That's why I came to you."

"I know, and that's why I'm telling you this. Don't go it alone like I did. Talk to the police. Sheriff Ilsley is a good man. He'll lead you in the right direction. If you want, I'll go with you."

Peter recoiled at the thought of approaching the police. Many of the New York policemen had been bribed by the owners of the gambling halls and brothels. "I don't know. What if Vince gets mad? What if I'm wrong?"

The pastor grasped Peter's shoulder. "That's why you need friends to stand with you. Don't claim more than you know. Just tell the sheriff what Vince asked you to do and state your concerns. Do you have any proof that the compartment might be used for liquor?"

Peter recalled Blake Kensington's comment, but neither man had mentioned liquor. No proof. Just guessing. He shook his head.

"Well, the size of the compartment might tell us if liquor would fit inside."

"Maybe," Peter said, "but how do we know what size they'd need to haul liquor?"

"The sheriff would probably know. If not, he can contact the federal prohibition agent. One way or another, we'll get the dimensions. Shall we go there now?"

Peter hesitated. Years ago, the policeman he'd talked to about his dead friend said he couldn't do a thing, even when Peter gave him the thugs' names. But Pearlman wasn't New York. If Pastor Gabe said the sheriff could be trusted, maybe he could.

"I'll be with you the entire time," Pastor Gabe added.

Fear battled against doing the right thing.

Pastor Gabe must have sensed why Peter hesitated. "The sheriff can protect Minnie. He helped save Felicity."

That testimony had to be good enough. Peter couldn't think of another choice that wouldn't put Minnie in peril.

"All right." Peter stood. "Let's go."

Chapter Fourteen

Blake and Beatrice came for Mother and Daddy early in the morning. Blake had used his influence to drag the telegraph operator into the office to send a wire to New York late last night. Jen would check for a response from Ruth and Sam at noon. If nothing arrived then, Minnie would close the shop early to get the reply.

On this crisp early-April morning, Mother had bundled Daddy in layers of clothing and his heaviest winter overcoat. Even with all that bulk, his thin frame couldn't be hidden. He wheezed and coughed every few steps. Blake had to assist him down the staircase, with Mother hovering over every step.

"I'm all right," Daddy stated between coughing fits. "Stop fussing over me, Helen."

Minnie and Jen stood their posts at the bottom of the stairs like twin guard dogs. When he reached them, Jen took his arm. "Walk with me, Daddy."

He stood a little straighter. "Someday I'll walk you down the aisle, Genevieve."

Jen didn't even flinch at his use of her much-hated first name. "I'll hold you to that."

He'd smiled then but had to sit a spell at the kitchen

table and again in the living room. That was where he addressed Minnie. "I understand you got a part in the upcoming musical revue."

"Yes, Daddy." Minnie sat at his feet, like she'd done as a child.

"You always were quite the songbird."

"I was?"

He smiled softly, dim eyes seeing only the memory. "I remember you singing when you were on that old rope swing we put in the oak tree out back. I'd wait behind the shed on my way home from work so you wouldn't see me. You never wanted anyone to hear you singing." He coughed. "Now think, my little songbird is going to sing in front of the whole town. I'm so proud of you."

Minnie blinked back tears. She couldn't tell him that she'd already decided to decline the spot. How could she waste hours in frivolous entertainment when her family needed her?

Beatrice gently touched his arm. "It's time to go. Blake has the car ready out front. I had him move it so the passenger door is at the end of the walk."

"Dear Beattie." He pecked her cheek. "Always making sure things are just so."

Minnie couldn't tell if her oldest sister was pleased or upset by his statement. Together, the sisters got him to his feet and onto the front porch. Minnie was surprised to see Peter waiting with Blake.

"We'll take him from here," Blake said, hurrying forward with Peter on his heels.

Peter gave Minnie a look of sympathy before assisting her father down the porch steps. She battled tears as they followed, Mother first with the blanket.

When they reached the car, Daddy held on to the roof.

"Thank you, Blake. Peter—" he grasped Peter's hand "—you're a fine young man."

Minnie's throat nearly swelled shut, and she had to blink furiously so she wouldn't burst into tears.

Daddy lowered himself onto the passenger seat, and then Mother tucked the blanket around his legs before getting in the back with Beatrice. Blake shut all the doors and got into the driver's seat. Daddy leaned his head back and closed his eyes, his face ashen. A pang tore through Minnie, like ripping a piece of cloth in two. Her father was leaving. She might never see him again.

"Daddy!" She waved and called out as Blake pulled away from the house.

She and Jen ran after the car. The morning light gilded the Cadillac's windows so she could not see inside. Blake honked the horn. Then he turned onto Second Street, and they were gone.

"Play along," Sheriff Ilsley suggested. His steely gaze bored through Peter. "Galbini already trusts you. What we need is an insider."

Last night's visit to the sheriff's office had led to this afternoon's interview. Sheriff Ilsley had wanted to call in the prohibition agent from Grand Rapids before they discussed the situation further. Mr. Fallston arrived on the afternoon train. At least Pastor Gabe had come along with him again. Peter looked to him for encouragement. He didn't like the sheriff's suggestion one bit.

Neither did Agent Fallston. "Pearlman's pretty far away for an outfit like Torrio's to show any interest. They're mostly getting their supplies close to home. But that doesn't mean a change isn't in the works. We're counting on you to find out if it is."

"Torrio?" That was a new name to Peter.

"The most powerful gang leader in Chicago. Capone is his next in command. Infiltrating their organization would be a coup." Fallston leaned forward. "Can you do it?"

Peter looked from the tall, strong sheriff with his uncompromising stance to the comparatively meek federal agent, who looked more like an accountant than an officer of the law. If he had to put his faith in one or the other, he'd go with the sheriff every time.

He licked his lips, still recalling Minnie's anguish this morning and her determination not to break down. He could not fail her. He glanced at Pastor Gabe. The minister had said Felicity nearly died because he didn't trust the law. Peter couldn't risk that. "This sounds dangerous. What if something goes wrong?"

"One step at a time," Fallston said.

The sheriff shook his head. "Peter has a right to ask. In my experience, preparation is key. Prepare for any eventuality, and you're likely to succeed."

Fallston clearly disdained what he viewed as trampling on his territory. "We don't even know yet if there's any bootlegging involved. Once we have proof, we can make a plan. Until then, it's wasted time."

Peter did not need the two lawmen bickering between themselves when lives were on the line. "I want to prepare now."

Ilsley nodded his approval. "Here's what I suggest. First we measure the compartment. That should give us an idea if it's even possible to transport liquor in it. If it's too small to hold much, it wouldn't be worth the trouble."

"Unless it's high-grade liquor from across the border," Fallston countered. "Beer is transported in trucks. An automobile would most likely haul the expensive stuff. I'll check with my cohort in Detroit to see if he knows of any connection between Chicago and suppliers there."

"And I'll make sure Hermann Grattan isn't up to his old tricks."

Most of this was flying right over Peter's head. He recalled Mr. Grattan going to jail for bootlegging back when Peter first arrived in Pearlman. That was how Peter had ended up with Mrs. Simmons instead of the Grattans, who'd selected him at the orphan distribution. But the rest of the conversation didn't make much sense. He was trying to concentrate, but all he could think about was Minnie.

The sheriff glared at Fallston. "It doesn't matter what kind of liquor they're hauling if it's bootleg." He turned back to Peter. "If it looks suspicious, try to get a job. Tell Galbini some hard-luck story, whatever it takes."

Fallston added, "Guys usually start in delivery. You can drive. Galbini knows that. And you're pretty big. Are you good with your fists?"

Peter balked. "I don't fight." Not since turning his life over to Christ.

"Too bad. Does Galbini know that?"

"Well, no." Vince would remember him as a scrappy street urchin.

"Good. Let him believe you still like to fight."

Peter glanced at Pastor Gabe. "But that's lying."

Fallston looked disgusted. "It's playing a part."

The pastor said, "You don't have to lie. I suspect Vince wants you to join him. He wouldn't have come here otherwise. What you need to ask yourself is if this is worth the risk."

Fallston clearly did not appreciate the pastor's interference. "Do you want us to keep Pearlman out of the bootlegging trade or not?"

Peter looked from one man to the other. "I don't want anyone getting hurt."

Sheriff Ilsley stepped in again. "These gangs don't take no for an answer. You're not going to be able to back out of this if Galbini thinks for a moment that you know what he's doing."

Peter swallowed hard. He'd already accused Vince. If Sheriff Ilsley was right, he was already trapped. He might be able to save Minnie, though. "What do I do?"

"See if you can get in as a driver," Fallston said.

"And Minnie?" Peter had to make sure she was safe. "I gotta have your word that Minnie won't be charged and that you'll make sure she doesn't get hurt."

"You have my word on it from the county standpoint," the sheriff said. "I'm sure Agent Fallston will agree to the same."

Agent Fallston did not appear at all agreeable. "If she is an accomplice—"

"An unwitting one," the sheriff interrupted. "If I'm reading Mr. Simmons correctly, you must agree to this stipulation in order to get his assistance."

Peter nodded.

Fallston mulled it over for a few seconds. "All right."

"Very well," Pastor Gabe said. "Are you ready, Peter?"

Pastor Gabe was asking if Peter was ready to go, but as Peter stood he felt the impact of what he'd just agreed to do. In a couple of days, Vince would show up to pick up the car. Peter would have to ask for a driving job. What Vince said next would change his life forever.

The sheriff stood beside Peter. "You all right, son?"

Peter squared his shoulders and nodded.

"Good, let's head on over to the garage and check out the size of that compartment."

One last hope. One last chance. Peter prayed that when they measured, the compartment could only hold luggage.

Though no taller than Minnie, Mrs. Eugenia Kensington always intimidated her. The woman led virtually every church and civic women's group in town. Even Beattie found her formidable, and Mrs. Kensington was her mother-in-law.

The next day after work, Minnie stood on the porch of the Kensingtons' imposing house with its huge columns and circular driveway, her knees knocking and her heart pounding through her rib cage while Mrs. Kensington stared at her in disbelief. Minnie had stated her case, but Mrs. Kensington had yet to accept it.

In the distance, Minnie heard the squeals and laughter of Beattie's children, who were staying with their grandparents until their parents returned from Grand Rapids.

"I'm sorry," she repeated for the fifth or sixth time.

Mrs. Kensington finally found her voice. "Do you know what you're turning down? Other girls would give anything to have this opportunity."

"I'm sorry. I want to. I really do, but I can't make the rehearsals, at least not until Ruth and Sam get back from New York, and that won't be until Sunday or Monday. I'd miss the first rehearsal, and you said we had to attend every rehearsal or lose our spot."

"I see." Mrs. Kensington's sharp nose seemed to poke right into Minnie. "I suppose I could make an exception to the rule in your case, considering the extreme circumstances, but don't let it happen again. Another missed rehearsal, and you'll be cut. Understand?"

Minnie couldn't promise to attend every other rehearsal. She had already committed to return to her old housecleaning clients when Ruth got back. That meant working on Saturdays. Then there was the work for Mr. Galbini. She was supposed to go to the garage tonight to help Peter put together the compartment. Another car might arrive tomorrow. And Ruth would expect her to continue her apprenticeship at the dress shop. Moreover, they'd have the housework to manage with Mother gone. No, she couldn't promise.

"I—I think you should offer it to someone else," she stammered out.

Mrs. Kensington's gaze narrowed. "You intend to let your community down?"

Minnie tried to swallow, but her throat was dry. "I don't have any choice."

"Very well. I'll find someone else, but don't ever expect to receive another chance, Miss Fox."

Minnie hurried off. The loss of her dreams hurt. Why must she always give up what she wanted? Beattie married the man she loved. So did Ruth. Jen got to keep her beloved job at the airfield. Whenever something interesting was happening there, she got to attend, while Minnie had to watch the dress shop. It wasn't fair.

By the time she reached the motor garage, her mood had grown black. She pulled on the office door. It was locked. Peter was there, though, because the lights were on in the work bay. She pounded on the closed barn doors. As if everything else going wrong wasn't bad enough, now Peter was shutting her out.

"Open up!" She banged with both fists until the wood door nearly shook off its hinges. The crush of fist against wood felt good. Painful. Mr. Peter Simmons would hear about locking her out. "I know you're in there. I can see the lights on."

He pushed open the door enough to admit one person. "Calm down. There's no need to shout."

"I wasn't shouting." She brushed past him and made a beeline for the car. "Let's get this put together so it's ready for Vince."

He cringed, probably because she'd used Mr. Galbini's given name, but she didn't care. She walked over to the worktable where he usually piled the boards before assembly. The surface was empty.

She whirled around to face him. "Where are the boards? We're supposed to put the compartment together. What have you done with them?"

"It's done."

"What? Done? When?"

"Yesterday."

She rushed to the car and looked in the back. Sure enough, the seat was in place with no sign of the compartment underneath. "How could you? We were supposed to do it together."

He wiped his hands on a rag. "I had some extra time, so I took care of it." But he wasn't looking at her. "I figured you were busy, with rehearsals and everything."

The reminder of what she'd just given up stung. "I'm not doing the revue. All right? You ought to be happy. You didn't want me to audition in the first place."

He stared at her and swallowed. "Maybe not at first, but when you sang, well, you've got the prettiest voice I've ever heard. You deserve to be in that revue."

"Well, I'm not." She crossed her arms. "I already resigned."

"Why? Because of the upholstery work? Don't quit on account of that." He waved at the car. "It might be the last one anyway. If not, I can do the work."

"Then you don't need me, either?" Angry tears burned in her eyes.

He looked stricken. "Of course I do."

"No, you don't. You just said you could do everything yourself. Well, fine. Do that." Even though she knew she was being unfair, she couldn't stop. The upheaval of the past few days had built to the point that she couldn't stand it anymore. "See if Vince likes your stitching as much as he likes mine."

"What do you mean? I can't sew, and even if I could, I couldn't do it as good as you."

The words salved the wound a little, but she wasn't ready to let go yet. "It doesn't matter. I'm more than a seamstress. I'm going to be famous one day."

He did not look pleased. Still, he said softly, "Maybe you will be. You can do anything you set your mind to." He swallowed. "But you gotta know that I care for you."

Minnie could not hear this. "Like a friend."

"No. More than that. I'd give anything to take care of you the way you deserve."

Maybe it was the look on his face. Maybe it was the earnestness of his words. But something broke inside her. Shattered. No one outside her family had ever said such a thing to her. Certainly no man had ever done so. Peter truly did care. Not a crush. Not something silly and insignificant. Though she'd guessed at his feelings for some time, hearing them spoken aloud scared her.

At first, she trembled. Then the tears came, so fast they blurred her vision. Embarrassed, she stumbled away, but she couldn't find her way out and away from the confusing emotions. Instead, she fell apart right in front of him.

She felt his arms draw her in. That only made her cry harder.

He rubbed her back, whispered in her ear that it would be all right.

That took the fight out of her. She collapsed against his shoulder and wept. She had abused him, yet he didn't scold. He just held her. Comforted her. Told her everything would work out. How strong he was. Such integrity. Peter would never betray her to anyone. He would never hurt her. His arms felt so right. Why hadn't she noticed that before?

Chapter Fifteen

Peter could have held Minnie for ages, but sense kicked in. It was late. No one was around. If anyone did see her there with him, the gossips would tear her to shreds. Plus he had to keep her as far away from the car and Vince as possible. So after she wiped her eyes and blew her nose, he said good-night and saw her home.

The next morning was Saturday. Peter dreaded meeting Vince. Would his friend take one look at him and know he was working with the law? Though the compartment had measured out big enough to haul liquor, it wouldn't hold more than a few cases. A case of whiskey might fetch a hundred dollars on the wholesale market. That wasn't worth the risk, unless it was premium stuff. The hidden compartment intrigued Fallston, but he couldn't come up with a logical use for it beyond cash or valuables. It was too shallow for more than a flask.

In the end, even Fallston conceded that the compartment was most likely for luggage, but the federal agent wanted proof. That meant Peter had to get into the operation—if there even was an operation.

The day dawned cold and clear. Peter went to the motor garage early and slid open the bolt to the work-bay door.

He was too nervous to stand around, so he slipped outside and paced out to the street, where he looked for Vince before heading back.

A watched pot never boils, Mariah would always say. Apparently watching for someone had the same result. After several looks, he huddled by the work-bay door. Maybe Vince wouldn't show up. Maybe he'd worried for nothing. His palms sweated. His throat was parched. He walked out to the street and shot another look toward State Road.

Nothing but the glimmer of sun on frosted rooftops.

He stomped his feet to keep them from going numb and paced back to the garage. Had Vince gotten wind of the law's involvement?

Peter hunched his shoulders against the wind and dug his hands into his pockets. How had he gotten himself into this, and how could he get out of it?

Only the memory of Minnie sobbing in his arms could distract him. She'd acted crazy last night, and he'd got plenty peeved. Then she broke down, and he realized she'd lashed out at him because she was worried about her pa. His heart about broke. He wanted to help. He wanted to tell her he'd take care of her if the worst happened. And he would. If he could get out of this mess.

At exactly eight o'clock, Vince pulled up next to the side of the garage in a recent-model Maxwell. He stepped out of the car, dressed in the usual dapper suit and jaunty fedora. "Hey, Stringbean! How's business?"

Peter dug his hands deeper into his jacket pockets. "Slow."

"That so?" Vince lit a cigarette and looked both ways down the street and then at the garage, as if expecting to see someone jump out at him. "Whatcha doin' standing out in the cold?"

Peter's pulse raced. Did Vince suspect something? After all, Peter had accused him of breaking the law. This was never going to work. He stared at the street, empty of traffic this early on a Saturday. "Looking for you."

Vince grunted, but Peter couldn't tell if he believed the explanation.

He tried again. "Sure do appreciate the extra work you're givin' me."

"Sure thing, kid." Vince measured him up.

"It's helpin' out a lot."

Vince tapped ash onto the ground. "Glad to see you've come to your senses."

Peter ignored the jab and pushed forward with the plan. "I'm hopin' to get together enough to ask Minnie to marry me." Saying it aloud made him blush.

"You don't say." That broke the ice. Vince even laughed. "No wonder you look so nervous. Ya had me worried."

Peter forced a laugh. It sounded hollow. "Yeah. I don't know what she'll say, but I don't have a chance if I can't get together enough to at least rent an apartment."

Vince grinned. "Good to see you got your priorities straight. She's a right fine gal."

Peter shoved aside the memory of Vince flirting with her. "These jobs are helping, but I sure could use a little extra. I'm hopin' you got more for me."

"If the work on the Lincoln's anything like the Pierce-Arrow, there'll be more."

"Good." Peter pushed out a sigh of relief even though he wasn't at all relieved. He still hadn't asked the big question. He tried again. "That'll help, but like I said, business is slow. I was wondering if…well…do you think you'd have anything else I could do? Like maybe I could bring the finished car to you and pick up the next one? I'm a good driver. Nothing would happen to the car, I promise, and then you wouldn't have to drive here all the time. I mean, if I was busy like you, I'd hate to take away time just to drive cars around." That sounded idiotic. He hoped Vince didn't notice his nerves.

Vince didn't say anything for a while. He drew in on his cigarette and blew smoke into the cold air. His other hand tapped on the roof of the Maxwell, the fat gold ring sounding like a telegraph signal against the metal support.

Long minutes passed.

Peter shivered. "Dumb idea. I'll show you the car." He pulled open the heavy work-bay door, and they stepped inside.

The Lincoln waited in the dim interior, its paint polished to a gleam. Peter never sent a car back to its owner looking less than perfect.

Vince nodded in appreciation. "Not that dumb an idea." He stubbed out the cigarette in the bucket of sand before approaching the car. "If the inside is anything like the outside, the owner will be pleased."

It didn't take long for Vince to approve the new luggage compartment. He ran his hands along the padding and tugged on the wood frame. He checked the hidden compartment. After a few more taps, he signaled Peter to help him move the seat back into place. Then he stood.

"It's better than the last one." Vince closed the rear door. "First-rate."

"Then there'll be more work?"

"Sure thing, kid. I got a few guys interested in this kinda customization."

"Good." Peter grinned. He hoped he looked pleased.

Vince bought it. "That delivery idea of yours might work out, too. See, I got this other project in mind. A truck that needs some engine work. Sound like somethin' you can do?"

"I work on truck motors all the time. What kind of work are you talking about?"

"Need to install a new engine. The old one gave out. It was never powerful enough, and we got a twin-six that'll give it more pep."

Peter removed his cap and scrubbed his brow. "I could give it a shot. We've replaced a couple engines here." He didn't mention that Hendrick had done the work.

"Terrific! Now, the guy who owns the Maxwell—" Vince poked a thumb out toward the car he drove up "—wants it right away. Same kind of compartment. Can you get it done in a week?"

"A week?" Peter choked.

"Say by next Friday. He wants to use it for a little week-end tour."

Peter couldn't very well refuse. Agent Fallston's whole plan depended on him getting this driving job. Now that it was in place, he had to move forward, no matter how difficult. He'd just have to put in extra hours.

"All right." He could construct the compartment, but he wasn't sure how to handle the padding. He didn't want Minnie involved anymore. Maybe she'd sell him the material and tell him how to fit it properly. "I'll do it."

"Good. Got a piece of paper and a pencil?"

"For what?"

"I'm gonna tell ya how to get to the drop-off spot. Why don't we make it Friday night at ten o'clock? That'll give you time to close up like normal and still get there."

Peter didn't like this plan. Instead of daylight, he'd have to deliver the car in the dark. "The owner will be awake?"

Vince laughed. "Don't worry. We'll take care of business, and then I'll take you to the truck. Put you up for the night."

On the surface it all sounded reasonable, but the hairs

rose on the back of Peter's neck. If this wasn't completely legitimate, he was stepping into some pretty dangerous stuff. When Vince laid out the directions and Peter realized that he'd have to cross the state line into Indiana, the one lawman he trusted, Sheriff Ilsley, fell out of the picture. Jurisdiction belonged to federal authorities or policemen he didn't know. That didn't make him feel any too safe.

After that embarrassing breakdown in front of Peter, Minnie avoided the motor garage. She didn't even look his way at church on Sunday.

"What's wrong?" Jen asked as they hurried home after the service. "Peter was trying to catch your attention, but you walked right past without saying a word."

Minnie wasn't about to tell Jen that she'd made a fool of herself in front of Peter. Moreover, she'd treated him abominably.

His words still rang in her ears. He cared for her. He wouldn't ever stop caring for her. No one had ever said such things to her before. The very thought sent her insides tumbling like a stone down a cliff. Maybe he was just saying that because she was upset. Maybe he thought better of it later. She ought to concentrate on helping out the family instead of these crazy feelings for Peter Simmons.

"Hello," Jen said, punching her in the upper arm.

"Ouch! Why'd you do that?"

"Because I asked you the same question five times and you didn't answer."

"Oh. I was deep in thought." Minnie shrugged, hoping her sister would let it go.

"Mired in thought is more like it."

"So? Ask the question again."

Jen gave her a look of disgust. "I asked if Peter had more work for you."

"I don't know." That was the truth. She hadn't asked and hadn't stopped by to check. After what she'd said to him, how could she? "Besides, he said he could do it all himself."

"Even the upholstery?"

"That's what he said."

"Hmm. Maybe Mariah volunteered to do it."

Minnie hadn't thought of that. "She sews?"

"I don't know. Don't most women?"

"You don't," Minnie pointed out.

"I'm not like most women." Jen carried that like a badge of honor. "Maybe that's why Peter wanted to talk to you today. Maybe he needs your help."

Minnie's pulse quickened. Work beside Peter again? She wanted to, but… "I don't know if I'll have the time."

"Ruth is arriving today. She'll take over the dress shop. That should give you plenty of spare time."

"I'll be busy cleaning houses."

"That's only part-time," Jen pointed out. "And the rehearsals are in the evening. You'll still have plenty of time to work on upholstery."

Minnie hadn't yet told the family that she'd refused the role in the musical revue. Part of her hoped Ruth's arrival would indeed give her back the evenings, but deep down she knew that wouldn't be enough. She couldn't do everything. "Daddy needs me."

"Daddy?" Jen slowed her pace. "What do you mean?"

"I mean that work comes before pleasure."

Jen nodded thoughtfully. "Then why don't we stop by the garage on the way to the train station to see if Peter has another car for you to work on?"

"It's Sunday," Minnie pointed out. "The garage is closed."

Jen linked her arm through Minnie's. "Then why is

Peter heading that way?" She nodded toward the other side of the street. About a block ahead, Peter strode away from them and toward the garage.

Minnie felt her stomach flip-flop again. "Maybe he's dining out."

"Instead of eating Sunday dinner with the family?" Jen laughed. "Besides, Lily's is closed on Sundays."

"He might be expecting a shipment on the train."

"Good." Jen grinned triumphantly. "Then we'll be able to talk to him at the station." She tugged Minnie forward. "Come along. You have a date with destiny."

"I have no such thing. I'm going to meet Ruthie. That's all."

"Sure you are."

"Stop it, Jen." Minnie playfully punched her sister's shoulder, but she still watched Peter Simmons with a flutter of eager anticipation. If he'd tried to catch her attention at church, maybe he wasn't sore at her after all.

When Peter paused to look in the mercantile window, he happened to see Minnie and her sister headed his way. After the way Minnie had ignored him at church, he was surprised to see Jen waving at him. Even a block away, he could see the blush in Minnie's cheeks.

Naturally he waited for them.

"We're on our way to the depot," Jen said when they drew near. "Ruthie's supposed to arrive either today or tomorrow morning."

Minnie cast her gaze downward but peeked up at him once or twice. Each time her cheeks got pinker.

Peter tried to concentrate on the conversation, but he kept noticing Minnie's perfume and the pretty stitching on the collar of her dress.

"We'll help with her bags," Jen continued.

That caught his attention. "Won't her husband do that?"

"Sam's staying in New York. Apparently he's close to making a deal on Ruthie's designs."

Peter offered to help with the luggage. Jen refused, but he didn't hear anything else because Minnie chose that moment to smile at him. The shy glance and anxious nibbling at her lip meant she was worried. Maybe that was why she'd snubbed him, not from anger but from fear. The realization rolled through him with tremendous strength.

"I hope you can help me with another car," he blurted out in the midst of Jen saying something.

The older sister stopped talking and backed away.

Minnie looked at him tentatively. "You still want my help after what I said?"

Oops! He hadn't said that right. He'd only meant to ask her how to pad the boards, but she clearly expected to do more.

He forced a smile. "Of course."

"I said awful things."

"Forgotten." Not entirely, but holding her close had wiped most of them away.

She blinked rapidly. "I'm sorry."

His throat swelled. "It's all right." He wanted to hold her hand but didn't dare, not with her sister standing right there. "I'll stop by the dress shop tomorrow and show you what needs to be done." At least he could keep her away from the garage.

"I won't be there. I'm going back to housecleaning."

"Oh." He couldn't seem to keep her out of this. "Stop by the garage, then, when you're done."

She flashed him a dazzling smile, and he plumb forgot to tell her they had a tight deadline. Considering the bounce in her step as she hurried toward the train depot, she must be pleased to work with him again.

Peter plucked a yellow daffodil and hurried after her.

Chapter Sixteen

Something had changed in Peter. Minnie first noticed it on Monday at noon, when she stopped at the garage. The door was propped open to let in the balmy spring air. Peter sat at the desk in the office reading what looked like a telegram. He was so deep in thought that he didn't notice her enter.

After waiting a moment, she cleared her throat.

He looked up, and his frown deepened. He stood and shoved the piece of paper into his overalls pocket. "Oh. You're here for the first board."

Without even saying hello, he walked out of the office and into the work area. Puzzled, Minnie followed. Something on that piece of paper must have bothered him. Maybe he'd gotten bad news from New York.

The work area was full. Mr. Evans's car occupied the spot inside the work-bay doors, and Peter had squeezed an unfamiliar sedan into the area next to it.

"Is something wrong?" she asked.

"Nope." He skirted around the first car. "Wait there. I'll get the board for you."

She paused at the front of Mr. Evans's car and looked over the dusty sedan. It must be the one Vince had dropped off. "This car's not as pretty as the last one Mr. Galbini had us work on."

"Pretty?"

"You know. Shiny and all. It doesn't even look new."

"Probably not." Peter headed for the wood-shop worktable in the back.

Minnie edged closer to the sedan. "It's not a Pierce-Arrow, is it?" Maybe she could sound knowledgeable enough to impress him.

"Nope. It's a Maxwell."

"Maxwell. I never heard of it, but I don't like it as well."

"It doesn't cost as much as a Pierce-Arrow." Peter picked up a board off the worktable. "A regular guy might be able to afford a Maxwell if he works hard enough."

The way he'd snapped that out, she must have offended him. "I didn't mean anything by it. I could never afford either one. We don't even have a Model T."

"Yeah. I know." He sighed. "Sorry. I got a lot on my mind these days."

"Like what?" Minnie surveyed the uncharacteristically messy work area. Sawdust and scraps of wood littered the table and floor. He'd already cut three of the boards. One was ready for her. The other two lay on sawhorses and reeked of fresh varnish. "You've got a lot done already."

"Yeah, we've got a tight deadline. The owner wants the car Friday night."

"This Friday?" she gasped. "That's impossible."

"If you can't get the padding done, we'll have to do without."

"No, I'll do it." She wasn't about to give up this job, not after throwing away her dream of the stage. "But why Friday? Mr. Galbini always shows up on Saturdays."

"Not this time."

Minnie had missed seeing Peter's friend when he

dropped off this car. The way Peter was moping around, she had to remind Mr. Galbini how much they needed the work. "When do you expect him?"

Peter frowned. "He's not coming here. I'm delivering the car."

"You?"

"I can drive," he snapped.

She cringed. "I know you can drive, but why do you have to deliver the car? Doesn't your friend usually drop off the next car when he picks one up?" She sucked in her breath as a thought occurred to her. "Is this the last job he's giving us?"

"Let's get this one done before we worry about the next. I'll carry the board to the dress shop for you."

"Actually, Ruthie wants me to do the work here."

"What?" He drew up short. "But your father insisted you work in the dress shop or with a chaperone. Is Jen going to come here with you?"

"No. Ruthie says she doesn't have to." Her sister's pronouncement had come as a surprise to Minnie, too. Ruth had always been so strict, but she'd come back from New York both radiant over the coming baby and filled with shocking new ideas. "She said as long as you keep the doors wide-open and you put a table out front for me to work on, it'll be all right." Peter did not look convinced, so Minnie explained further. "She needs all the work space in the dress shop for customer orders and some new designs she's working on."

He set the board on the worktable. "It's quite a change."

"It surprised me, too, and that's not the only change. Apparently Sam ordered a telephone for the dress shop. He says it's so he can keep in touch with suppliers and so Ruthie can reach him until he gets back from New York, but we'll also be able to contact Mother and maybe even talk to Daddy."

"That'll ease your mind."

She sighed. "I hope it's installed soon. I'd like to hear Daddy's voice."

"No word from your ma yet?"

Minnie shook her head.

"Maybe that's good news. Maybe he's getting better."

"I hope so." But she didn't want to talk about her father's illness when she was still irritated about Peter delivering the car. He'd managed to avoid answering her question about more work. She had to emphasize how much she needed this work. "I'm just glad you asked me to do the upholstery. The extra money is going to help a lot with the medical bills."

He bowed his head, but not before she caught the distressed look on his face.

Her heart sank. He must think this customization business was over, but it couldn't be. She'd given up so much for this. Daddy needed it. The whole family needed it. "You have to tell Mr. Galbini that we can get the work done a lot faster. Now that Ruthie's back, I can easily finish one job a week."

"I can tell him, but he's the customer." Peter not only looked downright miserable, but he also wouldn't look her in the eye. He glanced at the car, the boards, pretty much anything but her. "This job might be the last."

"It can't be. You said Vince had a lot of people who wanted a luggage compartment in their cars. We could even do it for people in Pearlman."

He shook his head.

She couldn't give up. "Don't you see? It's a new business, something lots of people will want. We could even advertise. People would come from Kalamazoo and Grand Rapids and Holland."

"Maybe."

His reluctance infuriated her. "What's wrong with you? Why are you giving up so easily? That's not the Peter I know. The Peter I know would fight until he got what he wanted. What happened to you?"

"Nothing. You just don't know the whole story."

"It's that telegram, isn't it?"

He flushed. "I gotta get to work now. Mr. Evans needs his car by the end of the day."

Minnie felt everything slipping away. "Aren't you going to let me start on the first board? I can bring the material and supplies if you'll set up the table. There's a spot behind the Maxwell that'll be out of your way and meet Ruthie's stipulations."

"Go help your sister at the shop. You can work on the boards tomorrow."

"Tomorrow? But I thought we had to finish this by Friday."

Instead of answering, Peter got into Mr. Evans's car and started it. The roar of the engine drowned out all further attempts at conversation.

Peter couldn't very well tell Minnie that Vince's wire had asked him to pick up a package tonight at the rear door of the drugstore. The place had only one back door, and it led to the speakeasy. That was no place for nice girls. No place for Minnie. If she knew he was going there, she'd have an even lower opinion of him than she already did.

He did not want to set foot in the place. Years ago, he'd gone in the back doors of New York clubs to deliver messages. Tobacco smoke hung thick as fog in the dark rooms humming with violence and vice. Gambling, money, things he didn't want to know about. Sometimes people disappeared from those places. More often they lost their souls. Peter wanted nothing to do with clubs.

On the other hand, this was Pearlman. Mrs. Lawrence ran a good, clean drugstore up front. The speakeasy out back was probably more respectable than the clubs he'd seen, but it was still against the law. Why Sheriff Ilsley didn't do anything about it puzzled him. The lawman occasionally raided the place, but he never shut its doors.

Why would Vince ask him to pick up a package there? Shouldn't it be at the post office? The telegram made no sense. It also didn't say what would be in the package, just that Peter needed to pick it up and bring it with him Friday night. Put in hidden compartment, the wire had stated. That sure didn't sound like anything legitimate.

Peter considered going to the sheriff with this, but the man's permissiveness toward the speakeasy bothered him. He also couldn't tell Fallston, since the prohibition agent had returned to Grand Rapids until Friday, when he planned to tail Peter to the drop-off spot. That left Peter on his own. The only thing he knew for sure was that he had to keep Minnie out of this.

Peter would deliver Mr. Evans's car early and stop by the drugstore on the way back. If the package turned out to be liquor or anything illegal, he'd refuse to take it. Vince could find someone else to deliver his dirty merchandise. Either way, going there early meant Minnie would be hard at work at the dress shop and never know that he'd gone into a speakeasy.

Minnie returned to the dress shop, perplexed by Peter's behavior. She was sure it all had to do with that telegram. If the news came from New York, then Mariah probably got a wire, too. She still kept in close contact with the former director of the closed orphanage there. As the day went on Minnie grew more and more convinced that Mariah would know what was troubling Peter. To help him, Minnie had to know the problem.

After assisting Ruth until four o'clock, she headed for Constance House. On a day like today, the children would be playing in the large backyard after school. Mariah would be able to talk, and Peter wouldn't be back from work yet.

Motorcars and people clogged Main Street. With the fine weather, everyone seemed to be out. So many people stopped her to say hello that she feared Mariah would have taken the children to the park by the time she got there.

Fortunately, the orphanage director answered the door on the second knock.

"Minnie! What a pleasure." Mariah always welcomed people as if she'd been longing to see them for ages. "Have a seat in the parlor, and I'll put together a tea service."

Minnie glanced at the formal parlor, kept tidy for visitors and potential parents to meet with a child. "If you don't mind, I'd rather talk in the kitchen."

Mariah laughed. "You're a woman after my heart. I'll be able to keep watch on the children from there."

"Is Anna helping?" Peter's foster sister occasionally assisted at the orphanage.

Mariah swept through the house with calm authority. "She's at the bookstore today but will be here tomorrow. Did you want to see her?"

"No, I was hoping to talk to you."

"Excellent. I always enjoy a visit."

Once they reached the kitchen, Minnie sat at the table while Mariah heated the teakettle on the oil stove and pulled a couple of teacups and saucers from the cupboard. "Cookies?"

"No, thank you." Minnie couldn't take sweets from the children. "Mother doesn't like us to eat between meals."

Mariah settled into the chair beside her while the tea-kettle heated. "How are your mother and father? I heard they had to go to the hospital in Grand Rapids."

"No word yet."

Mariah squeezed her hand. "We'll take that as good news. The whole church is praying for your father."

"Thank you."

Mariah looked deeply into Minnie's eyes. "Now, what brought you here today?" She was always direct but managed to be so without offending.

Minnie considered how to say this. After all, Peter was the foster brother of Mariah's husband and lived with them at Constance House. "I wondered if there was bad news from New York."

"From New York?" Mariah blinked. "Why would you think that?"

"Oh, good." Minnie breathed out a sigh. "What a relief. I saw Peter reading a telegram, and he looked so distressed by it that I figured something awful had happened."

"Not that I know of," Mariah said slowly.

"Oh, dear, maybe I shouldn't have said anything. Maybe it was personal."

"Perhaps." But Mariah still looked concerned. "I don't know who would wire Peter. He has no relations or connections in New York. Are you certain it came from there?"

Minnie vaguely recalled Peter saying he had an uncle, but maybe the man didn't live in New York. "I figured it had to be from New York. Where else could it come from?"

"Hmm. I don't know. Are you certain it was a tele-gram?"

"It was the same color of paper they use for telegrams." The way Mariah was looking at her made Minnie feel uncomfortable, as if she'd been eavesdropping, which she hadn't. "You're probably right. I'm sure it's nothing. I let my imagination run wild."

"Perhaps."

Minnie felt sick. She should never have pried. "I'm just so used to bad news lately. I jumped to conclusions."

"That's all right."

Despite Mariah's gracious understanding, the knot in the pit of Minnie's stomach didn't loosen. What if Mariah told Peter that Minnie had asked about the telegram? He'd be furious with her. He'd think she was interfering where she shouldn't.

Minnie stood abruptly, scraping her chair against the wood floor. "I should go. Ruthie will want help closing the shop."

"Of course." Mariah started to stand.

"No need to get up. I can show myself out." Minnie pushed her chair in and backed away. "Promise you won't tell Peter I asked about this? I'd be so embarrassed if he knew."

"Perhaps you should talk to him about your concerns. I'm sure he wouldn't be offended."

Minnie knew better. If he'd wanted her to know what was in the wire, he would have told her when she asked. She said her farewells and hurried from the orphanage, thoroughly embarrassed. Why had she stuck her nose in where it wasn't wanted?

She stepped onto Elm Street and waited to cross. A car was traveling down the hill at a rapid rate of speed, a cloud of dust behind it. That was Blake's Cadillac. She blinked to make sure. She couldn't see if Beattie was in the passenger seat. If she was, her sister would have a conniption over such reckless driving.

Minnie waited for him to turn onto Main Street and

head for the mercantile. Instead, he drove past and turned into the alley, tires churning up gravel. Why on earth would he drive down the alley? Main Street would get him to the mercantile more quickly, unless he wasn't going to work. What if something was wrong? The children! Oh, dear. What if he was headed to Doc Stevens's office with one of the children?

She changed course for the alley. By the time she reached it, the Cadillac sat parked behind the drugstore two blocks ahead. Minnie's heart thudded in her chest. Illness or injury would have been terrible enough, but racing to get to the speakeasy? Poor Beattie. Minnie's oldest sister had enough to handle with two children and demanding in-laws without her husband visiting the saloon.

Minnie took a deep breath. Maybe she was wrong. After all, she'd been wrong about Peter's telegram. Maybe it wasn't Blake's car. Pearlman had a Cadillac dealer. Someone else could have bought the same model of automobile. She might be jumping to the wrong conclusion again.

She hurried down the alley, but as she crossed Fifth Street, she knew she hadn't been wrong. That was Blake's car all right.

Oh, dear. What should she do? Tell Beatrice? Her sister would be crushed. Yet this wasn't something Minnie could keep to herself. What if authorities raided the saloon? What if Blake went to jail? What would Beatrice do then?

Minnie felt shaky, and she leaned against the back corner of the bookstore to steady herself. Empty crates were stacked high there, shielding her from view. She drew in a deep breath and collected her thoughts.

Barging into the speakeasy was out of the question. Once inside, she wouldn't know what to do. If Blake was there, he'd deny it in front of Beattie, forcing her to choose between husband and family. Minnie's head hurt.

Whatever Blake was doing there, she could not go near the place. She'd go back to Fifth Street and head up to Main. With shaky legs, she ventured back to the cross street. One final glance, just to be sure, before she left.

What she saw shocked her even more. Peter Simmons was leaving the speakeasy.

Chapter Seventeen

Minnie couldn't very well ask Peter what he was doing at the speakeasy. Plenty of townspeople visited it, but she had never imagined him going there. It was wrong. Forbidden. Illegal. Peter always seemed so honest.

It didn't make sense.

Neither did his silence while she worked on the boards the following days. Every day she expected him to explain. He didn't.

Oh, he set up the table like she'd asked, but other than asking after her father, who had rallied somewhat since arriving at the hospital, he practically ignored her. By Thursday, she couldn't stand it anymore. Tomorrow night this stream of income would dry up if she didn't convince Peter to fight for more jobs. Surely Vince would understand the business possibilities. He could promote it to everyone he knew in Chicago. She could bring the idea to Grand Rapids when she visited Daddy next week. It made perfect sense. Everyone would win, if she could just convince Peter. If that didn't work, she'd have to go straight to the source.

Changing a situation meant taking a risk.

When Minnie finished the last board Thursday afternoon, she called Peter over to help her carry it back to the wood-shop workbench.

"I'll help you put the compartment together," she offered. "We can do it right now or after you close the garage."

"Don't need help," he muttered, again not looking at her.

"Maybe I *want* to help."

"Maybe I don't want any help."

"It'll go faster. We'll have it put together by dusk."

Peter took the board from her and set it on the workbench. "I'm busy."

"After work? I thought we had to have the car ready by tomorrow."

"I'll put it together in the morning." He tried to skirt around her, but she blocked the way. He wasn't going to brush her off this time.

"What's wrong with you? You've been acting strange all week. We have a job to do. Let's do it."

He shrugged, his gaze downcast. "I got an appointment."

"That makes no sense. No one takes appointments after five o'clock. You're just trying to get rid of me."

That brought his gaze up. A look of consternation flitted across his face before he closed down again. "I would never try to get rid of you." His voice broke, and he had to clear his throat before going on. "I do have to see someone tonight. Please believe me."

That was the Peter she remembered. His hazel eyes looked black in the shadow of his cap, but his pleading spoke of deep anguish. Did he regret his trip to the speakeasy? Should she tell him she'd seen him leave there?

He gripped her shoulders. "You have to believe I would never willingly hurt you."

His touch recalled the warmth of his embrace when

she'd lost control and wept. How tenderly he'd held her then. How soft his words promising to always take care of her.

She looked up and saw so much compassion in his eyes that she trembled.

"It's all right." He gathered her into his arms and whispered, "I promise it will all turn out all right."

Though her emotions swirled into a tempest, no tears came. In his arms, she felt both secure and strong enough to accomplish anything.

He broke the embrace. "I talked to Mrs. Kensington. She'll still let you sing in the revue."

Her jaw dropped. He talked to the director? He arranged this for her? She didn't know whether to be angry or pleased. "Oh, Peter, you shouldn't have."

"Yes, I should. You deserve this. You deserve the world."

She swallowed the lump in her throat. "But the work."

"If there's more, we'll work around rehearsals."

What a wonderful man! Never mind that she barely thought about the musical revue any longer. He thought she did. He'd even faced down the imperious Mrs. Kensington to win back her spot in the show. That was love. Her heart swelled so much she thought it would burst. "Oh, Peter."

He looked confused. "You don't like it?"

"I love that you'd do that for me." Impulsively, she stood on her tiptoes and placed a kiss on his cheek.

His eyes widened, and he wrapped his arms around her. His face drew gradually closer, as if ratcheted ever so slowly together. She couldn't look away, couldn't draw a breath, couldn't stop the spinning in her stomach. Then, ever so softly, his lips brushed hers. The shiver started deep inside her and sped out with lightning force. Never had anything felt so right. She and Peter. He'd been there all along. While she chased after men who'd never given her a second look, he waited.

She stood a little taller on her toes and kissed him back.

He swept her into the embrace, and she gave in with abandon. This was what it meant to fall in love. Not the constant fear of rejection but the absolute assurance of devotion. Peter loved her through and through. Despite her harsh words. Despite her demands. Despite her tears. When other men laughed and walked away, he stayed. She reached her arms around his neck and hugged him close.

Then, for no reason at all, he stiffened and pushed her away. "This is wrong."

"What do you mean?" His reaction left her chilled.

He glanced toward the street. "You're supposed to be out there in public view, not back here. Your father and mother would never approve."

"But—" Words failed her. What could she say to that? Her family insisted on impossible restrictions that no one else had to follow. "Other girls go on picnics with a guy. Some even go on a drive together."

He stepped even farther away. "Don't measure yourself by other girls. You're better than them."

"If you think that, then why push me away?"

"Because I care about you." His Adam's apple bobbed. "I want to be with you."

Never had anyone's words sounded both so wonderful and so perplexing. "I don't understand."

"We have to do this right. Proper courtship. Your father's permission. All of it."

She understood. A little. "But what if he never comes home from the hospital?"

He gulped. "We won't think about that. The whole town's praying for him. That has to count for something."

Minnie wasn't so sure. She'd experienced plenty of

unanswered prayers. "I think he'd give you permission. Mother says he likes you."

"He does?"

She nodded. "So why not court? Guys and gals make that decision for themselves these days. Knowing Daddy already approves of you should be good enough."

"I suppose." Hope flickered in his eyes. "Maybe I could place a long-distance telephone call and ask him."

"Then all of Pearlman would know we're courting, since Cora Williams listens in on every telephone call," she teased.

He grinned and even blushed, which warmed her so much that she dared broach the risky subject. "Take me with you tomorrow night."

His smile evaporated. "No."

"Why not? We're courting for all practical purposes."

"I thought I made that clear." He pulled off his cap and raked a hand through his hair. "Because it's wrong. That's why not. Besides, you have a chance to sing. I thought that's what you wanted."

That dream had lost all its power, becoming no more substantial than a paper lantern. "Not anymore. I want love, Peter. I want someone to love me the way Valentino loved Lady Diana in *The Sheik*."

He looked incredulous. "That's a moving-picture show. That's not real love."

"Yes, it is. Don't you see? That's why I want to be with you every day and through everything, no matter what happens."

Peter took her by the shoulders, the old determination back in place. "That's why I have to refuse."

Minnie gulped. She'd given him the chance to declare love. She'd practically said the words herself, but he hadn't taken the bait. Instead, he refused to even consider a tiny little thing like letting her ride with him to deliver the Maxwell. "I thought you cared." She felt the angry tears burn in her eyes.

"I do." He squeezed her shoulders. "I can't explain. Not now. You'll have to trust me."

That was the last thing she could do. He hadn't earned her trust.

Peter should have gone to the sheriff before Thursday. Minnie's request to join him on the delivery cemented his decision to do so after closing the garage. He'd already gotten her too involved. Maybe the package Vince had him pick up at the speakeasy would give the police enough proof of wrongdoing that he wouldn't have to deliver the car tomorrow.

He had to wait for the sheriff to return from a reported theft from Hermann Grattan's dairy farm. Considering the sheriff's decision to investigate Grattan's operation, this could either be a smoke screen to divert the sheriff from what was really going on or proof that Grattan was clean.

Peter kinda hoped the sheriff would find some sign of bootlegging there, but the sheriff returned alone.

"Was anything stolen?" Peter asked.

Sheriff Ilsley sat down at his desk with a grunt, a frown creasing his brow. "Some copper piping."

"Why would someone steal that?"

"For homemade stills, for one."

Peter sucked in his breath. Maybe he'd be able to wriggle out of this deal. "Think he's got one?"

"Not that I can find. Had my deputies scour the area." Ilsley scrubbed his forehead. "Nothing. Grattan's clean."

Peter's hope deflated. "Sorry about that."

"Me, too. Now, what you got? You said yesterday you had something to show me."

"Yes, sir." Peter slipped the package wrapped in brown paper from his coat pocket. It sure wasn't the liquor he'd expected to be waiting there. It felt more like a small book, all wrapped up and tied with string. On the front were scribbled *Mr. Brown* and a Chicago address.

The sheriff turned the small package over and over. "Brown? Does the name mean anything to you?"

"No, sir, but it is addressed to someone in Chicago."

The sheriff set the package down and leaned back in his chair. Steepling his fingers, he tapped a forefinger against his lips, deep in thought. "You said Mr. Galbini asked you to pick it up."

"Yes, sir."

"Hmm. There aren't any postal stamps or cancellations on it. Where did you go to pick it up?"

"Uh…" Peter considered how to say this. "The back door of the drugstore."

The sheriff's gaze narrowed. "I see. Since there isn't any sign it went through postal delivery, we have to assume someone either brought or delivered it there. Who gave it to you?"

"No one."

"What do you mean? Someone had to open the door and hand it to you."

Peter didn't see the point in naming Mrs. Lawrence. Everyone knew she operated the place. Moreover, she'd only let him in the door and waved toward the package. "Actually, it was sitting on this sort of counter, kinda like a little hotel counter, with my name on it."

The sheriff examined the package again. "I don't see your name anywhere."

"It wasn't written on the package, sir. It was on a piece of paper tucked under the string."

"Do you have that piece of paper?"

Peter blanched. "No, sir. Didn't think of it at the time. Just wanted to get out of there fast as I could."

"You didn't go past the counter?"

"No, sir."

"No one went in or out while you were there?"

"No, sir. It only took a couple minutes. I didn't see anyone except Mrs. Lawrence. She opened the door." Peter would admit that much, but he couldn't bring himself to mention that Blake Kensington's car was parked outside. Kensington visited the speakeasy a lot, if his car was any indication. Peter saw it there three or four days a week. Blake was married to Minnie's oldest sister. Peter sure didn't want to bring any more hurt to that family.

"Did you hear anyone?"

Peter held his breath. He'd heard Reggie Landers laugh. At least he thought he had, but he wasn't gonna name anyone without proof. "Not that I could put a face to."

"All right." The sheriff tapped a finger against the package. "The question is whether to open it or not."

"Isn't it breaking some sort of law to open a package addressed to someone else?"

The sheriff ignored his question. "The string will have to be cut. But we can retie it in the same manner. If we're careful to use the same creases when repackaging, no one will know anyone ever opened it."

Peter swallowed hard. This felt wrong. On the other hand, the sheriff ought to know the law. Maybe it was all right. Either way, he hoped Vince wouldn't suspect they'd opened the package.

It took Sheriff Ilsley only seconds to cut the string and remove the brown paper. Inside, as Peter suspected, was a book. The greasy leather cover was worn at the edges. The sheriff flipped it open. His brow creased, and he turned another page. Then another.

Peter couldn't stand the suspense. "What is it?"

"I'm not sure." The sheriff slid the small notebook across the desk. "Looks like an account book, but for what?"

The pages were divided into columns filled with numbers and cryptic words like *bootstrap* and *monkey*.

"Makes no sense," the sheriff muttered as he leafed through the rest of the notebook.

"Did you find anything else?"

"It's all the same. Numbers and odd names. It could be a bookie's tally book, but most of these don't sound like horse names. Siloview? What's that?" He flipped to the front and then the back. "Also, no one put his name in it. No telling who it belongs to. Is this Mr. Galbini's writing?"

"Don't know," Peter admitted. "I've never seen him write anything."

"Not even the directions to the drop-off spot tomorrow night?"

"He told me and had me write it out. I figured he wanted me to be able to read the handwriting."

The sheriff leaned back with a sigh. "Well, this was a dead end."

Peter's hope faded away. "Then I'll still have to deliver the car tomorrow?"

"There's no way around that." The sheriff must have sensed Peter's discomfort, because he rounded the desk and perched on the corner in front of him. "Agent Fallston's a good man. He'll be there as promised. I also took the liberty of tipping off my compatriots down there. They won't interfere, but they'll be on the alert. Peter?"

"Yes, sir?" He gulped. The sheriff sounded even more serious than usual.

"This going to be dangerous. I won't lie to you. Apparently the route Galbini gave you heads into some pretty remote area. Do you own a gun?"

Peter's pulse ground to a stop. "No, sir."

The sheriff walked over to his gun case. "I want you to have a rifle with you, just in case. Do you know how to shoot?"

The sound of gunshots ringing from out back of the New York club pierced through the haze of memory. He'd run far and fast, but he couldn't outrun the screams. "No, sir."

"I'll show you the basics, but without practice, you're not likely to hit the target. Keep it hidden. Use it only if necessary."

The sheriff proceeded to show him how to load and fire the weapon, but Peter couldn't keep his attention on the instruction. His thoughts swirled elsewhere.

"Forget it." Peter pushed the rifle away. "I'd never use it, and it'll only get in the way."

"Your life could be in danger."

Peter took a shuddering breath. "I know, sir, and I'm willing to risk it, but I gotta know that Minnie will be safe. She asked to come along. I thought I had something lined up that would keep her busy, but she didn't go for it. Can you make sure she's safe?"

The sheriff sat down again. A smile tickled his lips. "I can't lock her up, if that's what you're asking. Perhaps some social engagement? Our families don't socialize. Do yours?"

Peter thought hard, but he couldn't recall one instance of the Foxes dining with the Simmonses. "Not exactly."

"You might want to enlist the aid of one of her sisters."

Peter shook his head. "They don't know anything, and I don't want them to."

"Is it fair to assume Miss Fox wants to join you because you two are courting?"

Peter felt his face heat. "Yes, sir, a little."

The sheriff leaned forward, elbows on the desktop. "You could break the courtship."

"What?" After waiting for Minnie for so long, Peter couldn't imagine driving her away.

"Temporarily. Until you're back and all is well. Hopefully, this will turn out exactly like Mr. Galbini told you. When you return, you can let Miss Fox know why you had to make the trip by yourself."

Peter hated to break Minnie's heart, but the sheriff did make some sense. If Minnie was angry with him, then she wouldn't want to go on the delivery. She also wouldn't suffer if the worst happened. None of his new family would if he did this right.

He stood a bit shakily. "Thank you, sir."

"Sure you don't want the rifle?"

The offer was tempting. If Peter was still the scared boy on the streets, he might've taken the gun and relied on something he couldn't operate. But he'd given his life to God. Faith would see him through.

He squared his shoulders. "No thank you, sir."

Trust me, Peter had said right after telling her she couldn't deliver the car with him. Trust him? That was all he could tell her? Minnie fumed all night and into the next day. The truth was that Peter didn't trust *her.* That was why he wouldn't take her along. That was why he'd gone out of his way to make sure she was preoccupied with rehearsals. That was why he wouldn't say that he loved her in return. Something was going on, and he wasn't telling her one bit of it.

A man courting a woman needed to tell her everything. He needed to trust her. Clearly, Peter didn't.

"I don't know what's wrong with him," she said to Ruth as she sorted through scraps of cloth in the dress shop. Larger pieces went into the cubbyholes by color. Small scraps went into an old flour sack that Mrs. Grozney would pick up for the quilting guild at church. She probably wouldn't stop by today, not with rain threatening.

"With whom?" Ruth adjusted the lamp over the worktable so she could see better to sketch a new ball-gown design.

"Peter." Minnie looked over her sister's shoulder. "That's pretty. I like the sash."

"It is nice, isn't it?" Ruth held the piece of paper up to the light. "What's wrong with Peter?"

"He's acting odd. Did you know he asked Mrs. Kensington to let me back into the musical revue?"

Ruth gave Minnie one of those knowing smiles. "How sweet."

"It's not sweet. He did it to distract me."

"If you ask me, he did it to *attract* you."

Minnie plopped onto the stool across from her sister. "You don't understand. He doesn't want me hanging around the garage anymore."

Ruth showed little sympathy. "I don't know why you'd want to spend time there anyway. You've never been interested in mechanical things, like Jen is." She began sketching again. "Besides, I could use your help. Now that you're finished with upholstery, you can work on dresses. Mrs. Lyman's gown needs hemming."

"I'm not finished with upholstering. I can't be. Do you realize how much money that brings in? Mr. Galbini paid four hundred dollars the first time and two hundred the next."

"I heard." Ruth barely looked up. "Mother said the amount was outrageous. She thinks it should have gone to Peter, but he's so taken with you that he handed you the whole amount."

"No, he didn't. I asked, and he said he'd already been paid."

"How much?"

"I didn't ask. That's not a polite question."

"Mmm-hmm." Ruth's pencil scratched furiously over the paper. "A man in love does things like that."

"He's not in love." The fact that he hadn't taken her hint confirmed it. "If he was, he'd tell me everything."

Ruth chuckled. "I used to think that, too. Remember how Sam concealed his real last name?"

"How could I forget? We had no idea he was opening a department store next door. You were furious."

"I was mistaken."

"What do you mean? He lied to you. I remember you saying that."

"My mistake. I let emotion overcome good sense." Ruth shook her head. "I knew better, too. That's the sorriest part. I treated him abominably and almost ruined everything."

"But it all worked out in the end."

"Because Sam is a forgiving man." Ruth looked over her glasses at Minnie. "My point is that I should have trusted him enough to accept his word. Circumstances forced him to conceal the truth, even though he wanted to tell me. He even hinted at it, but I refused to listen. Maybe Peter is facing the same dilemma."

"This isn't the same at all. Sam had to hide the truth from you because of his father. Peter's an orphan, and he doesn't have an inheritance to lose."

"Parentage is not the point. I don't know what Peter

is facing, but he might risk losing something important to him."

Minnie groaned. "Since you know so much, what would that be?"

Ruth shrugged. "I'm just saying you ought to give him a chance. Listen to what he does tell you and let him know you'll stand up for him no matter what."

"I don't see why I should do that if he's not being honest with me."

"Then maybe you're not ready for courtship."

That stung. "Of course I am. I've been ready for ages."

Ruth looked ready to rebuke her but was cut off by Jen rushing through the door.

"You won't believe what happened," Jen said between gulps for air. "It's chaos."

Minnie stood. "At the airfield?" That's where Jen was working today.

Ruth dropped her pencil. Her color drained. "The planes. Did someone crash?"

Jen shook her head. "Everyone's safe." She leaned against the worktable and caught her breath. "It's Peter."

"Peter?" Minnie gasped. "What happened to Peter?"

"He quit."

Chapter Eighteen

"He what?" Minnie screeched. "Why would he do that?"

"I don't know." Jen recoiled at Minnie's ferocity. "Don't kill the messenger. All I know is he told Hendrick and Mariah this morning at breakfast. Hendrick's furious. He told Peter to get out at once, but Mariah made him promise to let Peter pack up his things and settle business at the garage."

Minnie's head spun. "But why would Peter just up and quit? Where would he go? Why would he leave his family?"

Ruth seconded Minnie's questions. "This makes no sense."

"If you'd just let me explain," Jen said, "you'd understand. Apparently Peter got a job offer from that friend of his, the one that's been bringing him the cars to work on."

"Mr. Galbini?"

"That's the one," Jen said. "According to Mariah, the job pays more, and Peter's heading down to Chicago tonight with the Maxwell you two just finished. Once he gets there, he's going to take the new job."

Minnie tried to wrap her mind around this. No wonder Peter had been acting strangely all week. No wonder he didn't want her to ride with him. No wonder he wouldn't commit to her. But then why lead her to believe he was only waiting for her father's permission to court? It made no sense. "You mean he's not coming back?"

"That's what taking a job in Chicago would mean," Ruth said before turning to Jen. "What I don't understand is how you learned all this. I thought you were at work."

"Mariah stopped by the airfield to ask Mr. Hunter to keep an eye on the factory. With Peter quitting, Hendrick had to go back to working at the garage."

Minnie sank onto the nearest stool. "Then it's really happening."

"Oh, Minnie." Ruth gave her a hug. "I'm so sorry. And after I tried to convince you that Peter was sweet on you. I didn't know, or I would never have said those things. Honestly, we all thought he liked you, didn't we?"

Jen nodded.

"Me, too," Minnie whispered.

"You poor dear." Ruth said. "You have such a bad time with men. First Reggie. Now Peter."

Minnie clapped her hands over her ears. "Stop it! Peter is nothing like Reggie Landers. Peter is good and considerate and honest. He always put me first." She choked back a sob.

Ruth hugged harder, which only made Minnie feel like bursting into tears.

Jen, on the other hand, spat, "Why would he do this? It's totally out of the blue."

Minnie sucked in a shuddering breath. She knew why. It was clear as could be. Ruth had said as much earlier. Yesterday Peter asked her to trust him. Instead of doing so, Minnie had thrown his words back in his face and stormed out of the garage. She was the reason. She'd forced him to leave.

"I don't know," Ruth was saying. "We may never know."

Minnie couldn't leave it at that. She had to change Peter's mind. "I have to go." She grabbed her coat and threw it over her shoulders, not even taking the time to stick her arms in the sleeves.

"Go? Where?" Ruth asked.

Jen understood. "Do it, Minnie! You can stop him!"

Minnie dashed out the door and raced for the motor garage. Hopefully, she'd get there in time.

This had to be just about the worst day of Peter's life. His parents died when he was too young to fully understand. Aunt Ursula's death brought fear. This situation tore him apart. The Simmons family had been so good to him. It was bad enough facing Hendrick's wrath, but when Anna brought Ma Simmons to the garage a little later, he pretty near broke down.

Ma took his hand and looked into his eyes. "Is this what you want, Peter?"

That was all she asked, but it knifed through him. He couldn't look at her when he nodded.

He didn't want to leave. He didn't ever want to leave. Ma was the best mother since his own. But he couldn't let them suffer if tonight went wrong. Better they never know. If it turned out better than he figured, then he could come back and beg forgiveness.

"All right, then," Ma said with a sigh. "Give me a hug, dear."

He stooped low to embrace her. For a second he lingered in her arms like a little boy. "I'll never forget you." He pulled away before emotion overcame the tough facade.

Ma patted his arm. "You're a good boy. Write to me every Sunday, all right?"

That was a command, not a suggestion. "Yes, ma'am."

"And make sure you eat properly. Launder your clothes regularly and stay out of trouble."

"I'll do my best, ma'am."

"Remember that you always have a home here." Her pale eyes swam in tears.

His throat narrowed. "All right, Ma."

Anna walked her mother out, but not before giving Peter a scathing glare. He had broken her mother's heart. He knew that. It hurt him, too, but he didn't have time to think much about it before Minnie stormed into the garage.

"There you are." She plunked her hands on her hips. "Tell me Jen was wrong. Tell me you aren't taking a job with Vincent Galbini."

Peter barely had time to swallow his tears. He sure didn't want to talk to Minnie. If only he'd waited until late in the day, but he hadn't wanted to leave Hendrick in the lurch.

"Well?" she demanded. "Speak up."

He lowered his gaze. "I am."

"You're what?"

"Taking a job with Vince."

"You can't!"

Her strong reaction made him look up. "Why not? I don't have ties here. I'm an orphan, remember?"

She shuddered, as if he had struck her with an arrow. "Not anymore. You're a Simmons now. You're part of the family."

Her words echoed what Ma had just said, but he couldn't change course now. "Ma Simmons accepts that a man has to make his way in the world. Why can't you?"

"Why?" She hugged her arms tight against her midsection. "Didn't anything I said yesterday mean a thing to you?"

She'd more or less said she loved him. Her words had

rung over and over in his head. That was why he had to do this.

He looked away from her. He had to. "I don't know what you mean."

"I love you." The soft plea stood in such contrast to her earlier indignation that it nearly undid him.

He wanted to tell her that he loved her, too. He did. He had for ages and ages. But he couldn't risk her life for a moment's indulgence. He took a deep breath and hoped she didn't hear how ragged it sounded. "I'm sorry. I should have told you then that it would never work."

He heard her gasp, heard her step backward. Every cell in his body wanted to run to her, to take her in his arms and hold her forever, but he'd gotten her in too deep. Sheriff Ilsley might not know what that notebook was, but he had a strong suspicion. He'd seen something like that once, when he was running errands to the clubs. It tallied the receipts from gambling and money laundering and other forms of vice. Vincent Galbini was involved in something terrible. Tonight would not end well.

"I'm sorry," he repeated.

For some reason, that rallied her. "Don't be sorry—stay. Don't you understand? You're better than all of them by a million miles. Reggie Landers is a cad. Vincent Galbini? Nothing. Less than nothing. Don't do this, Peter. Don't leave everyone who loves you."

It was more than he could bear, yet he had to do it. He had to hurt her in order to save her. Summoning all his courage, he looked at her. "I'm going, Minnie, and there's nothing you can say that will change my mind."

The fight went out of her slowly, like a leaky tire deflating. First, the fire died in her eyes. Then the confidence wavered. Lastly, the tears came.

Throwing her hands at him, she cried, "I hate you," and ran from the garage.

Peter collapsed against the Maxwell and wept.

He couldn't mean it.

Minnie wiped away the tears and stormed all the way across town to the Grange Hall in the spitting rain. Never work? How could he say that? All this time he'd let her think he cared for her. He'd hounded her, asked her to everything. Then she finally fell for him, and he refused her. How could he? It must be her. She could never choose the right man. Every one of them turned on her.

One block she fumed. The next she wept. By the time she worked her way back, the drizzle had cooled her temper enough to let her figure out that he must be hiding something from her. She'd seen fear in his eyes. He would barely look at her. His shoulders slumped. This wasn't a man eager to set off on a new adventure. No, he was doing this for another reason.

But what? Peter treasured his new family. He wouldn't hurt them like this without an overpowering reason. Take a job with Vince? Impossible. She hadn't even heard Vince offer Peter a job. If he had, one of them would have said something. Plus, Peter wouldn't go on and on about courting her if he'd intended all along to leave town.

That was why she had to do something.

Minnie Fox did not quit. Neither did the Peter Simmons she knew and loved. He'd fought and scrapped to stay alive as an orphan. Something else was going on.

She reached the end of the alley facing the garage. The rain had stopped, and the Maxwell was parked outside now, all shined up and ready to go. Peter walked out of the garage carrying his wood toolbox, his shoulders bowed and his gaze low. She pressed against the cold bricks of the corner building and watched as he opened the car's rear door and set the toolbox inside. Then he closed the car door and ambled toward Main Street, never once looking up.

He looked like a man defeated.

She wanted to run after him to plead her case, but he'd proven unmovable. The time for talk was over. She had to act.

Again her gaze landed on the Maxwell. He refused to take her along, but he couldn't object if he didn't know she was there. The luggage compartment was big enough for a small person—for instance, one determined woman. If Peter Simmons wouldn't listen to her, maybe Vincent Galbini would. She would put an end to this nonsense about taking a job in Chicago.

She would stow away.

Chapter Nineteen

The sun had dropped below the trees before Peter drove out of Pearlman. He parked by the bridge and tugged the telegram from his coat pocket.

Change of plans, the wire read.

Arrive at midnight. Stop.

New route. Stop.

Vince hadn't just given him a different route; the new directions took him almost due east instead of south. He wouldn't leave Michigan at all. Peter had stopped by Sheriff Ilsley's office, but he and Agent Fallston were already gone. The deputy promised to give them the new directions if either man returned or placed a call to the office. Peter took the time to copy them down for the deputy, but worry dogged him from that moment forward.

He had thought Agent Fallston was going to tail him. If he and the sheriff were already gone, then they couldn't. So where were they? Had they gone ahead based on the old directions, or were they waiting for him somewhere? Peter hoped the latter was the case, but no automobile followed him out of town and none passed him at the bridge. For all he knew, Fallston could be on his way to Indiana.

His palms sweated, and his pulse thrummed. Somehow he'd have to finish this without help.

Concentrate.

He had to memorize the directions before it got dark. He didn't own a flashlight, and Hendrick refused to lend him one. Peter couldn't blame him. Hendrick thought Peter wasn't coming back. He sure hoped his foster brother was wrong.

Peter repeated the directions one more time, trying to visualize every turn of the unfamiliar route. *Out of town heading east and then turn right and follow that a short distance. Left and then straight for miles. Right. Left. Left. One after another. Look for a pitchfork in the ditch.* Simple enough except in the dark. At least there was a three-quarter moon.

He put the car in gear and drove over the Green River and away from home. Regret tugged at his heart. If only he'd refused Vince that first day, he wouldn't be in this mess. If only he hadn't been swayed by money. He'd thought it would impress Minnie. Instead it had driven her away. After the abominable way he'd treated her today, she'd never forgive him.

By the time he reached the first turn at the whitewashed silo, darkness had settled in. The road was straight here, cut through flat farmland. With the fields newly turned and planted, nothing blocked his view except for the occasional grove of trees. Peter kept glancing behind, hoping to see the headlamps of another automobile. Once, he spotted some, but the vehicle turned off. If Agent Fallston got the right directions, he was keeping his distance.

Perspiration beaded on Peter's upper lip even though the car was icy cold. He'd worn several layers of clothing under his overalls, knowing this would be a long and cold drive, but no amount of clothing could ward off the cold sweats.

After one last glance, he turned onto the next road. He sure hoped Agent Fallston was coming. He wasn't sorry to leave the tooth-rattling "corduroy" road. The slabs of wood kept the car from sinking into the mud, but they were rough on the suspension.

By the time he turned again, he'd left open farmland and plunged into thick woods. The road narrowed, and branches scraped against the car. The ruts grew deeper, and he had to swerve constantly to avoid muddy potholes.

Still no headlamps behind him.

He drove past the last turn. Anyone would miss it. The road was so overgrown that Peter doubted it had seen a car since last spring. This couldn't be right. A man willing to pay good money for a luggage compartment wouldn't pick up the car in the wilderness. Yet there wasn't any other place to turn, and he could see the handle of a pitchfork sticking out of the ditch just like the directions said.

The hair rose on the back of his neck. Heading down this road was sure to lead to trouble. He ought to turn back. Drive anywhere else and abandon the car. He could slip into a boxcar on a train and disappear forever. It was tempting, but that left Minnie in danger. If he didn't fulfill this delivery, Vince might blame her.

Regret tasted bitter. Too late to get out. In too deep to ever get the one thing he wanted most

He closed his eyes and took a deep breath. *God, please help me. I don't know what to do. I don't know what's right anymore. I'm sorry for failing You. Take me, if You want, but keep Minnie safe. Please.*

It wasn't much of a prayer, and he probably didn't use the right words, but he felt a little better afterward.

Then he put the car in gear and crept onto the overgrown road.

If Minnie had known she would ride in the luggage compartment, she would have put in thicker padding. Every bump and dip hurt. That ghastly washboard road chattered her teeth, and she accidentally bit her tongue. She braced her hands against the sides so she wouldn't roll and alert Peter to her presence, but she couldn't keep it up the entire time. When the road smoothed out for a bit, she relaxed. Then the car would hit a pothole, and she'd get another bruise.

The compartment was as small as a coffin. She could push up the seat cushion, but there was no place to go. Peter had stopped the car once soon after getting started and again much later, but he didn't get out either time. The motor was running, but the car wasn't moving. Was he lost? She lifted the seat cushion just enough to peek out, but that was when the car lurched forward. The cushion bounced up and nearly slid onto the floor. Only a quick grab and a lot of effort prevented disaster.

He'd nearly discovered her back at the garage. She'd snuck into the car while Hendrick was closing the garage. He and Peter had argued something awful, but she couldn't make out what either one said. Sometime later, the car door opened and the seat cushion lifted. She froze. It wasn't dark out yet. Surely Peter would see her.

Something soft yet heavy struck her on the shoulder. She grabbed what felt like a hard and lumpy pillow. She had to pull it down over her head so Peter didn't reach into the compartment. Thankfully, he set the seat cushion back in place without noticing her. Then he opened the shallow hidden compartment underneath her and put something in there. What? She was dying of curiosity, but he'd gotten into the driver's seat, and she had no opportunity to get out and look.

A deep pothole bounced her against the underside of the seat cushion and then against the floorboards. Why hadn't she thought to bring a blanket? It was freezing back here. She'd shivered for hours. Surely they must be there by now.

Almost on cue, the car stopped. This time Peter turned off the motor. They'd arrived.

Now she had to convince Mr. Galbini not to hire Peter. From inside the compartment, she couldn't hear anything except the car door slam. That had to be Peter getting out.

While lying on her side, she pushed up on the seat. It lifted a little before her arm started to ache and she had to give up. This was going to take more than one arm. She wiggled around until she could get a knee and two hands on the bottom of the cushion. Up she pressed. The cushion lifted enough for her to scoot up and push it off the pegs so she could lean it against the seat back.

Her legs were cramped, and her arms ached, but she managed to crawl to her knees and look around. No one was in the car. Peter's toolbox was still on the floorboards. The full moon illuminated everything. He'd driven into a wooded area with an old, ramshackle henhouse that looked about ready to fall down. No house. No barn. No sign anyone lived here.

She could hear voices. It took a minute to spot Vince and Peter near another car. Minnie squinted. It looked like the Pierce-Arrow. Vince was talking to Peter, who kept glancing around nervously.

This was her moment. She gripped the door handle,

opened the door and crawled out. Unfortunately, her legs had lost feeling from being cramped up in the compartment, and she stumbled to her knees.

"Peter!" she called out.

He whipped around.

She was met with the sharp sound of guns preparing to fire.

"Minnie? What? How? Why are you here?" Peter stammered.

Vince eased off his revolver. "It's all right, boys. I know the gal."

The three thugs who'd shown up with Vince reluctantly backed off.

Peter had the distinct impression they were disappointed not to fire their shotguns. Well, he wasn't going to give them the chance to get near Minnie. Before Vince could say another word, he rushed to her side and helped her to her feet. "What are you doing here?"

She jutted out that defiant chin of hers, apparently unfazed by the guns that had just been pointed at her head. "Helping you."

"I don't need help."

"I can see that," she said with deserved sarcasm. "You have things completely under control."

He ignored the jab. "How did you get here?"

She gingerly hopped from foot to foot. "The luggage compartment."

"What? But I put my clothes in there."

"So that's what that is."

Peter raked a hand through his hair. This was bad. Very bad. Vince did not look pleased. Though he'd already said enough to imply he was bootlegging, he hadn't yet divulged the details. Peter needed that admission in order to turn Vince over to federal agents. Minnie was not only unwittingly ruining that, but she was also in tremendous danger. Vince's willingness to protect her could end at any moment. Peter wished he'd brought that rifle of the sheriff's after all.

Minnie, on the other hand, seemed to grow more confident by the second. "Mr. Galbini. How good to see you again. I hope I can have a word with you."

Vince must have been stunned by her forwardness, because he didn't say a thing.

"I'll take that as a yes," she said. "As you know, Peter is an important member of our community. People rely on him." Her voice wavered a little. "I rely on him."

Embarrassment mixed with horror. What was she doing? Vince didn't respond to emotional pleas. Not anymore. The old Vince might have, but he'd changed. If Peter had fallen in with him, he would have changed, too.

"Minnie," Peter pleaded, trying to tug her back. "Stop it. Vince doesn't want to hear that kind of talk."

Vince's lips curled into a sneer. "Naw. Let her talk. We could use a gal like her." He gripped Minnie's chin and forced her to look at him.

Peter balled his fists. "Let her go."

Vince looked surprised. "Didn't mean nothin' by it, kid. Just gotta figure out what ta do with her. She wasn't in the plans." He patted her cheek.

Peter gathered the now-frightened Minnie into his arms. "We let her go home."

"Can't do that, kid. You know that."

Peter held her tighter. "Minnie has nothing to do with this, understand?"

"C'mon, kid. A gal like that, all innocent, is just the ticket for us. Give her a Bible ta hold on to, and none of those revenuers would think ta stop us."

"You will not use her," Peter growled, pulling her behind him just to be sure.

Vince laughed. "What exactly you planning to do? Make her walk home?"

"Drive her?" he croaked.

Vince laughed. His henchmen joined in. Then Vince stopped. "No. Either she's one of us, or she can say her prayers."

Peter felt Minnie tremble. *He* was trembling. *God, I could use a little help here. And it'd sure be nice if You'd answer real quick.*

Pastor Gabe's tale flickered to mind. What had he said? That he'd mistaken Felicity's father for a bootlegger? What if the same was true for Vince? Peter had a tough time wrapping his mind around that, considering the way Vince was acting, but his old friend had called off the trigger-happy thugs. Maybe if Peter treated Vince as if he was honest, he'd act that way.

Minnie had squeezed against his back so tightly that he felt the pounding of her racing heart. Somehow he had to calm her. Panic wouldn't help them.

He put his hands over hers, where they gripped around his waist. "Have faith," he said loud enough for everyone to hear. "Nothing is impossible for those who love the Lord." He hoped he got that scripture right or at least close enough.

Vince sneered, "What happened ta ya, kid? Ya turn inta one of them Bible-thumpin' preacher fellows? Maybe I better put ya in the backseat with the missus."

Though Peter's legs wobbled with fear, he managed to reply. "Yes, I gave my life to Jesus Christ."

"You hear that, boys?" Vince guffawed. "We got us a born-again fool."

Humility. Pastor Gabe said that his pride had put Felicity in danger. Peter had to stay humble.

He cleared his throat. "That's right. I'm a fool, but I'm willing to work out a deal."

"You? Offer me a deal?" Vince screeched derisively. "You ain't in no position to be makin' deals." His hand twitched near his holster.

Despite the danger, Peter stood a little taller, his confidence growing as the plan grew clear. "Just hear me out. What you want is someone who'll help your business. Sure, Minnie's a pretty face, but she don't know the ways of the world, if you know what I mean. She's just a country girl."

Minnie kicked his shin from behind.

"Wholesome and raised up in Sunday school," Peter continued. "You aren't gonna get much outta her except trouble, so why not let her go? I'll join you. Do everything I can to help grow your business." He heard her gasp, but he couldn't explain. He might never be able to explain. "What you need is a mechanic and carpenter. I'm both. I'll handle all the outfitting for you, get the vehicles ready, whatever you need...*if* you let Minnie go."

Vince narrowed his gaze, but his hand moved away from his holster. "She'll talk."

"No, I won't," Minnie said from behind Peter.

"She'll never know where we went," Peter said. "Leave her here."

Minnie squeaked and buried her face against his back. Her arms wrapped a little tighter yet.

"Here?" Vince asked. He looked at the thick woods. "That just might work. The doll said she hid in the luggage compartment." Vince grinned. "That means she didn't see how ya got here."

"Right." Peter held his breath. This just might work. It wasn't the perfect solution, but at least Minnie would live.

"Hey, Jacko. Get that rope outta the car." Vince drew a silk handkerchief from his pocket. "You and me are gonna get the little lady ready for a good night's sleep."

Peter wasn't sure he liked the sound of that, yet something inside him said to trust. Pastor Gabe ended up having to trust the man he'd pegged a criminal. Peter wasn't sure he could trust Vince, but he did trust God. The feeling that everything would turn out all right had to come from God. It sure didn't come from Vince or his cronies.

"God will be with you," he whispered as he removed Minnie's hands from around his midsection, "and I'll come back for you."

She was shaking violently, so he slipped off his coat and placed it on her shoulders. She put her arms through the sleeves. It was huge on her, but at least she'd be warm.

He allowed himself a single touch to her jaw. "Have faith."

Her eyes were wide, her face ashen in the moonlight. Her lower lip quivered, as if she was hovering between tears and wanting to tell him something.

He couldn't let fear be the last thing she saw in his eyes, so he leaned down and kissed her.

Chapter Twenty

"All right, doll," Vince said. "It's time ta go." He yanked her from Peter's grasp.

This couldn't be happening. She reached for Peter and silently pleaded for him to save her. He took a step toward her, but the thugs held him back. Peter mouthed something. He probably meant to encourage her, but nothing could cut the fear. The woods loomed dark and cold. How would Peter ever find her again?

She resisted, and Vince tightened his grip until it hurt.

"Ya go back ta the kid," he warned, "and they'll shoot ya."

Minnie's heart thudded to a stop. Numb, she stumbled along as Vince dragged her into the woods. He didn't take her far. In fact, Minnie could still see the two automobiles and the men milling about.

"Hold out yer hands," Vince growled.

A voice in her head screamed to run, but Peter said he'd come back for her. If she left the area, he'd never find her. So she fought off instinct and held out her hands.

Vince wrapped the coarse rope around her wrists several times and tied a knot. He then blindfolded her and pushed her against a tree. He pressed against her, and she shuddered at the thought of what he might do while she was defenseless. To think she'd once tried to attract his attention. What a fool she'd been! The real hero had been in front of her the whole time. A whimper threatened. She steeled herself for the worst. For Peter's sake, she would not cry out.

"Wait until after we leave," Vince whispered in her ear.

Minnie recoiled from his stale breath.

He grabbed her chin and forced her face forward.

She cringed at the thought of his lips pressing against hers. "Please don't." Her heart pounded in her ears. She prayed it would stop entirely before he did anything to her.

Instead of feeling his lips on hers, his breath tickled her cheek. "Don't make a sound. There's a farmhouse a half mile back."

She lifted her hands to push him away, but he stepped back on his own. Her hands met air. A second later his footsteps crashed through the undergrowth.

"Let's get going, boys," he barked out.

Minnie's legs gave out. She slid down the rough tree trunk until she sat on the cold ground. The damp earth soaked through her skirt and stockings. She didn't care. Vince Galbini hadn't forced himself on her. Peter had promised to come back for her. She took deep gulps of air to steady her spinning head. She would survive.

Would Peter?

Soon they would leave, and Peter had promised to join Vince's operation. Everyone except Peter had a gun. How would he ever get away from them to come back for her?

Since Vince had tied her hands in front of her rather than behind her back, she could easily push up the blindfold. She looked around. One of the men was moving crates of something out of the ramshackle henhouse. Two men removed the seat cushion from the back of the Maxwell, while Peter and the other thug did the same with the Pierce-Arrow. Even from a distance, she could see that the crates would fit into the luggage compartments. It wouldn't take long to finish the job. If she didn't want to be left behind, she'd have to act quickly.

She crept forward into a patch of moonlight. There, she noticed that Vince hadn't tied the knot very tight. Using her teeth, she loosened the knot and slipped her hands from the rope. The coarse jute scraped the sensitive scar from when she'd cut her hand removing the battery cable on the Pierce-Arrow.

She rubbed the irritated skin against her dress and planned her next move. Escaping had been easy. Now how could she stop Vince and save Peter?

She crouched in the shadows behind a scraggly pine sapling. If any of the men shone a flashlight in her direction, he'd spot her, but she couldn't find anything better. The plants hadn't leafed out yet. She had to hope that they were more interested in carting off their cargo than checking on her.

"I'll drive the Maxwell," Peter volunteered as he joined Vince outside the henhouse.

"Good. Jacko, you take the other car."

Minnie pressed her sore hand to her lips and calculated her options. If she could stop the second car, then she could sneak into the Maxwell and escape with Peter. But how could she disable the Pierce-Arrow?

All at once, the answer came. Her hand! Thanks to Peter and that cut, she knew exactly where to find the battery cable on the Pierce-Arrow and how to get it off. She'd need a wrench, but Peter's toolbox was sitting outside the Maxwell, on the opposite side of the car from all the men. She could skirt the clearing in the shadows and

grab the wrench. Then she'd come back around and disconnect the cable.

Her plan had just one problem. She didn't dare open
the hood. On the other hand, she remembered leaning way
over to reach the cable. Maybe she could get at it from
under the car.

She had to hope she could find it.

Peter had trouble thinking about what he had to do.
Minnie was out there in the woods somewhere. It was getting real cold. There'd probably be frost. His fingers already ached. Even though she was wearing his coat, she'd
never last the night. Somehow he had to get back to her.

He wanted to go to her right now. Grab her and run.

That would be stupid. Vince and his cohorts had guns.
Vince might spare him, but those thugs wouldn't.

Peter felt sick.

He didn't want to think about what Vince might have
done to Minnie. His friend's parting words, that he'd get
Minnie ready for a nice long sleep, ran over and over in his
head, like a moving picture with only one frame.

Vince couldn't have taken her far. He hadn't been gone
all that long. Neither had Peter heard a thing. Minnie hadn't
cried out. No gunshot. Vince might have conked her over
the head, though. She might be bleeding to death.

Peter had to get away from these men. At least Vince
had agreed to let him drive the Maxwell. It wasn't as fast
as the Pierce-Arrow, and there was no way they'd let him
trail them to their destination, but maybe he could outdrive
the thugs and then double back for Minnie.

He glanced back at the overgrown road. If only Fallston
would show up. He'd have his proof, and Peter could fetch
Minnie.

He had to stall them until Fallston arrived, but how?

Peter didn't have any means to slow the crooks down. Someone like Reggie Landers might joke around and get the guys distracted. A good speaker like Pastor Gabe would try to talk sense into the men. Peter didn't have any of that. He couldn't even pull a gun on them.

Use your faith.

The thought needled him, but how could faith help? Vince had laughed at him the last time he mentioned it. Compared to guns, faith seemed puny. Then again, a shepherd boy had killed a giant with five small stones and some mighty big faith. If it had worked for David, maybe it could work for him. Still, what could he say? He wasn't Pastor Gabe. Then again, the Bible said that the Holy Spirit gave the disciples the words they needed. He had a tough time believing that could happen nowadays, but maybe if he got Vince talking, he could slow him down.

"Hey, Vince." Peter hurried to join him after helping remove the Maxwell's seat. "How'd you meet up with this Capone fellow?"

If Vince was suspicious, he didn't show it. "Through channels, kid, like you're doin' now. Play your cards right, and you might get noticed, too."

Peter helped lug a case out of the henhouse. From the weight and jiggling sound, he had little doubt the crates contained liquor.

After setting it down, he pretended to be winded. "Whew. Not used to hefting this kinda weight."

That drew Vince's skepticism. "Thought you were a mechanic, kid."

Peter cringed. He should have known better than to try that ploy. He coughed. "Maybe I'm getting a touch of a cold. It's been running through the kids at home lately."

Vince bought that. "Kids are good for that. Leave the hauling to the boys. We'll get 'er knocked out in no time."

"Yeah." Disappointed, Peter tugged on his cap. Instead

of slowing things down, he'd got them to speed up. He had to try something different. Maybe if he shot straight to the heart of the matter. "Don't see how this little bit's gonna bring in much money."

Vince laughed. "This ain't home brew, kid. This is prime whiskey from across the border."

Peter's skin prickled. Fallston and the sheriff had guessed right. "That's a long way away. How'd you get it all the way here?"

Vince tapped his coat pocket, where he'd stowed the rewrapped notebook. "I got my connections, too." He clapped Peter on the back. "Stick with me, kid. We're going places."

Peter hated to think where those places were. Jail. Prison. Death. Eternal damnation.

Have faith. He'd told Minnie that. Maybe it was time he followed his own advice. Vince had started to walk away to supervise the loading of the liquor.

Peter trotted after him. "What happened to you, Vince?"

His friend whipped around, his expression wary. "What d'ya mean?"

"In New York. You were different then. You went to church and cared about the kids. I looked up to you. You showed me I could do something decent. Respectable."

Vince's expression hardened. "Decent don't put food on the table."

"But your faith—"

He jabbed a finger into Peter's chest. "I give more than a tithe to the local church, so don't you go telling me that I'm not pulling my fair share. Now shut up and get to work."

The conversation was over, and still no federal agents were in sight.

While Peter talked to Vince, Minnie crawled underneath the Pierce-Arrow, wrench in hand. Since it was dark, she had to guess the cable's approximate location and feel around until she found it. That took too long.

Her first attempt landed on something round and covered in grease and dirt.

"Yuck," she muttered before catching herself.

Next she found something square, but there weren't any cables coming off of it. This was not going well.

Worse, one of the thugs approached with a flashlight, which he was waving all over the place. The beam of light danced between the car, the ground and the trees. At any moment, it would land on her.

Minnie pulled her feet in and prayed he wouldn't see her. She held her breath. *One, two, three...*

The man stopped at the open rear door. "Put it in on this side. We'll go around with the next one."

Oh, no. She had to find that battery cable before they came back with the next crate. She looked up, and the beam of the flashlight shone at the perfect angle to reveal the battery. It was within reach, but it had two cables. Fiddlesticks. Peter had said something about making sure she took them off correctly, but she didn't remember which came first.

"Hope it'll start this time," one of the men said. "Want me ta try it?"

Minnie yanked her hand away at the thought of electricity pulsing through her when he started the car. Then the beam of light moved, and she realized she'd better stick her hand near the battery before she lost its location.

"Naw," the other man said. "No need. We got a mechanic now."

Minnie let her breath out slowly.

The two men moved off, taking the flashlight with them.

Now Minnie had to unhook the battery cable without

any light at all. She felt along the length of the cable until she reached the end that attached to the battery. If she did something wrong, she could get hurt. She remembered that much. And it had to do with the wrench, but she didn't know exactly what. After a quick prayer, she felt around and found the bolt. It was loose!

Thank You, Lord. No wrench was needed. She yanked off the cable.

Before the thugs returned, she scooted out from under the car and inched up the door to check where the men were. Vince and one of the thugs were hauling a crate to the Maxwell while Peter set aside his pillowcase of clothing. The other two thugs had just picked up a crate and would soon head back here. There were just two crates left outside the henhouse.

"That's the last one here," Vince said, stepping back from the Maxwell. "Peter, you help Jacko put the seat back in place. Then you two help out Fritzy and Bugs. We gotta get going."

Minnie slipped into the woods before Fritzy and Bugs got to the Pierce-Arrow. Since they were going to load that case on the side closest to her, she skirted around to the scraggly pine and hoped the man with the flashlight wouldn't shine it in her direction.

Next she had to get into the car Peter was going to drive. To her dismay Jacko slammed shut the rear door of the Maxwell that faced the woods. To get in, she'd have to open it, which would alert everyone to her presence. Peter, meanwhile, had grabbed his pillowcase to put it in the back.

Jacko grabbed Peter's arm. "Forget it. We got more important stuff ta do."

Thankfully, neither man closed the other rear door. But to get to it, Minnie would have to cross the clearing in full view. Even though the moon had sunk a little lower in the sky, it still lit the open area. There was no way she could get into the car without being seen.

The three thugs and Peter hauled the last two crates to the Pierce-Arrow while Vince supervised. If everyone's attention stayed focused on the Pierce-Arrow, she could chance making a run for the Maxwell, but Vince kept sweeping his flashlight around the clearing. She couldn't risk it.

As the men replaced the seat cushion, hope slipped away. In seconds, they'd all get into the cars. Peter would drive away, but the men in the Pierce-Arrow wouldn't. They would still be there, and they'd be mad. Hopefully, they'd blame it on the starting problem they'd mentioned, but Vince might think she had something to do with it. If so, she'd be in deep trouble.

She glanced at the Maxwell with its open door. She had to get into that car. Somehow. If only she could distract the men. She shifted to ease her stiff knees and knelt on something hard and round.

Ouch! Her first instinct was to cry out, but then she realized what that small round object was. Acorns. They would do the job nicely. She ran her hands over the ground and scooped up two handfuls. If she moved a little to her right, she would have a clear shot at the Pierce-Arrow. All five men stood together in a huddle near the henhouse as they got their marching orders from Vince. All the flashlights had been extinguished. No one would notice her.

She slipped into the open and threw the acorns with all her might.

Bang. Bang. Bang.

The rattle of nuts against metal sounded like gunshots.

Every man whipped around toward the Pierce-Arrow. The thugs drew their guns.

Minnie darted across the clearing behind them and scrambled into the backseat of the Maxwell. The toolbox sat on the floorboards behind the driver's seat, but she had enough room to squeeze between it and the backseat. Then she curled into a ball, Peter's coat covering all but her head and feet. Soon enough she'd know if they'd heard her. Through the open car door she could see the men looking around the Pierce-Arrow. Flashlights bobbed around and scanned the clearing and woods.

"Nothin'," one of the thugs said.

"Those nuts didn't come from nowhere," Vince growled.

Peter pointed up. "We're under an oak tree."

Yes! What a wonderful guy to think of such an explanation. Minnie held her breath and hoped the men didn't realize all the acorns would have fallen by now.

"Must be it," Vince said. "Let's get outta here. Jacko, you and the boys take that car. Me and the kid'll take the Maxwell. We'll head out first. You follow."

Minnie's heart sank. She'd planned to tell Peter she was in the car once he drove away from the clearing. Now he'd have Vince with him, and from what she'd heard, he wasn't about to let Peter walk away.

The men broke up, with Peter and Vince heading straight for her. Oh, no! Peter's pillowcase of clothing sat just outside the open doorway. If Peter put it in the backseat, she'd be all right, but if Vince did, they were sunk.

Chapter Twenty-One

Peter desperately scanned for headlamps. If Fallston had gotten the news that the drop-off location had changed, he should have been here by now. Peter had been listening for a car motor or the crunching of tires on gravel the entire time they loaded the cases of liquor, but he'd heard nothing. This place was plumb deserted. Not one lawman would find them.

He was on his own.

The obstacles kept mounting. Minnie was back in the woods, bleeding to death from a blow to the head or freezing in the icy night air. Not only wasn't he alone in the Maxwell, but Vince had also gotten more and more tense by the minute. With the faster Pierce-Arrow following and three armed thugs inside, he'd have no chance of escape.

Please help me, Lord. Keep Minnie safe. Bring someone to help her.

He had no choice but to trust her to God.

As he picked up the pillowcase and slung it into the backseat, he eyed Vince. The stocky man was shorter than him but solid. He'd boxed back in New York. Won a lot of bouts, too. Peter could never take him down. Moreover,

Vince kept his hand close to his holster. He could draw the weapon in a split second. Presumably, he'd fire just as fast.

Nope, Peter couldn't do this on his own. He had to rely on God giving him an opening and play along in the meantime.

He rounded the car and opened the driver's door. "Thanks for lettin' me drive."

Vince got in the passenger's side. "Sure thing, kid. I'll get a good idea of your skills."

As Peter got in, the hair prickled on the back of his neck. Instinct told him something was wrong. He'd seen newspaper stories out of Chicago about guys found dead in a cornfield with a bullet in the head and no idea how they'd gotten there. He'd figured the poor souls had taken a ride—willingly or unwillingly.

Peter started the engine and put the car in gear. At least with him driving, Vince wouldn't put a bullet in his head. He hoped that'd hold once they stopped. Or if the federal agents showed up. He gripped the wheel.

"Nervous, kid?"

Peter let out his breath. "A little."

Vince laughed, but it wasn't friendly. "Drive like normal. If ya see someone tailin' us, let me know."

"You mean, other than the Pierce-Arrow?"

Vince guffawed, and Peter hoped the joke eased the man's wariness. He also noticed there weren't any headlamps behind him, but then maybe the thugs had decided to go without. Peter almost asked if he should douse the headlamps, too, but since Vince said to drive like normal and didn't say anything about them, he decided not to say anything. Besides, he wanted Fallston to spot him, if the agent was waiting on the main road.

With a final scrape and bump, he pulled to a stop at the end of the overgrown road. "Which way?"

"Left."

So they were headed away from the route Peter had taken to get there. If Fallston was waiting for him, he'd better be close to this intersection or he'd never find them. As Peter turned onto the road, he scanned for any sign of an automobile parked alongside the road. To his dismay, he saw nothing.

He was truly alone.

Please, Lord. Show me what to do.

At least Vince didn't say anything. He must not have noticed the lack of headlamps.

Peter glanced at his friend and saw the man scowling. Was he thinking at all about what Peter had said earlier, that he'd changed since leaving New York? Maybe that was the way to get to him.

"You sure used to be able to do wonders with wood. Do you still make things?"

Vince's jaw tensed. "Too busy."

"It was fun, wasn't it?"

Vince paused long enough that Peter knew he'd gotten to him.

Peter pushed harder. "Remember that little car you made for Luke?"

"Yeah," Vince grunted.

"He loved that. Wore the wheels off. Did you know that Pastor Gabe took him in and he's talking and everything now?"

"Pastor Gabe?"

"Yeah, Gabriel Meeks. You remember him. The whole family volunteered at the orphanage. He's a pastor now. At my church in Pearlman."

"Do-gooders." Vince snorted. "Society folks like them like ta throw themselves around places like the orphanage for publicity."

"Not Pastor Gabe or Mariah. They're like family to me. Mariah opened an orphanage in Pearlman. That's where I live." Peter was no longer ashamed to admit that.

"In an orphanage? Then nothing's changed."

"Yeah, it has. Now I help kids the way you used to help me. I want to make enough to set up a wood shop so I can teach the older boys to work with their hands so they can get a good job after they finish school."

Vince must have sensed his passion, because he didn't make a snide remark this time. "You think I'm some kinda hero, kid?"

"I used to." Peter heard Vince snap back in the seat. "Then I learned that we all make mistakes."

"You think what I'm doing is a mistake? Is that it? Let me set you straight, Stringbean. This operation's gonna get me places. Back in New York, I was a nobody. I'm important now. I got nice things for the first time in my life. Fancy clothes. Expensive watch. Nice place ta live. I even got a gorgeous dame. People respect me when I walk into a club."

"I respected you back at the orphanage."

Vince snorted. "What good is that? A bunch of lousy orphans and street urchins? Ain't one newspaperman in the country that'll write about an outta-work carpenter helpin' out orphan kids. They'll write about Vincent Galbini now, kid. You'll see my name splashed across the headlines."

Peter hoped it wouldn't be because Vince was dead. "Maybe life's not about getting noticed."

Vince snorted derisively.

Peter pressed on. "Maybe it's about doing the right thing. Helping people. Loving them and honoring God."

"You been spendin' too much time with them do-gooders. They're twistin' your head around, kid. Stick with me, and you'll see the way the world really works.

I'll take ya places and show ya things ya never dreamed of. I've always had a soft spot for ya, kid. Together we'll make one unbeatable team."

Peter shivered. He knew without a doubt that this was not what he wanted, but he had to play along in order to find a way back to Minnie. "Is that why you came to me? You could have any carpenter make these compartments. You could have made them yourself. Why go to all the trouble of searching for me?"

Vince clapped his shoulder. "Because you're like a son to me."

Peter suppressed a shudder.

"You know who got me into the operation?" Vince asked.

"Mr. Capone?"

"Naw. He'd already left for Chicago by that time. The guy who got me into this is a little more personal to ya."

The hairs rose on the back of Peter's neck again, as if a gunman was seated directly behind him, ready to shoot. "Who?"

"Yer uncle Max. In fact, you two'll get reacquainted when we reach our destination."

Peter's grip could have snapped the steering wheel in two. Uncle Max was ruthless. He spared no one, not even kin. Peter had worked so hard to get away from him. He'd run away after Aunt Ursula died and lived on the streets in a different part of the city. He'd changed his last name and refused to give his real name to the orphanage. He'd changed his age. He'd asked to go with the other orphans on that train and would've gone to anyone who'd take him, even that mean Mr. Coughlin who'd squeezed his biceps to see if he was strong enough. When he'd ended up with Mrs. Simmons, it had been an answer to prayer. Surely God had saved him.

Now Uncle Max had found him. Not only that, but he also knew where Peter lived and who his new family was. He'd enlisted Vince to find him. After all Peter had done to escape, Uncle Max was reeling him back in. Peter couldn't think. He couldn't breathe. How was he going to get out of this? Could he? He sure didn't want Uncle Max to go to Pearlman. He would destroy decent folk like the Simmons family and the Foxes.

Minnie! His heart stopped. What if Uncle Max found Minnie?

No, no, no! Peter would risk his life before he let his uncle near her.

"What's the matter, kid?" Vince laughed cruelly. "Nerves got ya?"

"N-no, sir." Peter snapped back to attention and whipped the wheel to the left. He was shaking so badly that he'd nearly driven off the road.

Minnie could hear fear in Peter's shaking voice. Something was really wrong. He'd been jumpy at first but seemed to calm down once he and Mr. Galbini started talking about old times. The two seemed like opposites. She had a hard time imagining Vince as a carpenter. She'd always thought of carpenters as quiet men, strong and solid. Vince was more interested in how he looked and who noticed him. What had she ever seen in him?

Peter, on the other hand, impressed her with his strong, quiet faith. He'd defended Pastor Gabe and Mariah. He'd shared his faith under the most dangerous circumstances.

Then Vince mentioned an Uncle Max, and Peter's steely nerves frayed. Minnie vaguely recalled him mentioning that his aunt had a no-good brother. Peter clearly feared the man.

"It'll be a grand reunion," Vince was saying with that

nasty laugh of his that she'd come to despise. "He's been lookin' forward ta seein' his nephew again."

Peter didn't answer for a while. "All right." His voice still wavered. He cleared his throat. "I'll join up with you, if you promise never to set foot in Pearlman again. Not you or Uncle Max or anyone in your operation."

What? Minnie clapped a hand over her mouth before the exclamation snuck out. What was Peter doing? He'd kissed her before Vince led her away. She'd seen love in his eyes. Then why ask Vince never to go to Pearlman? If Peter joined him, he wouldn't return home, either.

"Sure, kid. You got my word."

"And Minnie has to get home safely."

He was abandoning her. She could have wept.

"Do you promise?" Peter demanded. "I won't do a thing until you promise that Minnie will get home safely."

Her throat swelled as the truth hit her. He wasn't abandoning her. He was giving up his freedom and possibly his life to save her. All along he'd acted unselfishly. She was the one who'd thought only of herself, of her wants and desires. How foolish she'd been!

Vince snorted. "I'll personally bring her back."

Minnie shivered at the thought of him touching her again.

"No." Peter was firm now. "I do it or no deal."

"You expect me to let you go back to Pearlman alone with your gal? What kinda idiot do you think I am?"

"One with a heart. I don't think the old Vince is dead. I think he's still inside you. It's just that Uncle Max has twisted things around until you forgot who you are."

"Shut up," Vince growled in a low voice.

Minnie heard the threatening edge to his words, but Peter didn't seem to notice it. If anything, he got bolder.

"You're a child of God. He loves you and wants you to come back to Him—just like the prodigal son."

"Shut up, kid! I ain't no prodigal son."

"We all are. I made my share of mistakes, too. Thought I was too far gone to ever get back in God's good graces. Then a lot of good folks showed me how God forgives all the bad things we've done, washes us clean."

This time Vince didn't say anything, but Minnie could see his posture stiffen. He was either struggling over whether to take this to heart or coiling up like a snake waiting to strike.

Peter didn't notice. "All you gotta do is admit you did wrong and ask God to forgive you."

"That all?" Vince said derisively. "Maybe I'm waitin' until I get all my sinning done."

"Don't wait," Peter urged. "Do it now before it's too late. Confess and turn yourself in to the police. I'll put in a good word for you."

"Forget it!" Vince yelled.

In a flash his hand shot up. Minnie nearly yelped when she saw the silhouette of a gun in the moonlight.

Vince pressed it to Peter's head. "Drive faster, kid. I better not learn you've called in the law or your dear uncle will be saying hello to his nephew's corpse."

The cold muzzle of the gun made Vince's point. Peter had run out of options. He'd pushed too hard thinking God had given him the opportunity, but it had backfired. Now his life was in danger, and Vince might retract his promise to save Minnie.

The whole thing was spiraling out of control.

Help me, Lord. That was all he could think to pray. Over and over and over.

Finally, Vince lowered the gun, though he didn't put it back in the holster. "Turn left at the next intersection."

Peter glanced in the rearview mirror. Still no headlamps. If the Pierce-Arrow was following, he couldn't see it. Neither could he see anyone else, such as the federal agents. If the Lord was sending help, it hadn't appeared yet.

Trust in the Lord.

Hadn't he faced that same stumbling block over and over the past couple months? Well, now he had no choice. He could do nothing to save those he loved.

"It's all in Your hands, Lord," he whispered.

Minnie had to do something. With Vince holding a gun on Peter, he couldn't get them out of this mess. That left her. Neither man knew she was in the back. She was the only one who stood a chance of stopping this car, but how?

All her life she'd messed up at the big moments. Misjudging Reggie. Losing the envelope of receipts from the dress shop. Running away from the auditions. Whining about her petty problems when Daddy's health was slipping away. What made her think she could succeed now, when the stakes were even higher?

Peter said he trusted God to help him. Could she?

Peter started singing, so off-key that she cringed at first. Then she realized he was singing "Amazing Grace," the song she had sung at the audition.

As she listened to the words, she realized it all came down to faith. Despite having a gun trained on him, Peter trusted God's plan.

So could she.

The car hit a pothole, and the cargo jiggled inside the luggage compartment. That definitely sounded like bottles. They were heavy enough to knock out a man. So were tools. She felt around Peter's toolbox but couldn't figure out how to open it. On the other hand, she could lift the seat cushion enough to get a bottle out and strike Vince before he knew she was back there. But she'd have to do it quietly.

Peter's singing seemed to distract Vince.

"They sing that sometimes in church," Galbini said between verses.

At least he didn't demand that Peter stop. Once Peter resumed the next verse, Minnie wiggled to her knees and carefully rolled the pillowcase off the seat and onto the floorboards. It landed with a thud.

Minnie held her breath.

Peter continued to sing. Vince started humming along.

Whew! She wedged her hands under the front edge of the seat cushion. This was going to be heavy, and she didn't have enough room to slide the cushion forward. She'd have to brace it on her shoulder while she pulled out a bottle. She sure hoped the crates weren't nailed shut.

Naturally she couldn't see a thing. Moonlight had flickered into the car when they were in less wooded areas, but they'd entered some sort of evergreen forest on a rutted, bumpy road. On the positive side, that meant Vince couldn't see her. Unfortunately, she couldn't see under the seat, either. She'd have to do this by touch.

At the next bump, she lifted. Oh, my! The cushion was heavy. She barely hung on to it before slipping her shoulder underneath. Panting, she waited as Peter continued into the next verse. He mixed up the words, but it didn't matter to Vince, who hummed along.

She felt around in the compartment. The crates were open. Her fingers grazed bottle tops. The corks or stoppers were pushed down below the rim. Minnie didn't know much about spirits, so she had no idea what they might be, but the bottles felt fairly large. She could probably squeeze one through the opening, though.

She grabbed one and lifted.

My, oh, my! That was heavier than she'd expected. At this awkward angle and already balancing the heavy seat on her shoulder, she struggled to pull the bottle free of the case. She'd have a time of it bringing the bottle up high enough to hit Vince on the head. Then what if she accidentally killed him? Would the police call it murder? Would she go to jail?

Her resolve faltered, and she nearly let the seat cushion slam down when the car pitched into a particularly large pothole.

Shaking, she gathered her wits. *If God be for us, who can be against us?* The memory verse from Romans came to mind at exactly the right time. God would give her strength. He would guide her hand.

This time when she pulled up on the bottle, it came out of the compartment right away. After bracing it between her knees, she eased the seat cushion down and prepared to strike. She could get a better shot by crawling up onto the rear seat.

Slowly, carefully, she eased onto the seat directly behind Vince, bottle in hand. Now all she had to do was strike him solidly enough to knock him out but not kill him. She lifted the bottle overhead, but her arms shook too much, and she had to set it down.

She'd never be able to hit a man. Never. Even to save them.

Peter finished the song.

"Keep singing," Vince said, sounding agitated.

"I'm not a good singer, and my throat is dry," Peter said.

Vince pressed the gun to Peter's head. "I said to keep singing."

Minnie drew in her breath. Vince sounded crazed enough to kill Peter. She had to act. But if she missed,

Vince would shoot them both. She squeezed her eyes shut. Peter began "Amazing Grace" again from the beginning. *Was blind but now I see.*

She opened her eyes and noticed that Vince had lowered the gun and leaned back on the seat. His neck was within reach. At that moment, she saw the answer. She didn't have to knock him out. She just had to convince him that she had a gun. The mouth of the bottle was about the right size. With the cork pushed in, it would feel like the muzzle of a gun. If she shoved it against Vince's neck and pretended to be a policeman, she might startle him enough that he'd drop the gun.

Slowly, carefully, she raised the bottle.

The car jostled on the rutted road. Peter kept singing. Vince had dropped his hands to his lap. His fingers still curled around the trigger, but he was relaxed.

Minnie waited for the right moment. She had one chance. One opportunity. She'd better get it right.

Lord, I do trust in You.

Peter finished a verse. The road smoothed out. The moon had sunk below the trees, leaving them in complete darkness. The moment had arrived.

She pressed the mouth of the bottle against Vince's neck and in as gruff a voice as she could manage shouted, "Hands up!"

Chapter Twenty-Two

What was that? Peter jumped at the odd voice. He whipped around to see who was in the car with them. Had Fallston somehow gotten into the backseat? When? The car had been in view the entire time they loaded the liquor. He hadn't seen anyone, even when he threw his clothes in the back.

Vince yelled something about driving.

Peter turned back to discover the car had veered left and was headed for the trees. He yanked the wheel to the right. The rear tires spun out on the gravel, and the car fishtailed. Before he could regain control, Vince whipped his gun past Peter's head to the backseat.

This was his chance. Peter lunged for the gun with one hand and missed, but he caught Vince's arm. The gun fired. A woman screamed. Peter let go of the wheel completely. With all his weight and both hands, he bent Vince's wrist backward, trying to shake loose the gun.

"Let go," he spat out between clenched teeth.

Vince pummeled him on the back with his other fist. "Never."

Peter smashed Vince's hand against the dash. Vince

punched Peter in the back of the head. Peter's head snapped forward. He blinked but didn't let go.

"Stop it," a woman screamed over and over.

A woman? Agent Fallston brought a woman? The voice sounded familiar, but Peter didn't have time to think about that. He jabbed an elbow into Vince's throat. The man gasped but didn't let go of the gun.

The woman let out the most ear-piercing screams. Something large and heavy flew past Peter's head and landed harmlessly on the floorboards, where it rolled from side to side with the wildly careening vehicle.

Peter wrestled Vince's hand toward the dashboard again.

Someone crawled over the backseat behind Peter and grabbed onto the steering wheel. Peter forced Vince's hand forward. The man's grip was loosening. If he could smash his hand against the dash one more time... Peter summoned all his strength and pushed.

Vince fought back.

The car spun...once, twice.

"Watch out," the woman shrieked as she lost hold of the steering wheel and fell into the rear seat.

The automobile dipped and then shot up. Peter held on to Vince's hand, which cracked against the dashboard on the forward pitch. The impact sent the gun flying. He heard it hit metal moments before both men slammed back against the seat.

A split second later, the car crunched to a sudden stop. Metal screeched. Wood splintered. Dirt flew everywhere. Vince shot forward through the windshield, shattering it in a spray of glass. Peter's left shoulder hit the steering wheel. His head cracked against the dash.

Then nothing.

* * *

"Peter, Peter!" Minnie shook him, but he didn't wake.

In the dim light, she just could make out her surroundings. Peter was slumped sideways over the steering wheel, his head lying on the dashboard. He'd been battling Vince when the car dipped into the ditch and then crashed into the trees. Vince lay halfway out of the car, unconscious and possibly dead, but Minnie cared only about Peter, who wasn't moving.

The car had hit a large evergreen tree hard enough to crumple the front of the car and pop the driver's door open. Minnie couldn't push open the rear door, so she crawled over the seat behind Peter and got out that way.

Something crunched beneath her feet. Probably glass. She leaned in and tugged on Peter again.

"Wake up, please, wake up."

What if he'd died? No. *Please, God, no.*

She pressed her ear to his back. Her heart was pounding so hard that she didn't hear anything at first. Then she held her breath and closed her eyes. Yes, there it was. A faint heartbeat. He was alive.

"Thank You, God," she murmured, kissing him on the side of the head. "Thank You for sparing Peter." She wrapped her arms around him. "Please wake him up. Please let him be all right."

Minnie's voice pierced through the blackness that had closed around Peter. She was there with him. She was alive, and she was crying.

He fought the fog that threatened to swallow him again. No, he wouldn't give in. He had to get to Minnie. He had to console her.

He drew in a breath to clear the fog and gasped as sharp pain ripped through him.

"Oh, Peter, Peter," she cried, kissing the back and sides of his head over and over. "You're alive. You're alive. I prayed, and God answered."

He drew in a smaller breath this time, but it still hurt. "Minnie?"

"Yes, I'm here."

He tried to wrap his mind around where he was and why he hurt so much. He opened his eyes but could see little. "Where? How?" He gasped again at the pain.

"Don't talk. Gather your strength, and then we need to get out of here. I don't know if Vince is alive or just knocked out. And I can't find the gun."

Vince. Gun. It all came back. Vince had tried to shoot the person in the backseat. A woman had been screaming. Minnie. He'd almost killed Minnie!

"You hurt?" Peter managed to ask between bursts of pain.

"No. No, I'm all right." She smoothed a hand over his head. "But you're hurt. You're bleeding." She pressed something to his head. "Not too much. A little pressure ought to stop it, but we need to get away from the car." She sounded unnerved.

Why? The gun. Must be because of Vince and the gun.

"I'll try," he murmured, but the blackness was closing in again.

"Peter! Don't fall asleep again." Minnie shook him.

Peter groaned, but he sounded so groggy.

The bleeding from his scalp had slowed but not their troubles.

Though Galbini hadn't woken up yet, he could at any moment. What would she do then? She had to find that gun. It must have fallen onto the front floorboards. She rummaged around Peter's feet and came up empty. Maybe it was on the other side. She rounded the car and felt the floorboards around Galbini's limp and dangling legs. The liquor bottle was there, but no gun. Maybe it had flown out of the car when they crashed. If so, it could be anywhere. In the dark, she'd never find it.

She'd better get Peter out of the car and walking so he wouldn't drift off again. Hadn't she heard something about making people stay awake when they'd hit their head? Oh, yes, Beattie had mentioned that years ago when her friend Darcy hit her head in an aeroplane crash. They'd kept Darcy awake for hours. She'd have to do the same for Peter.

"Stay awake, Peter," she called out as she scrambled out of the ditch to round the car again.

He mumbled something.

Good, he was still awake.

Once she reached the road, she stretched her limbs, amazed at how stiff they'd become in the short time she'd crouched beside the car. She looked down the road, and in the distance, headlamps appeared. A vehicle was headed their way. She waved her arms, hoping they'd see her. Peter needed to get to a doctor.

"Help is on the way," she said. "Stay awake, Peter. We'll get you to a doctor soon."

She waved her arms again. They must have seen her, because the car looked to pick up speed. "They're hurrying. They'll be here soon."

"Other car," Peter gasped.

"Other car? What other car?"

"Pierce-Arrow."

Oh, no! The thugs. She'd forgotten about them. They knew where Peter was going. They would have been able to fix the car by now. A dangling battery cable would be obvious. If she could do it, anyone could. Peter was right.

This car was probably the Pierce-Arrow. No one else would be traveling such a desolate road in the middle of the night.

She scrambled down the ditch on the driver's side. "Get out! Get out of the car! We have to run. Now."

With a groan, he twisted forward and then slumped back against the seat, motionless.

She reached the driver's seat and put her arm around his shoulders. "You can do it, Peter. I'll help." She tugged on his trousers. "First one leg and then the other. You can do it."

Slowly, he slid his left leg out of the car, followed by a sickening moan.

"Good. Now the other one." She glanced up. The head-lamps lit the trees now. "They're getting closer."

He got the other leg out of the car and turned toward her with a shuddering gasp.

"All right." She put her arms under his and hugged him tight. "Lean on me, and I'll help you up."

She pulled. He moved a little. She tugged harder as the headlamps brightened.

"They're almost here." She panted from the exertion. "Help me. I can't lift you alone."

He gave a push. She pulled. For a second, she had him mostly upright and out of the car. Then his full weight pressed onto her. She tumbled backward, and he landed beside her with a groan.

"We have to get into the woods." She shook him. "Crawl if you have to."

She got to her hands and knees. The shards of glass bit into them, and she gasped from the knifing pain.

"Go," he gasped. "Run."

"No, I won't leave you."

"Save yourself."

She couldn't. This time she would not run away. She

would stay with the man she loved and face whatever came next. Even a bullet to the head. A sob slipped out, and she buried her face in Peter's shoulder.

He was shaking. Oh, dear, he must be freezing. She was wearing his coat. He had nothing. She wrapped her arms around him and held on tight.

"Go," he gasped.

"No. We face this together."

"Trust God." He barely got the words out.

"I do."

The automobile stopped, its headlamps illuminating them. In the light, she could see the welt on Peter's temple. She choked back a sob.

Car doors opened. Someone got out.

"There they are," a man said. "Follow me."

Minnie squeezed her eyes shut, held Peter close and prepared to die.

Chapter Twenty-Three

"Are you hurt, miss?"

That was awfully polite for a thug.

"Miss Fox? What are you doing here?"

That was Sheriff Ilsley's voice.

Relieved, Minnie lifted her head. "Sheriff. I'm sure glad to see you." Light from the headlamps revealed four other men, a couple with guns drawn. "Peter's hurt. We need to get him to a doctor."

A short man, who looked more like an accountant than a lawman, directed the other men to check Galbini. From the way he barked out orders, he must be in charge.

"He's out cold," one of the men shouted back. "But still alive."

"Handcuff him," the man in charge said.

Meanwhile, the sheriff helped Minnie get Peter to a sitting position.

"He hit his head," she said. "I got the bleeding slowed, but something else is wrong. He's having trouble breathing."

"Ribs," Peter gasped out.

The sheriff nodded. "All right, Peter. Miss Fox and I will help you to your feet. We need to get you to the car."

"I'll help," the accountant said.

"No." Minnie wasn't about to let any stranger near Peter.

"Federal Agent Fallston," the man barked out. "I'm not here to hurt Mr. Simmons."

Though relieved to learn he was a lawman, she wasn't ready to leave Peter's side. "I can handle this, sir."

The sheriff chuckled. "I expect Miss Fox means what she says, Agent. Help your men with Galbini."

Minnie stood on one side, and the sheriff took the other—and most of Peter's weight. Together, they got Peter out of the ditch and to the policemen's automobile. While the sheriff was getting Peter situated, Minnie noticed another car traveling toward them.

The thugs!

"Sheriff, the rest of Mr. Galbini's men are heading this way. We have to get out of here now."

The sheriff looked back. "Looks like Sheriff Everson has Galbini's men well in hand."

The car pulled over, and the officer inside told Sheriff Ilsley they were headed to the county jail.

"Fallston will follow you with Galbini," Sheriff Ilsley said. "I've got an injured man here. Which way to the closest doctor?"

While the sheriff got directions, Minnie waited beside Peter in the backseat of the police car.

"Sheriff Ilsley will get you to help." She slipped off his coat and laid it over him.

"You'll get cold," he protested.

"You need it more than I do."

"I'm all right."

She hugged him. "You're so brave. I should have seen it sooner." She bit her lip. Would he remember saying he loved her? Would he forgive her for yelling at him and not trusting him? "I'm sorry."

He squeezed her hand. "Me, too."

Once before she'd risked declaring her feelings only to have her words thrown back in her face. Now she truly understood what Ruth had been trying to tell her. The risk was worth it. Even if Peter didn't ever love her, she would always love him.

She took a deep breath and looked him in the eye. "I love you, Peter."

His lips curved into a smile. "I love you, too."

No words had ever sounded sweeter. "You do?"

"It hurt to pretend I didn't." He winced.

"Hush now." That was all she needed to hear. His earlier rebuke had been a ruse. He'd loved her all along. She laced her fingers through his and leaned her head on his shoulder. "I could stay right here forever."

He kissed the top of her head. "Me, too."

"Minnie?" The familiar voice jolted her from the moment. "Where's Minnie? I have to see my sister. Is she all right?" Those hysterics sounded like… Impossible.

Minnie swiveled around. Sure enough, another car had pulled alongside them. In the headlamps of the local sheriff's vehicle, a woman argued with Sheriff Ilsley.

Minnie stuck her head out the window. "Beattie? What are you doing here?"

Sheriff Ilsley wouldn't fill them in on the details until Peter received treatment at a nearby doctor's office. Agent Fallston and his men took Vince into the back with Peter and the doctor. Peter had balked, wanting Minnie to get her scrapes and cuts cleaned first, but she would hear nothing of it. Peter's condition was more serious. Her little nicks had already stopped bleeding. She would wait.

Beattie sat in one of the room's two chairs. Pastor Gabe, who for some unfathomable reason had brought Beatrice here, stood chatting with the sheriff. Beatrice sobbed and begged forgiveness, but she wasn't making any sense at all. Nor could Minnie keep her attention on anything when Peter was hurting. She paced the small waiting area until he reappeared, bandaged up but looking more alert.

His gaze went straight to her. "The doctor says it's just some cracked ribs. They hurt, but there's nothing to do but be careful and let them heal."

Minnie threw her arms around his shoulders and hugged until he grimaced. "I'm sorry." She touched the thick bandage on his head. "Does it hurt?"

"It's fine." He grinned sheepishly. "Apparently I have a hard skull. Unlike Vince. They have to take him to the hospital. Agent Fallston is talking to him now, while the doctor finishes up."

Minnie looked to the sheriff. "Will Mr. Galbini be arrested?"

"Already is. Sheriff Everson took the rest of the men into custody with the assistance of federal agents. When Mr. Galbini recovers, he'll join them in jail."

Minnie breathed out a sigh of relief and noticed her sister clenching her hands together so tightly that her knuckles had turned white. Now that Peter was safe, her curiosity returned. "Beattie, I still don't understand how you found us."

Beatrice bit her lip. Her eyes were red and swollen. She looked drained.

When she didn't answer, Sheriff Ilsley stepped in. "Once we realized you weren't headed for the initial drop-off site, we placed a call to the office. My deputy told us the location had changed. He also said Mrs. Kensington and her husband had an urgent matter to discuss that had a direct bearing on this case."

"Blake?" Minnie looked to her sister, who lowered her

gaze. "Where is Blake?" She glanced at Pastor Gabe, who gave nothing away. "Shouldn't he have driven you here?"

"Let me explain," the sheriff said. "Mr. Kensington agreed to testify against Mr. Galbini in exchange for lesser charges."

The impact of his words hit like a brick. "Charges?" She'd never particularly liked Blake, but a criminal?

"It's my fault," Beattie sobbed, wringing her handkerchief. "I should have told you. I should have told all of you. You're my family. But I was so ashamed. How could I have made such a horrible mistake? I should have known. I'm the oldest. I'm supposed to know better." She pressed a handkerchief to her eyes.

Minnie turned to the sheriff. "I don't understand."

"Apparently Mr. Kensington ran up a large debt."

"Gambling," Beatrice interjected.

The sheriff nodded. "Unable to get money from his father, who had apparently gotten tired of funding his son's excesses, he got tangled up in a scheme to coordinate a bootlegging ring running Canadian liquor from Detroit to Chicago."

"Capone," Peter said. "Vince mentioned working for Al Capone."

"Agent Fallston and I suspect your friend was trying to get in on Torrio's operation by impressing Capone with a new source for high-end alcohol. That notebook you picked up for Galbini contains all the coded information on hiding spots along the proposed route. Mr. Kensington is the one who brought the notebook to Pearlman and left it for you at the drugstore."

So that was why Peter went to the speakeasy. Minnie breathed out with relief.

Beatrice, on the other hand, sobbed quietly.

"Then Blake is in jail?" Minnie asked.

"At the moment," Sheriff Ilsley said.

No wonder Beatrice was distraught. Minnie felt for her. It did explain why Beattie never had any money to help out the family. Her excessive concern with propriety also made sense. She didn't want her little sister to suffer the way she had.

Minnie left Peter to join her sister. "It's all right, Beattie."

"I could have gotten you killed." Beatrice sniffled. "I knew Blake was gambling. I knew he owed a fortune. I knew he was keeping bad company, but I thought I could fix things so no one would find out." A sob wracked her shoulders. "I was wrong."

This was going to be hard for Beatrice. Even though Blake's father owned half the town, he didn't control the newspaper. They would leap to publish this story. Those who held grudges against the Kensingtons would lash out. Beatrice would take the brunt of their vitriol. Minnie looked at Pastor Gabe, who nodded. His wife, as Blake's sister, would bear some of the scorn, too.

"I think we should keep the family in prayer," Minnie said.

Pastor Gabe seconded the suggestion, but it was Peter who pulled a chair up to Beatrice. Taking her hands, he said, "God can turn bad into good. You have to believe that. He did for me. I did rotten things back in New York, but God gave me a second chance with Ma Simmons. He'll give you that chance, too."

Beatrice's lip quivered. "But it's going to hurt. People will talk. My children…"

Peter looked sad. "Sometimes the innocent suffer, but they'll pull through. I did, and I didn't have a mother like you. They can count on your love and ours. No matter what happens, keep loving them. Hold them close and teach them about forgiveness."

Agent Fallston reappeared. "My men have Galbini ready. It's time to go, Mr. Simmons."

"Go?" Minnie turned to Peter. "Where are you going?"

"To finish the delivery." Peter stood.

"But you're hurt. The car is smashed. You can't go."

"Mr. Simmons must identify the ringleader," Agent Fallston said.

Minnie didn't understand. "But you already have Mr. Galbini."

Peter shook his head. "Vince isn't the leader. My uncle Max is."

Minnie swallowed. She'd heard Vince threaten Peter with his uncle, but in all that had happened afterward, she'd forgotten. "Do you have to?"

"If I'm ever going to be free of him, I do."

In a way, Minnie understood. She'd battled her fears and overcome them. He had to do that, too. She turned to Fallston. "I don't suppose I can talk you into taking me, too."

Fallston's mouth curved into a wry grin. "If we needed someone to disable a car, I would."

"You?" Admiration shone in Peter's eyes. "You disabled the Pierce-Arrow? I wondered what happened."

She shrugged as if it was unimportant. "I just disconnected the battery cable. But I wouldn't have known how to do it if you hadn't shown me."

Peter swept her into his arms. "Minnie Fox, you're the most amazing, resourceful woman I've ever met. What would I do without you?"

"I can't imagine," she teased before poking a finger into his chest. "You'd better come right back. I don't want to hear you've run off on another adventure without me."

He cupped her face in his hands and gazed deep into her eyes. "You're the only adventure I want. You're the first thing I think about when I wake up in the morning and the last thing on my mind when I go to sleep. No other gal's ever come close to you. Ever. I will love you until the day I die."

Minnie felt the tears build, but before they could fall, Peter leaned over and kissed her, right in front of the sheriff, the federal agent, her sister and even Pastor Gabe. They were more than almost engaged. He'd declared undying love. For her! This time her love had not been misplaced. This time she'd chosen the right man.

When he broke away, his smile could light up the darkest night. "I'll be back, Miss Fox."

She smiled right back. "I'm going to hold you to that, Mr. Simmons."

Chapter Twenty-Four

Six weeks later

Peter's ribs had almost completely healed by the time Daddy came home from the hospital. Though Minnie pestered her mother that Peter wanted to speak with him, Mother insisted Peter wait two more weeks until Daddy settled in after the long trip home.

This time, they didn't attempt the stairs, instead transforming the parlor into her father's bedroom. The sofa came out and Ruth's old bed went in. Ruth and Sam helped set up the room, complete with lovely sheer curtains that allowed Daddy to look out but gave him a measure of privacy. Then they moved to the apartment above the dress shop, which Sam rented using the money from the sale of one of Ruth's designs.

Each morning, Minnie and Jen brought breakfast to their father before heading to work. He looked pale and weak, but it was better having him home than far away at a hospital.

"I understand you had quite an adventure," he said to Minnie one morning.

Jen scooted out of the room.

Minnie sat beside her father's bed. "Yes, Daddy."

He struggled to hide a smile. "And that a certain young man is itching to speak with me."

"Yes. Peter won't even have a soda with me until he talks to you."

"Hmm." He drew his eyebrows down in an attempt to look serious. "I suppose I ought to respect that."

Minnie held her breath. She'd waited patiently, knowing that their love wouldn't change in a few weeks. Maybe at last the time had come.

"Tell him to stop by after the church service on Sunday. Your mother is roasting a turkey. The whole family will be here."

Minnie could have groaned. She did not want the entire family to witness this. It would make Peter doubly nervous. And then if Blake came with Beatrice, it would be terribly awkward. Though he was out on bail awaiting trial, the newspapers had covered the story with rabid fascination, and the repercussions had to hurt. Beattie seemed to bow under the weight of public scorn and spent most of her time huddled inside her house.

Daddy tipped up her chin. "Penny for your thoughts."

"Nothing. Thank you for seeing Peter."

"You're worried about Beattie. We all are, but she's strong. Her faith will see her through this, and they'll come out of it better off than they went in."

Minnie hoped he was right.

"If there's any lesson to be learned from this, dear child, it's not to take marriage lightly."

Her heart sank. How did Peter stand a chance now that Blake had predisposed Daddy to thinking ill of the men who married into the family? "Sam's a good husband."

"Yes, he is. A good Christian with his heart in the right place. Take care you find someone like that."

Oh, dear. If he was suggesting she find the right kind of man, then he must not think Peter was good enough for her. She left their conversation feeling worse than ever. Why did Peter have to be such a stickler for getting her father's permission? Why couldn't they just announce they were getting married like Reggie Landers and Sally Neidecker had?

By the time Sunday afternoon arrived, she'd worked herself into such a state that Mother held her back when Peter walked into the parlor to speak with Daddy.

"You can't go with him, dearest." Mother wrapped an arm around Minnie's shoulders.

"But I have to explain. Daddy doesn't know all Peter did, that he's a hero, that he testified against his uncle."

"He knows." Mother steered her toward the kitchen. "Come help us with dinner."

The kitchen was a frenzy of activity. Jen was mashing the potatoes while Ruth made the gravy. Beatrice set the table. She looked away when Minnie entered. Sam and Blake stood at the bottom of the stairway, the only place that was out of the way.

Minnie balked. "There's nothing to do and too many cooks in the kitchen already. I have to hear what Daddy says."

"Me, too," Jen said, dropping the masher. "The potatoes are ready. Come along, Minnie. We can watch through the crack in the door."

Mother frowned. "Why do I have the idea you've done this before?"

Jen grinned. "Only for important things like Christmas."

Mother threw up her hands. "I surrender."

Minnie and Jen crept to the door and peered through the crack. It didn't give a full view. She couldn't see Peter, for instance, but the gap was wide enough that she could hear the conversation.

"I see," Daddy was saying, "and your uncle is behind bars now?"

"Yes, sir," Peter answered without hesitation.

Minnie groaned. Daddy must have grilled Peter on every detail of his past. If he'd been leery of Peter before, he sure wouldn't feel any better knowing there was a criminal in the family.

"Well, we can't choose our relatives," Daddy said.

"No, sir, but we can choose how we treat them. The Bible says to forgive your enemies."

"Have you forgiven your uncle?"

"Yes, sir, but it's harder to forget."

"That it is, son. That it is." Daddy cleared his throat. "I get tired easily these days. We'd best get down to business. I understand you have something to ask me."

This was it. Minnie held her breath.

"Yes, sir." Peter also cleared his throat. "I love Minnie, sir."

"Wilhelmina."

"Wilhelmina, sir. Sorry."

She could imagine how red Peter's face must be.

"Are you certain it's love and not infatuation?" Daddy asked.

Minnie was mortified. How could he ask that after all they'd been through?

"Yes, sir," Peter answered. "I would give my life for her."

"Hmm. I understand you almost did. That took courage."

"No, sir. Minnie's the one with courage. I was just worried that she might get hurt. I couldn't let that happen. And

I won't. I promise. I'll love her and take care of her the rest of my life if you'll give me your blessing to court her."

"Courtship, eh? Suppose I refuse?"

Minnie groaned.

"That won't change how I feel. I'll still love her, but I'll respect your wishes."

This was getting worse and worse. She had to talk some sense into Daddy. He couldn't measure Peter against Blake. It wasn't fair. She grabbed the doorknob, but Jen leaned against the door so Minnie couldn't open it.

"Minnie!" Daddy called out. "You might as well come in. I know you're listening at the door."

Now she turned beet-red.

Jen ceremoniously opened the door, and Minnie edged into the living room, head hung low. Peter took her hand and squeezed it. That gave her the courage to look up. Peter's smile radiated warmer than sunlight, sending hope deep into her heart.

Daddy chuckled. "That's all I needed to see. You have my blessing, Peter."

"I do?" he said.

"We do?" she said.

"Now, don't go rushing into things," Daddy said. "I want a nice long courtship. You two are youngsters. You need to prepare yourselves. A couple years ought to be sufficient."

"A couple years?" Minnie cried.

Peter's jaw dropped, too, but he clapped it shut again. "Yes, sir. Whatever you want."

"Good," Daddy said. "Give it time, like Helen and I did."

"Wait a minute," Minnie said. "You and Mother got married right out of school. You didn't give it any time at all."

Daddy got a silly grin on his face. "You're not supposed to remember that."

"Well, I do." Minnie braced her hands on her hips. "So why make us wait?"

"Because I don't want you to go through the trials we did. If you truly love each other, it'll stand the test of time."

"A year?" Minnie suggested. "Maybe less?"

"A year. No less," Daddy confirmed.

A year seemed like forever, but Daddy had already yielded a little. In time, he might see how much they loved each other and let them marry sooner.

"Well?" Daddy said. "Aren't you going to kiss her, son?"

Startled, Peter flushed before stammering, "Y-yes, sir."

Then he softly and properly kissed her, sealing their promise for the future.

* * * * *

Dear Reader,

When I wrote *The Matrimony Plan* back in 2011, I was fascinated by how orphan trains sent children across the country in the hope of a better life. With this book, I wanted to see how a new home affected one of those orphans—Peter. Did he feel secure with his new family, or did his traumatic past follow him on that train? How would being an orphan affect falling in love and forming a lasting relationship?

That book also introduced prohibition and the problem of bootlegging. Sadly, too often a noble idea gets twisted into something that brings evil into people's lives. This amendment to the United States Constitution was born of the temperance movement, which sought to end the great harm wrought on families by alcohol addiction. Before long gangsters seized this new avenue to make money and fought over the lucrative profits.

Though the mentions of the Capones, the election day violence of 1924 and Johnny Torrio are factual, Vince Galbini and his plot are pure fiction. For Peter, Vince represents both the good and the bad decisions in his past. Minnie faces her own poor choices. Yet with faith and courage they overcome and step forth into a bright future.

I love to hear from readers. You can contact me through my website at christineelizabethjohnson.com.

May God bless you,
Christine Johnson

Questions for Discussion

1. Both Peter and Minnie initially think money will bring them the kind of life they crave. What do you think feeds that idea? Do you see any parallels in today's culture? If so, how do you think that can be changed?

2. Today we wouldn't think anything of a woman getting her hair cut short, but in the early 1920s, it was a sign of rebellion. How do today's young people display rebellion? Why do you think teenagers feel a need to rebel?

3. Minnie initially focuses her attentions on Vince Galbini. Why? What does this tell you about her character?

4. Minnie loses the envelope containing the day's receipts from her family's dress shop and then must tell her parents. Did you ever face something like that? What sort of emotions did you go through? Would you have handled it differently in retrospect? Should she have handled it differently? If so, how?

5. Early in the story, which of Peter's actions show his character? What events in his life do you think molded that character?

6. Minnie's family insists someone chaperone her whenever she works alongside Peter. That might seem very foreign today. How do you feel about such restric-

tions? Why do you think Mr. and Mrs. Fox imposed them? Why did Beatrice insist on them?

7. Peter gets sucked into doing work for Vince Galbini against his better judgment. How should he have handled the situation? Did he miss any opportunities to get out? If so, why do you think he didn't take them?

8. Minnie thinks she wants to become a star and sees the musical revue as a means to fulfill her dream. Why did she run away at the moment of success? Do you agree with her decision to give it up? Why or why not?

9. Peter takes a big risk by helping the law go after Vince Galbini. He claims he's doing it to protect Minnie. Do you think that's the only reason, or is there something deeper at work here? What might that be?

10. Why do you think Peter refused to take a gun with him?

11. Do you agree with Minnie's decision to stow away in the automobile? How do you think she could have handled it differently? Is there anything else she could have done that would have changed Peter's course of action?

12. Peter's past comes back to haunt him when Vince tells him they're going to meet up with Peter's uncle Max. How do you imagine their confrontation went? Do you agree with Peter's decision to go with the prohibition agent to put his uncle behind bars when he could easily have claimed he was too injured to do it? Why or why not?

13. If you were Beatrice, how would you deal with the news that your husband had been arrested? Could she have done anything to change the course of events?

14. Though Minnie has run away from trouble in the past, in the crucial moment near the end of the story, she is able to act. What do you think made the difference this time?

15. Both Peter and Minnie cling to faith in moments of crisis. How does faith see them through? Do you draw closer or further away from God during times of crisis? Why do you think you react that way?

HER HOLIDAY FAMILY
Texas Grooms
by Winnie Griggs

Eileen Pierce has shut herself off to life after living through tragedy. But when a stranded man and ten orphaned children seek shelter at her home, she finds herself opening the door to them—and to love.

THE BRIDE SHIP
Frontier Bachelors
by Regina Scott

Allegra Banks Howard is bound for a new life out West with her daughter. But when she is reunited with her first love—her late husband's brother—can they heal their painful past and forge a new future as a family?

A PONY EXPRESS CHRISTMAS
by Rhonda Gibson

A marriage proposal from Jake Bridges might be the solution to Leah Hollister's problems. If only he didn't already have enough on his hands between adopting his newly orphaned niece and mending his broken heart.

ROCKY MOUNTAIN DREAMS
by Danica Favorite

When Joseph Stone becomes guardian to his newly discovered little sister and inherits his late father's silver mine, he seeks help from the minister's beautiful daughter, who soon claims his love for her own.

———————

LIHCNM1014

REQUEST YOUR FREE BOOKS!

2 FREE INSPIRATIONAL NOVELS
PLUS 2
FREE
MYSTERY GIFTS

Love Inspired

HISTORICAL
INSPIRATIONAL HISTORICAL ROMANCE

YES! Please send me 2 FREE Love Inspired® Historical novels and my 2 FREE mystery gifts (gifts are worth about $10). After receiving them, if I don't wish to receive any more books, I can return the shipping statement marked "cancel." If I don't cancel, I will receive 4 brand-new novels every month and be billed just $4.74 per book in the U.S. or $5.24 per book in Canada. That's a saving of at least 21% off the cover price. It's quite a bargain! Shipping and handling is just 50¢ per book in the U.S. and 75¢ per book in Canada.* I understand that accepting the 2 free books and gifts places me under no obligation to buy anything. I can always return a shipment and cancel at any time. Even if I never buy another book, the two free books and gifts are mine to keep forever.

102/302 IDN F5CN

Name	(PLEASE PRINT)
Address	Apt. #
City	State/Prov.	Zip/Postal Code

Signature (if under 18, a parent or guardian must sign)

Mail to the Harlequin® Reader Service:
IN U.S.A.: P.O. Box 1867, Buffalo, NY 14240-1867
IN CANADA: P.O. Box 609, Fort Erie, Ontario L2A 5X3

Want to try two free books from another series?
Call 1-800-873-8635 or visit www.ReaderService.com.

* Terms and prices subject to change without notice. Prices do not include applicable taxes. Sales tax applicable in N.Y. Canadian residents will be charged applicable taxes. Offer not valid in Quebec. This offer is limited to one order per household. Not valid for current subscribers to Love Inspired Historical books. All orders subject to credit approval. Credit or debit balances in a customer's account(s) may be offset by any other outstanding balance owed by or to the customer. Please allow 4 to 6 weeks for delivery. Offer available while quantities last.

Your Privacy—The Harlequin® Reader Service is committed to protecting your privacy. Our Privacy Policy is available online at www.ReaderService.com or upon request from the Harlequin Reader Service.

We make a portion of our mailing list available to reputable third parties that offer products we believe may interest you. If you prefer that we not exchange your name with third parties, or if you wish to clarify or modify your communication preferences, please visit us at www.ReaderService.com/consumerschoice or write to us at Harlequin Reader Service Preference Service, P.O. Box 9062, Buffalo, NY 14269. Include your complete name and address.

LIHI3R

"**W**hat do you do besides work, talk and text on your cell phone, Dale Massey? What do you do for fun?" Faith stepped closer.

Simple fun? He couldn't remember. Every activity had a purpose. Entertaining clients, entertaining women, entertaining his next move as heir to Massey International. "I play tennis, remember?"

Faith shook her head. "The way you play doesn't sound fun at all."

"I play to win. Winning is fun."

She stared at him.

He stared back.

The overhead light bathed Faith in its glow, caressing her hair with shine where it wasn't covered by the knitted hat she wore. Dressed in yoga pants and bulky boots, she looked young.

Too young for someone like him.

"How old are you?"

Faith laughed. "Slick guy like you should know that's no question to ask a woman."

Her hesitation hinted that she might be older than he

thought. She'd graduated college, but when? He raised his eyebrow.

"I'm twenty-seven, how old are you?"

"Thirty."

Faith clicked her tongue. "Old enough to know that all work and no play makes Dale a dull boy."

"You think I'm dull?"

She'd be the only woman to think so. His daily schedule made most people's head spin. Yet this slip of a girl made him feel incomplete. Like something was missing.

Her gaze softened. "You don't really want to know what I think."

He stepped toward her. "I do."

She gripped her mittened hands in front of her. Was that to keep from touching him?

They were close enough that one more step would bring them together. Dale slammed his hands in his pockets to keep from touching her. No way would he repeat today's kiss.

"Honestly, you seem a little lost to me."

He searched her eyes. What made her think that? Lost? He knew exactly where he was going. His future was laid out nice and clear in front of him. But that road suddenly looked cold and lonely.

Will city boy Dale Massey find a new kind of home in Jasper Gulch, Montana, with the pretty Faith Shaw?
Find out in
HIS MONTANA HOMECOMING
by Jenna Mindel,
available November 2014 from Love Inspired.

*Texas Ranger Jake Cavanaugh turns to the one woman
who can help him find his kidnapped teenage daughter.
But there's a lot of history between Jake and Ella, as
well as between Ella and the Dead Drop Killer.
Read on for a sneak peek of
DEADLY HOLIDAY REUNION by Lenora Worth,
available November 2014 from Love Inspired® Suspense.*

"No, no, Jake. He's...he's gone. He hasn't killed anyone
in over five years because he's dead. The trail ran cold
after you found me. You know he was wounded and...he
had to have died in those woods, possibly drowned in the
lake. You were there the night—"

"I was there the night I found you half-dead and just
about out of your mind," Jake said. "But we never found
a body, Ella." He shook his head. "We assumed he was
dead but we never actually had proof."

His eyes held accusation as well as torment. He'd
never forgiven her for following her dream, but he'd sure
brought home the point he'd tried to make when they
broke up way back.

Jake got up and came to her. Putting his hands on her
arms, he stared down at her. "He's back. And he took my
daughter."

Ella refused to believe that. "How do you know it's
him?"

"He left me a note that led me to this."

Ella gasped, her gaze slipping over the necklace, a

delicate gold chain with a white daisy hanging from it. The chain Jake had given Ella for graduation their senior year of high school.

The chain she'd been wearing when the case they'd been working on together had gone bad and the Dead Drop Killer had taken Ella with the intent to kill her in the same way he'd killed four other young women. But she'd escaped because she had been trained to survive. Special Agent Ella Terrell.

He hadn't killed her, but she certainly hadn't been able to do her job anymore. And now Jake was asking her to step back into that world….

She slammed a fist against her old jeans, logic slamming against fear inside her head.

"I came to you because you're the only one who can help me find him." Jake pushed at the bangs falling over Ella's forehead. "I'm sorry, but I need you, Ella."

His touch was as gentle against her skin as a butterfly's fluttering wings. But the look in his eyes was anything but gentle. "And this time, when I do find him, I'm going to end it."

Don't miss
DEADLY HOLIDAY REUNION
by Lenora Worth,
available November 2014 from
Love Inspired® Suspense.